Natural IMPULSE

An Naturel Trilogy, Book Two

ANNA DURAND

JACOBSVILLE BOOKS · MARIETTA, OHIO

NATURAL IMPULSE

ISBN: 978-1-949406-34-4 (paperback)
ISBN: 978-1-949406-35-1 (ebook)
ISBN: 978-1-949406-36-8 (audiobook)

Manufactured in the United States.

Jacobsville Books
www.JacobsvilleBooks.com

Publisher's Cataloging-in-Publication Data
provided by Five Rainbows Cataloging Services

Names: Durand, Anna, author.
Title: Natural impulse / Anna Durand.
Description: Marietta, OH : Jacobsville Books, 2020. | Series: Au naturel trilogy, bk. 2.
Identifiers: LCCN 2020910189 (print) | ISBN 978-1-949406-34-4 (paperback) | ISBN 978-1-949406-35-1 (ebook) | ISBN 978-1-949406-36-8 (audiobook)
Subjects: LCSH: Nudism--Fiction. | Nudist camps--Fiction. | Japanese Americans--Fiction. | Man-woman relationships--Fiction. | Oregon--Fiction. | Romance fiction. | BISAC: FICTION / Romance / Romantic Comedy. | FICTION / Romance / Contemporary. | FICTION / Romance / Multicultural & Interracial. | GSAFD: Love stories. | Humorous fiction.
Classification: LCC PS3604.U724 N38 2020 (print) | LCC PS3604.U724 (ebook) | DDC 813/.6--dc23.

Praise for Anna Durand's Books

"[*Natural Passion* is] hilariously funny, irreverent. and steamy."
Debbie Orazi, Goodreads reviewer

"Wow! I'm so happy I picked up [*Natural Passion*]. [...] Refreshing, funny, and sexy, with a unique twist on a vacation spot. [...] Another author to add to my favorites list, and I can't wait for Ollie and Mara's story in *Natural Impulse*."
Sharon Clayton, The Eclectic Review

"Anna Durand adroitly sets the stage for a fun romantic comedy [in *One Hot Roomie*]. Durand's two main characters are perfect foils for each other; both are conflicted and for good reason. Seeing as they try to make being roomies for two weeks work is priceless entertainment."
Jack Magnus, Readers' Favorite

"[*Notorious in a Kilt*] is the book I have been waiting for! A great second-chance romance and one of my favorites in this series."
The Romance Reviews

"I loved the Scottish in Ian and the strength of Rae, but the love of one little girl makes [*Notorious in a Kilt*] something to behold."
Coffee Time Romance

"I have enjoyed this whole series, but Emery and Rory [from *Scandalous in a Kilt*] have stolen my heart and are now my favorites!"
The Romance Reviews

"An enthralling story. [...] I highly recommend the writing of Ms. Durand and *Wicked in a Kilt*, but be warned you will find yourself addicted and want your own Hot Scot."
Coffee Time Romance & More

"*Dangerous in a Kilt* by Anna Durand delivered! [...] It was the journey, characters, and smoking hot sex scenes that kept me turning the pages."
The Romance Reviews

"There's a huge hero's and heroine's journey [in *Dangerous in a Kilt*] that I quite enjoyed, not to mention the hot sex, and again, not to mention the sweet seduction of the Scotsman who pulls out all the stops to get Erica to love him."
Manic Readers

Other Books by Anna Durand

Natural Passion (Au Naturel Trilogy, Book One)
Natural Satisfaction (Au Naturel Trilogy, Book Three)
Dangerous in a Kilt (Hot Scots, Book One)
Wicked in a Kilt (Hot Scots, Book Two)
Scandalous in a Kilt (Hot Scots, Book Three)
The MacTaggart Brothers Trilogy (Hot Scots, Books 1-3)
Gift-Wrapped in a Kilt (Hot Scots, Book Four)
Notorious in a Kilt (Hot Scots, Book Five)
Insatiable in a Kilt (Hot Scots, Book Six)
Lethal in a Kilt (Hot Scots, Book Seven)
Irresistible in a Kilt (Hot Scots, Book Eight)
One Hot Chance (Hot Brits, Book One)
One Hot Roomie (Hot Brits, Book Two)
One Hot Crush (Hot Brits, Book Three)
The Dixon Brothers Trilogy (Hot Brits, Books 1-3)
Fired Up (a standalone romance)
The Mortal Falls (Undercover Elementals, Book One)
The Mortal Fires (Undercover Elementals, Book Two)
The Mortal Tempest (Undercover Elementals, Book Three)
The Janusite Trilogy (Undercover Elementals, Books 1-3)
Obsidian Hunger (Undercover Elementals, Book Four)
Willpower (Psychic Crossroads, Book One)
Intuition (Psychic Crossroads, Book Two)
Kinetic (Psychic Crossroads, Book Three)
Passion Never Dies: The Complete Reborn Series
Reborn to Die (Reborn, Part One)
Reborn to Burn (Reborn, Part Two)
Reborn to Avenge (Reborn, Part Three)
Reborn to Conquer (Reborn, Part Four)
The Falls: A Fantasy Romance Story

Mara

The forest raced by in a blur of green and brown, the blue sky seeming to melt into it, while I stared out the window of the taxicab without really seeing anything, too absorbed by my own thoughts. My life had become a blur too. Days bled into each other the way the sky bled into the trees, impossible to hold on to or to differentiate. This vacation was supposed to cure me of that.

Could two weeks at a birdwatching retreat do that for me? Maybe I was asking too much of the universe. Maybe I shouldn't moan about my life when so many other people had so much less than I did. But I needed a change. Something drastic. Nothing else might have a chance of breaking me out of these doldrums.

So here I was in Oregon, far, far away from my home in Philadelphia.

Where was I? Au Naturel Naturist Resort. Even the name sounded relaxing and blissful. When my travel agent had suggested I come here for my vacation, I'd jumped at the chance. The resort was for people who loved nature, she'd told me. It offered things like birdwatching and nature hikes. I could learn about the wildlife.

I had never left the city before, not in my entire life.

About time I expanded my horizons.

My parents would think I'd gone insane, so I hadn't told them where I was going.

The gray-haired cab driver leered at me over his shoulder. "So, you're one of those naturist freaks, huh?"

What about birdwatching was freakish? The driver had creeped me out from the moment I met him, but nobody else wanted to drive out here. Nobody at the airport would tell me why. They raised their eyebrows and smirked, like it was obvious and I was too dumb to understand.

"Not really," I said to the driver. "This is my first time at a naturist resort. I'm looking forward to communing with nature and stuff like that."

"Sure, communing." He leered at me again, snorting like he was trying very hard not to laugh at me. "Bet a pretty girl like you will commune with lots of other naturists."

Why did he say the word commune like it was filthy?

I returned my attention to the view outside the window. Out the corner of my eye, I spotted the driver still leering at me. It made my skin itch.

My phone made a blooping noise, indicating a new text message.

Sighing, I checked the text.

Nico: Where are you, Mar-Mar?

I growled under my breath. He knew I hated being called Mar-Mar. Hadn't he humiliated me enough? No, he had to taunt me with obnoxious texts. I typed, "None of your business."

Another bloopety-bloop. Another text from Nico. This one said, "I miss you."

My thumbs flew over the on-screen keyboard. *Should've thought of that before you dumped me.*

I made a mistake. Let's talk.

Another growl burst out of me. *Leave me alone.*

Talk later, then.

If I could've figured out how to block his number, I would've done it. I'd never been tech-savvy.

Another text came through, but I ignored it. At least they had cell coverage way out here in the boonies. Would the resort have Wi-Fi? Not that it mattered. I was getting away from the world, which meant no checking social media. Maybe I should've left my phone at home, but then what would I do in an emergency? What if there was a wildfire? An earthquake?

"Here we are," the driver said while he steered the cab down a gravel driveway that snaked through the woods. "Just a few more minutes until you can commune with the other freaks. You can get started now if you want."

I caught his leering gaze in the rearview mirror.

What was this guy's problem?

The cab rumbled down the gravel drive, emerging into a big, sunlit clearing. A modest-size house occupied the prime spot at the driveway's end, while a much larger, two-story building squatted to the right of that, a little further away. Other, smaller structures were barely visible behind the large building. I saw tents too, set up nearer to the woods.

I'd have to work up to sleeping in a tent. *Give me a soft bed and a plush pillow, please.*

The cab stopped near the small house.

"Here ya go," the driver said, leaning forward to peer out the windshield, squinting like he was trying hard to see something.

Someone rushed up to open the back door of the cab, but I couldn't see the person very well. The sun glinted on the windows, obscuring my view. Plus, it was so bright out and I'd left my sunglasses in one of my bags. Which were in the trunk. *What a hopeless ditz you are.* Maybe I had my spare pair in my purse.

I dug around inside it, hoping to find sunglasses. My hair fell around my face, tickling my cheeks and my nose. I scrunched up my nose, wishing with all my might that I would not sneeze on whoever was standing outside the car.

"Welcome to Au Naturel Naturist Resort," a male voice said.

A hand reached out to me. A hand that had been toasted in the sun, but not so much that the skin looked like leather.

I slung the purse over my shoulder and settled my hand into the stranger's, letting him help him out of the cab. His palm felt warm and soft. I lifted my gaze to his, and my tummy did a silly little flip-flop.

The gentleman holding my hand wasn't a drop-dead gorgeous hunk with enormous muscles, but I liked that he wasn't. He looked like a normal guy, though a uniform disguised his physique somewhat. The blue polo shirt had short sleeves that exposed a good bit of his biceps. This man wasn't ripped or shredded or whatever people liked to call it when a guy had bulging muscles rippled with veins. His physique seemed fit, but in a normal way.

He had the most beautiful face I'd ever seen, though I couldn't see his eyes with the sun glaring on his eyeglasses.

"Thank you," I said. "I'm Mara Severins."

Still holding my hand, the man stared at me. Not in an unsettling way, like the cab driver had. He stared like he couldn't believe what he was seeing.

Did I have lint on my dress? Or—*oh God, please say no*—did I have toilet paper stuck to my shoe? I had stopped at the restroom before leaving the airport.

"Is something wrong?" I asked. "Is this the wrong day? Sometimes I do that, I get the dates messed up and show up at the wrong time."

His lips worked for a second before he stammered, "I—whuh—"

A tag pinned to his shirt told me his first name.

I met his concealed gaze. "It's nice to meet you, Oliver."

He blinked several times, then glanced down at his shirt. Rolling his shoulders back, he let go of my hand. "Yes, I'm Oliver Jackson, the assistant manager. You can call me Ollie if you want. Let me get your bags for you."

"Thank you, Oliver." I liked the way his name slid off my tongue as smoothly as warm chocolate sauce.

He gestured to the cab driver. "Open the trunk."

The lid popped up, and Oliver hurried to get my bags. His brows shot up when he looked inside the trunk.

I winced. Yeah, I'd brought too much luggage. Four big suitcases and two smaller ones that held all my makeup and hair stuff, not to mention moisturizer and other necessities.

Oliver hoisted my bags out of the trunk and set them down alongside the driveway. He shut the trunk and the back door of the cab. "Thanks, man. See you next time."

The driver backed the cab up and turned it around, waving as he drove away.

Oliver waved back.

I eyed my luggage. My Prada luggage. Did nature lovers usually arrive with designer bags? Probably not. I also doubted they showed up wearing a designer, body-hugging dress and stilettos.

Such an idiot, Mara.

Oliver picked up two of my large bags, half stifling a grunt. He grimaced, but bravely soldiered on with my overstuffed bags. "Follow me."

I tried to navigate the gravel drive, but my heels kept tripping me up.

"Might be easier if you take off your shoes," Oliver said, slowing down so I could catch up.

"Right." I smiled sheepishly as I tugged my shoes off and held one in each hand. "I'm not used to the outdoors since I live in Philadelphia, but that's why I came here. To commune with nature or whatever."

"You can definitely do that here."

We were aiming for the two-story building, so I hurried ahead of him to open the door.

"Sorry, that's supposed to be my job," he said, lugging the suitcases across the threshold.

"My fault. I overpacked. Always do."

The door swung shut behind us.

Dragging in a deep breath, I let my eyelids ease half closed. The aroma of succulent foods wafted past me. Was that hamburgers? God, I'd kill for red meat. And did I smell fries? Maybe even sweet potato fries? *Please, yes, let it be.*

I blew out the breath I'd held. "Mm, I smell food. Haven't eaten since I left Philly early this morning."

"The other guests are having lunch," Oliver said. "Why don't you join them while I take your things upstairs? They're nice people, and they love meeting new guests."

"You don't mind? I mean, I'm leaving you to carry my bags. I know they're heavy."

"It's my job." He nodded toward the door a dozen feet down the hall. "Dining hall's in there. Go on, have fun."

A real smile stretched my lips. "Thank you, Oliver."

I trotted toward the doorway to food heaven, inhaling more delicious aromas, my eyes drifting partway closed again. My tummy grumbled. Oh lord, I was starving. At the doorway, I paused and opened my eyes all the way to survey the dining hall.

Men and women sat at tables, chatting, smiling, and stuffing fries in their mouths.

Naked men. Naked women. Not a scrap of anything resembling clothing on any of them.

A wave of ice cold flooded through me. I couldn't breathe. Couldn't budge even one-thousandth of a step.

Totally naked people.

Suddenly, the gaze of every single person in the dining hall veered to me.

And I screamed.

God, had I turned into the dumb chick in a B horror movie? Screaming? For heaven's sake, I was a grown woman. But I couldn't shake the ice-cold shock. What kind of birdwatchers ate lunch in the nude?

Pretty sure my jaw dropped. My eyes bulged too.

Something thumped behind me.

Everyone stared at me. They looked confused.

I stammered but couldn't piece together whole words, much less sentences.

Oliver appeared beside me, touching my arm. "What's wrong? Are you having an epileptic seizure or something? I can take you to the hospital if—"

"No, I'm not having a seizure." Why did my voice sound breathy? I squeezed my eyes shut and turned toward him, praying I could get a grip soon. "Why is everyone naked?"

"Oh. Yeah, that. I know at some naturist resorts the guests dress for meals, but here we have a less formal way of doing things. Are you sure you're okay?"

"Fine. Yes." The syllables were clipped. I pried my lids apart to look at Oliver. "Why would birdwatchers eat in the nude?"

"Birdwatchers? Some of our guests enjoy doing that, but what's clothing got to do with it?"

"Everyone is naked." Why did he not see how horribly wrong this all was?

"Uh, yeah, that's kind of the point." He laughed, sounding and looking a bit uncomfortable. "This is a naturist resort."

I threw my hands up, huffing. "Like that explains it?"

"Well, sure it does."

Seriously? He thought that explained the naked people scarfing down burgers and fries.

I stalked out into the hallway where I couldn't see into the dining hall anymore. Were my eyes on fire from what I'd seen? No, they were dry and hot because I'd been gaping at those people for…how long? An hour was what it felt like.

Oliver followed me. "I'm confused. Why are you so upset that all the naturists are naked?"

"Because—" I flapped my arms and huffed again. "Public nudity is illegal."

"This isn't public. It's a private resort." He held up his hands, his tone conciliatory. "Listen, you can dress for meals. Nobody will care."

"Oh, how generous." Christ, I sounded like a haughty bitch. How was I supposed to react to all of this? I scrunched up my face so hard my eyes watered. My lip probably curled. "I'm allowed to wear clothes if I want. Shouldn't you be more concerned about disturbing all the other guests who don't want to eat surrounded by naked people?"

"Um, those are all the other guests in there."

"Everyone eats in the nude?" What bizarre alternate reality had I stumbled into? I grasped my head in my hands, struggling to make sense of…anything. "What kind of place is this?"

"It's a naturist resort." He touched my arm again. "Relax. This is a clothing-optional resort, not a clothes-free one. You can take your time getting acclimated before you ditch the clothes. You haven't done this much, have you?"

"Done what?"

"Gone nude."

What on earth was he talking about?

I lowered my hands, narrowing my gaze on him. "What do you mean it's a clothing-optional resort? I thought this was a naturist retreat."

"It is." He raised his brows. "What exactly do you think a naturist resort is?"

"A place where people go to enjoy nature and see the wildlife."

He gave me a long-suffering look. "Miss Severins, you're at a nudist resort."

My eyes burned again, probably because I'd gone bug-eyed again. A new wave of icy shock crashed over me. My knees wobbled, and my face went subzero cold.

And I fainted.

Oliver caught me. "Miss Severins?"

My lids fluttered open, and I gazed into his eyes, now visible thanks to the lack of glare inside the building. He had gorgeous amber eyes. Cradled in his arms, I said, "Nudist?"

"Yeah, that's right. Some of us prefer naturist, though."

I closed my eyes and moaned.

He helped me to my feet. "How did you not know? It says right on our website, and on every travel site where we're listed."

"Never saw any website. I hired a travel agent to book my vacation. She said this was a place where birdwatchers and other nature lovers come to enjoy the outdoors."

"Sorry. I don't know where she got that idea." He glanced at my suitcases, where he'd dropped them on the floor when he hurried to my rescue. "You want to go home right away?"

"I can't." I threw head my back and moaned again. "I bought nonrefundable, round-trip airline tickets. Are there any motels in town?"

"Sure, but they're all booked up. The Renaissance fair is this week."

Oh great. I slumped against the wall. Sure, I could afford to buy another airline ticket, but that would mean crawling home with my tail between my legs to tell my parents I'd screwed up again.

"I'll take your bags up to your room," Oliver said. "And if you still don't feel comfortable eating in the dining hall, I can bring food to your room."

I managed a weak smile. "You're a good man, Oliver. How did you ever wind up working at a nudist retreat?"

His expression tightened a smidge, but only for a second.

"Never know," he said as he hefted my suitcases off the floor. "You might decide to give naturism a try."

I straightened and smoothed my dress. "I doubt that."

Then I lifted my chin and marched off down the hallway barefoot, having no fucking idea where I was going or how I would handle two weeks at a nudist resort.

Chapter Two

Ollie

I followed Mara down the hall, admiring her ass the whole time instead of watching where I was going. She had a great ass. I mean, epically great. Somebody should've sculpted a statue of her bottom, it was that fantastic. What wasn't great? Not paying attention to where I was walking.

Mara started up the stairs, but I didn't notice.

Holding on to two enormous and unbelievably heavy suitcases, I stumbled straight into the bottom step. My fingers popped open. The suitcases whumped down, and her shoes that I'd tucked under my arms clattered to the floor, but I tripped and tumbled forward right into Mara's fine behind.

She shrieked.

My face landed smack on her ass. I'd knocked her down, and now her legs were under me, but I wound up face-planting in her butt cheeks with only her dress and, I assumed, her underwear separating my nose and mouth from her body. Damn, she smelled good. Did she spray perfume on her dress or something? Nah, that wasn't a phony scent. It was all her.

"Get off me!" she hollered, trying to kick at me but not having any luck, what with all of me on top of half of her.

"Sorry," I mumbled into her ass.

I planted my hands on the step and pushed myself off Mara,

then offered her my hand. "Let me help you up."

The girl with the awesome ass glowered at me for a second. But then her features relaxed, and she accepted my hand. "Thank you, Oliver. I'm sorry I freaked out and kicked you."

"No problem. Sorry about the face-in-your-ass thing." Believe it or not, that wasn't the most embarrassing thing that had ever happened to me. I still remembered the day a porcupine had chased me out of the woods. Yeah, I'd screamed like a girl and run away from a pudgy creature that moved slightly faster than a snail. Not my finest moment.

"It's okay," Mara said, smiling shyly. "Probably my fault for making you carry those bags."

"Carrying whatever crap you bring is part of my job. Once, I had to haul a giant pet carrier with a Saint Bernard inside it."

Mara's eyes widened. "You allow pets here?"

"Sure. Only well-behaved ones, and they have to be on leashes."

"But Saint Bernards are..." She went pale, like she might faint again. "Their heads are huge. And their teeth..."

I grasped her elbow. "Whoa, take it easy. Don't pass out. There are no dogs here at the moment. Are you afraid of them?"

She squashed her lips between her teeth and squeezed her eyes shut, then sucked in a deep and noisy breath through her nostrils. Shaking off whatever it was, she squared her shoulders. "I am not afraid of dogs." She winced. "Most of the time."

Jeez, this girl was a tangled mess of phobias. Dogs. Naked people. What next? She was hot, and kind of sweet in a bat-shit crazy way, but completely neurotic.

I considered the stairs and the rooms they led to, rooms occupied by naturists. Lots of naturists. All of whom would be stampeding out of the dining hall anytime. How would Mara react to nude people playing miniten? She might freak when saw the thugs, the wedge-shaped boxes used to bat the tennis ball around in miniten. A thug kind of sort of resembled a Saint Bernard's head. If you squinted hard, and if you were an outrageously uptight city girl who was terrified of nudity.

"Tell you what," I said. "Why don't you stay in the little house, the one on the other side of the driveway? Val and Eve aren't here right now, so you can hang at their place until we sort out what to, uh, do with you."

Mara picked up her shoes. "Who are Val and Eve?"

"The owners of this resort."

She bit her lip. "Are you sure they won't mind?"

"Nah, they're cool. I've been staying in their house, but I can move if you'd feel weird about sharing a house with me."

"As long I have my own room, I'm fine with it."

"Yeah, you get your own room. With a door that locks." I hefted her bags off the floor, stifling a grunt. "Follow me. This is a family-friendly resort, so you don't have to worry about anything really crazy going on here. But it's probably best if you don't look into the dining hall."

She nodded gravely, still biting her lip.

Damn, I wanted to take that lip between my teeth and suck on it.

Instead, I led Mara out of the guest house and across the driveway to the little ranch house where Val and Eve lived. Until last summer, Eve had run the resort alone and cooked all the meals for all the guests in her kitchen. Ever since she and Val got together, and he became her business partner, they had loads of money to blow on improvements for the resort. Val was super rich, thanks to his previous careers as a soccer player and then a model. So now we had a big kitchen in the newly built addition to the guest house.

When we got to the door, I set down Mara's bags and dug the keys out of my pocket to unlock the door. I pushed it open, gesturing for Mara to go in first.

She peered inside with a hint of suspicion, but then smiled brightly at me and walked inside.

I lugged her bags across the threshold, kicked the door shut, and set the luggage down. "This is the kitchen."

Duh. Like she wouldn't know that if I hadn't told her. The room had a butcher-block island, two ovens, a double sink, a fridge, and pots and pans hanging from hooks.

Clearing my throat, I nodded toward the hallway. "Guest room's that way."

I headed down the hall with Mara behind me, pointing out the rooms as we went. The doors were all closed. "On the right is Eve's photo studio. Across from that is the bathroom. The other room on the right is Eve and Val's bedroom, which is where I'm staying, and this one on the left is the guest room."

Mara hurried past me to open the door.

"You've got a TV with satellite programming and DVR," I said. "There's also a clock radio with an alarm on the bedside table. This little desk here"—I ran my hand over the smooth wood surface—"has a drawer with notepaper and pens, plus a phone book. You also have a dresser with a big mirror on it, though I'm sure you figured that out on your own."

Yeah, the dresser was kind of hard to miss, being right there in plain sight. What an idiot I'd turned into today. It was her ass's fault. If she didn't have a shapely, enticing rear end, maybe I wouldn't act like such a dope around her.

Mara had stepped inside the room a few inches, but she eyed it with a hint of anxiety.

"Don't worry, nobody else is in the house." I tapped a finger on the phone on the desk. "If you need me, just press one. That rings the office in the guest house, which is where I'll be."

Her wide gaze flew to me. "You're leaving me alone here?"

"Relax, it's perfectly safe. You might not want to look out the window, but nobody will bother you here." I scratched the back of my neck. "Maybe I should hang around for a little while, to help you get settled."

Her tense shoulders sagged. "Oh thank you, Oliver. I'm so grateful there's one person here who isn't a nudist."

I almost winced. Not a nudist? She'd been assuming that because I was wearing clothes right now. If I told her I only dressed to greet new guests, she would panic for sure. Yeah, that was the reason I hadn't corrected her misconception about me. It had nothing to do with the fact I wanted to kiss her.

She inched toward the bed and cautiously settled her fantastic ass onto it. She bounced a little, like she was testing the mattress. "This feels wonderful. Very cushy."

Her breasts jiggled every time she bounced.

My brain went straight to a fantasy of Mara spread out on the bed, naked, moaning and begging me to—

"Oliver?" she said. "Are you all right?"

I coughed into my fist. "Yeah, fine."

The way she kept calling me Oliver made my balls tighten, but what the hell. Let's go with "I'm fine." If she called me Oliver again, I might develop a raging erection, but that was cool. I mean, it wasn't like she'd freak out and faint.

Ugh. At least this time, she would pass out on a nice soft mattress.

"Call me Ollie," I said for the sake of self-preservation. "Please. That's what everybody calls me."

My sister called me Liver, but she got away with it only because she was fourteen. No force on earth could stop a teenager from inventing insulting nicknames.

"Okay," Mara said. "Ollie."

That wasn't much better, but at least I'd averted a disaster. My dick had stopped twitching.

Until Mara stretched her arms above her head, smiled, and sighed. She flopped backward onto the mattress. "Mm, this bed is wonderful."

And then she glided her hands up and down her form-fitting dress.

Hard-on. Instant. Massive.

Shit, shit, shit.

I turned away from her, like I was about to leave. How could a woman who was terrified of naked people stretch like that right in front of me?

"You seem like you've settled in," I said, hugging the doorjamb to hide my hard-on. "I'll go make some calls to see if I can find a room for you somewhere else."

I made the mistake of glancing at her.

Mara, still lying on the bed, stretched her arms above her head again. "Thank you, Oliver."

Fuck. Would she ever stop saying my name?

I shut the door and ran out of the house.

Chapter Three

Mara

I lay there on the bed for several minutes, luxuriating in the softness of the mattress and the seclusion of this cozy little room inside this cozy little house. Curtains shielded the windows, so I couldn't see if nude people were having an orgy out there. Not that I believed they actually would do that. Ollie had told me this was a family-friendly place, and I believed him. He'd been so sweet and kind to me. Thank goodness I'd found one normal, non-nudist person to talk to at this resort.

He was cute too. And sexy.

I sat up and reached behind me to unzip my dress. Why had I worn this thing? It was tight and made it hard for me to kneel or sit down. I longed to strip it off and put on something comfy.

But I couldn't reach the zipper.

How stupid are you, Mara? Wearing a new dress for the first time when you're traveling.

When I'd bought the dress, the woman in the clothing store had helped me get out of it. Maybe that should've been a clue, but I hadn't been thinking clearly about anything. Get out of town, that's all I'd had on my mind.

I struggled to reach the zipper, contorting my arms into positions that almost hurt, but couldn't quite reach the damn thing. *Shit.* I flopped back onto the bed, glaring at the ceiling.

Footsteps drew my attention to the open doorway.

Ollie stopped at the threshold with two of my large suitcases and the two smaller ones in his hands, plus the other two big ones under his arms. Panting, he said, "Almost forgot your bags. They were still in the kitchen."

His gaze skimmed over me, and he licked his lips.

I sat up.

Ollie walked into the room and set my suitcases on the floor. "There you go."

He started to leave.

"Wait," I said, pushing up off the bed. "I, um… It's kind of embarrassing, but I need help."

It was completely humiliating, actually.

"Help with what?" he asked.

I hunched my shoulders and pointed at my back. "Can't get the zipper undone."

"Oh." He licked his lips again, his hands curling into loose fists. "I guess I can give you a hand."

"If it's too weird for you, I'll understand."

"No, it's not weird."

He came up to me, gesturing for me to turn around.

I did, but he made no move to unzip the dress. I waited, feeling more anxious with every second.

"Nice dress," he said, his voice huskier. "You look really good in it."

My voice refused to work, but my body warmed, starting with my cheeks.

He took hold of the zipper and eased it down, inch by inch, his warm fingertip grazing my skin. A sensuous tingle trailed down my flesh in its wake, and suddenly, I had trouble catching my breath. When he reached my bra, he pulled his hand away.

"I think you can do the rest," he said, his voice gruffer.

When I turned around, he was staring at me. Lips parted. Chest rising and falling visibly. Eyes darker somehow, probably because his pupils had enlarged.

My breasts lifted with every breath I struggled to suck into my lungs, and I had the most inappropriate urge to kiss him. Cool air teased my skin where the dress gaped open, the sensation making me a little bit crazy. I wanted to touch him. Press my lips to his. Slip my hand inside his pants.

Ollie's gaze wandered down to my breasts, and he scrubbed a hand over his mouth. "I should go make those calls for you."

He moved toward the door.

I rushed forward to grab his arm. "Oliver."

Though he stopped, he didn't turn to look at me.

A reckless urge overtook me, one so irresistible I couldn't prevent myself from doing what my body wanted. I stepped in front of him, caught his face in my hands, and kissed him.

He held stone-still for a few seconds, while I kept my lips glued to his and reveled in the warmth and softness of them. God, his mouth. I wanted it. Now. Wanted him to thrust his tongue between my lips and ravage me.

Instead, he took hold of my upper arms and pushed me away. "This is really not a good idea. You're still freaked out about the naturist thing, and I don't take advantage of vulnerable women."

Of course he didn't. Oliver Jackson was a good man. I'd known that when I screamed and fainted and he'd caught me. Despite my stupid behavior, he'd taken care of me. Maybe I was not quite myself, but I knew I wanted him, and he didn't want me. Rejection felt like crap.

"Sorry," I said, feeling my cheeks heat up, with embarrassment this time. Ducking my head, I sidled out of his way. "I didn't mean to—Oh God, I really am an idiot."

"No, you are not. But you've had a big shock." He touched my arm. "Take it easy for a while. Watch some TV and chill."

I nodded.

He hooked a finger under my chin and urged me to look up at him. "You're sexy, Mara. I want to kiss you, but not like this."

Ollie ran his thumb over my bottom lip, then he walked out the door.

I stood there like a statue for a minute or two, maybe longer, wondering why I always did such stupid things. Of course he wouldn't want to kiss me. Why would he? I'd freaked out when I saw naked people.

After changing clothes, I ventured out of my room, heading down the hallway and into the kitchen. Ollie wasn't around. He'd told me he was going to his office in the guest house, so I hadn't really expected to find him here, but I had hoped for it. What should I do? Going outside seemed like a horrible idea. The nudists might be out there, and though I knew I wouldn't pass out this time, I still didn't feel up to facing a bunch of naked people who'd heard me scream and seen me faint. God, they must've thought I was a lunatic.

My stomach grumbled.

Should I rifle through the fridge for food? This wasn't my house. I didn't feel like I should poke around in someone else's kitchen. Ollie was letting me stay here instead of in the guest house out of kindness and probably a desire to make sure I didn't faint in his arms again.

I leaned my elbows on the butcher-block island.

And that's when I saw the tented card standing in the middle of the island. It had my name written on it. I picked up the card and looked inside. It said, "Eat anything you want, then kick back and watch TV. I'll bring you dinner tonight." Ollie had signed the card.

Now that I had permission to rifle through the fridge, I did. The owners of the resort had lots of food on hand, some of it things I'd never heard of, like Minas cheese. I made myself a turkey sandwich, even putting cheddar cheese on it in spite of hearing my mother's voice in my head saying, "Dairy will make you gain weight, Mara, and proper ladies don't get chunky." Screw that. I'd had a horrible day so far, not to mention the entire year before today, so I deserved cheese, mayonnaise, and sour cream and onion potato chips.

And milk. Mm, it tasted so good.

Consuming a forbidden sandwich and chips made me want to go all the way, food-wise. I'd seen a tray of cupcakes in the fridge too, so I retrieved the tray and set it on the counter. The cupcakes looked like dark chocolate, tinged with red, and with vanilla frosting on top. Could they be red velvet? I'd never had that, though I'd dreamed of cupcakes like this often after seeing a case of them at the bakery across the street from my condo. Red velvet looked so decadent. So yummy. So…forbidden.

I picked up a cupcake, peeled back the wrapping, and sank my teeth into the dark, succulent flesh. The deep, dark chocolate melted on my tongue. The flavor of the cream cheese frosting melded with the chocolate in the most delicious combination. Sweet. Tangy. Rich. *Mmmmm, yum.*

An actual moan escaped my lips.

Swallowing, I closed my eyes and bit off another chunk of dark-chocolate heaven. Then another. And another. Once I'd finished off that cupcake, I dived into a second one, moaning even more deeply when the flavor of it filled my mouth.

A throat-clearing behind me made me jump and glance at the door.

Ollie still had his hand on the knob, the door halfway open. He wore a tight expression that seemed almost pained. "Sorry, I should've knocked first so I wouldn't scare you."

I quickly chewed and swallowed my bite of cupcake. Dropping the rest of it on the tray, I wiped my mouth with my hand. "No, I'm sorry. I shouldn't be wolfing down all the cupcakes. Bill me for the cost of them, please."

"No way." He shut the door and approached the island, standing near me. "You're a guest. All the food is included."

I gazed longingly at the cupcakes. "I just found out I love red velvet."

"Yeah, I could tell."

His voice was deeper, infused with something I couldn't quite identify, something almost…hungry.

I offered him a cupcake. "Want one?"

"No thanks. But you go ahead and eat all you want."

He still had that touch of hunger in his voice, but he said he didn't want a cupcake. Why did he sound that way, then?

Ollie raked his gaze over me from head to toe, taking in my capri pants and short-sleeve top. His tongue sneaked out to moisten his lips, and his eyes seemed to darken. When I got to my feet, he pulled in a long breath and exhaled it slowly, rubbing his jaw. "Pink toenails. I like it."

My sandals exposed my toes, and I always kept them painted. When he'd said he liked my pink nail polish, his voice had gotten deeper and huskier.

He lifted his gaze to mine.

The heat in those amber irises could've melted the clothes right off my body. It didn't, thankfully. But I did feel hot and wet in the most intimate way.

I suddenly realized the truth. When he'd looked hungry a minute ago, it hadn't been for cupcakes. He wanted to gorge himself on me.

No, it couldn't be that. *Stupid, Mara, jumping to conclusions.* If he'd wanted me, he wouldn't have pushed me away when I kissed him earlier.

His gaze skipped down to my chest and the modest amount of cleavage my top revealed. He licked his lips again.

"I should go," he said. "See you later."

And he left before I could form any words. How bizarre.

The door clicked shut behind him, and I went back to devouring red velvet cupcakes.

Chapter Four

Ollie

Pink toenails turned me on. Who knew? Not me, that's for sure. I'd never thought of women's toes as sexy, but one glimpse of Mara's pink-tipped digits had me fighting off a hard-on. It didn't help that she'd been enjoying a cupcake when I walked into the house. The blissful look on her face made me imagine her looking that way when I was fucking her. And the way she'd opened her mouth to take a bite, then closed her lips around it…

I'd pictured her mouth sealing around my cock the same way.

And that's why I'd needed to run away. Christ, the girl was terrified of nudity. How would she react if I developed a raging stiffy?

Oh yeah, I had one of those now. Luckily, I'd gotten out of the house before Mara saw it. I managed to sneak back into the guest house and up to the office without running into anyone. Most of the guests were out on the lawn playing miniten.

After half an hour of calling every hotel, motel, bed-and-breakfast, and campsite in the area, I realized I was never going to find another place for Mara to stay. I expanded my search to a hundred-mile radius, but still had no luck. It seemed like every person on the planet had decided to visit this part of Oregon this week. Calling all those additional places took another forty-five minutes. By then, I was feeling stiff all over—but at least not in the way I had been when I saw Mara earlier. My dick might've been relaxed, but the rest of me needed a massage.

I pushed up out of the desk chair and stretched, groaning when my muscles protested. My skin itched too. I really, really wanted to ditch the clothes, but I couldn't do that with Mara around. She was so happy to have one non-nudist to talk to. How could I turn up naked? She'd freak like she had when she saw the nudists in the dining hall.

Moving to the window, I stretched again and glanced toward the miniten court. The game had ended, but the net was still up. Guests lounged on outdoor chaises. Some lay on blankets, sunbathing or just talking to each other. My focus wandered toward the little house, the one where Eve and Val lived when they weren't visiting Val's family in Brazil. All the curtains were closed.

A flash of movement made me look at the guest-bedroom window. The curtain was partway open, at an angle like someone was holding it that way. My curiosity got the better of me, and I grabbed a pair of binoculars off the cabinet beside the window. Eve kept them there in case we needed to scout for bears or other wildlife that might wander into the main resort area. I aimed the binoculars at the window of the guest bedroom of Eve and Val's house.

Mara was standing there, holding the curtain slightly open, peeking out at—

A laugh snorted out of me. She was watching the guests who were hanging out on the lawn. Not so terrified of nudity, after all, I guessed. Maybe she'd worked up enough courage to take a peek, but I doubted she would scamper out there to join in the fun.

My phone made that silly tinkling noise it always made when I had a new text. While still holding the binoculars, I checked, and yep, I'd gotten a text from my best friend, Damian. He wanted to know when he could come for a visit. With Mara here? I had my hands full already, and Damian was kind of a player. He loved the ladies, and he'd never been shy about flirting with them—or stripping naked in front of them. I wasn't sure how Mara might react to him. He wasn't a nudist, but we had gone to an adults-only resort a couple years ago. Damian loved that.

I liked it here. With guests who were like family.

So I typed, *Not now. Too busy.*

Damian replied, *Maybe I'll surprise you.*

Please don't.

Okay. I'll wait. He typed an emoji of a winking face. *See ya.*

Just as I finished saying goodbye to him, the desk phone rang. I set down the binoculars and answered.

"Hey, Ollie," Eve said. "How are things at home?"

"Fine." I leaned back against the desk, where I could still see out the window, my attention fixed on the guest-bedroom window and the barely visible shape of Mara. "You know, you don't have to check in on me five times a day. I'm a big boy, Eve. I can handle everything on my own."

Yeah, I wasn't quite sure I could, but Eve didn't need to hear that. I mean, I could handle the guests. But then there was Mara...

"I know that," Eve said. "You're highly capable and very smart. But I got a text from Ruth Norris, and she seems to think you've got a bit of a problem on your hands."

Shit. Had Ruth blabbed to Eve about Mara?

"And I hear that problem is very pretty," Eve added.

"What? Come on, Evie, I'm a professional." Sure I was. I'd become super adept at acting like I knew what the fuck I was doing when I actually wanted to scream and pull my hair out. My career in computer systems engineering had gone kaput. What did I know about running a resort? Not much, but I was learning. The hard way, sometimes.

Like when I'd seen Mara and her pink toenails.

"I don't get involved with guests," I said.

"Never suggested you were involved with Mara Severins. It's interesting that you assumed that's what I meant."

The teasing tone in her voice told me she was enjoying ribbing me about this. So I ribbed her back. "I remember when you swore off sleeping with guests."

"Yeah, I stuck to that resolution for about five seconds after Val showed up." She laughed. "Oh Ollie, don't make the same mistakes I did. If you like Mara, tell her."

"I can't." I shuffled to the window, leaning my forehead on the glass,. "She's terrified of naked people, and I kind of, uh, let her sort of believe I'm not a naturist."

Eve laughed again, much louder than before. "Honestly, Ollie, you're the cutest."

"This isn't funny, Evie."

A male voice said something in the background, but I couldn't make out the words.

"Hang on," Eve said. "Val wants to talk to you, man to man."

Oh great. The notorious playboy, the guy who used to strip naked on the soccer field when his team won a game and the guy who'd starred in his own sex tape, was about to give me advice about women. One woman. A nutcase.

A really hot nutcase.

"Ollie," Val said in his Brazilian accent that women all seemed to love, especially Eve, "I hear you have a woman problem."

"There's no problem. Everything's fine."

He chuckled. "You're infatuated with a girl who's afraid of nudity. How is that fine? I can give you advice, you know."

"Thanks, but I'm good."

"Are you sure? I do have experience in this area."

"No, man, that's okay. I can handle things with Mara."

"All right. If you're sure."

We said goodbye, and I stood there with my forehead on the glass. Movement caught my attention again, and I glanced at Mara's window.

She had pulled the curtains halfway open and now held a small pair of pink binoculars.

I lifted my head, sure I couldn't be seeing what I thought I was seeing. Mara, the anti-nudist, could not be watching the naturists with binoculars.

But she was.

Maybe she wasn't as uptight as I'd thought. If she had a naughty streak... Just thinking about that made my hard-on return. Oh fantastic. I'd be spending who-knew-how-many days around a woman who gave me the worst case of blue balls in the history of mankind.

I sat down at the desk and forced myself to concentrate on work. Accounting was pretty much the most boring thing on earth, next to watching a golf game, so I focused on that for half an hour. My stiffy softened up gradually the less I thought about Mara, distracted by the complicated accounting software, until I felt reasonably confident I wouldn't look like a total perv when I walked out of the office.

Ruth Norris cornered me when I got to the bottom of the stairs, so close to escaping the guest house that I could see the exit sign down the hall. Of course I couldn't get away without an embarrassing conversation with a seventy-ish woman who loved to razz me. In a sweet old lady way. Like she was my naughty grandma.

"Ollie," she said, hooking her arm around mine. "I've been looking for you."

"Did you need something?"

She fixed me with a grandmotherly look of concern. "Are you all right, dear? Everyone can see how much you and Mara like each other, but the poor girl is afraid of nudity."

"How do you know if we like each other? You saw her for thirty seconds and never even spoke to her."

Ruth's mouth kinked up at the corners in a sly smile. "She came out of the house while you were hiding in the office."

"She—what?"

"Mara sneaked outside to have a look, from a distance, and I met her." Ruth urged me to walk, taking us down the hall toward the exit. "She's such a lovely girl, but I'm afraid she's full of anxieties. Mara needs a good man to straighten her out."

I had a sinking feeling in my stomach, like somebody had dropped a head-size boulder in there and it was tearing a hole in my gut, that I knew what Ruth would say next.

She squeezed my arm and tapped my chest. "You, Ollie. You are the man who can help her."

"When did I become the house therapist?" I shook my head. "Mara is crazy. She's cute, yeah, but totally out there. What do you expect me to do about it?"

Ruth waggled her eyebrows. "I'm sure you can think of something."

Yep, no doubt about it. A senior citizen was encouraging me to have sex with Mara in the hopes that would "straighten her out." I wasn't self-conscious about my skills in bed, but honestly, I kind of doubted I could fuck sense into Mara.

But I'd have fun trying.

No, I would not. Sex as therapy? Jeez, the girl was so uptight she'd probably shriek and hit me over the head with a baseball bat if I tried to seduce her.

Well, she had kissed me.

Oh no, I could not be seriously considering Ruth's insane suggestion.

Even though I was absolutely *not* considering that, I heard myself saying, "I'll see what I can do."

"Try singing for her. Women love men who have hidden talents."

"Uh, maybe. We'll see."

Ruth led me out of the guest house, then peeled off to go find her husband, Sylvester. I spotted him playing checkers with another senior guest, Gil Foster. The two silver foxes had become good buddies right off the bat when Gil had arrived a few days ago.

Other guests were playing volleyball on the court that had been set up for miniten earlier.

A trio of twenty-something girls had brought out butterfly nets and were jumping around trying to catch the little critters. Even the bouncing of their breasts couldn't rev my libido.

I scanned the area, looking for Mara.

She hugged the corner of the little house, not far from the kitchen windows, her expression pinched. I couldn't tell for sure if she had her eyes closed, but I thought maybe she did. I hadn't expected her to come outside at all, so this was a huge step forward for her. I walked toward her, seeing more of her face the closer I got. She held her palms to her cheeks, then slid them up to cover her eyes, only to peek out between her fingers.

"Enjoying yourself?" I asked, coming up beside her.

Mara jumped like she hadn't noticed me approaching. "Ollie, I—Well, I thought immersion therapy might be the best thing for me."

"Sounds like a plan. How's it going so far?"

"Think I need to go back inside for a while."

"No rush. Take your time adjusting to the naked people."

She smiled, her lips sealed, then retreated into the house.

I went back to doing my job, but several times I glanced out the office window to see Mara outside the little house, cautiously watching the guests who were hanging out on the lawn. And yeah, I got out the binoculars so I could get a closer look—at her facial expression, not her body. Okay, maybe I enjoyed taking a peek at that too. She seemed less anxious about the whole naturist thing, since she didn't squeeze her eyes shut anymore, though she still didn't go out onto the lawn to socialize. Baby steps, I guessed.

At lunchtime, I got a great idea. Well, it sounded like a great one to me. Mara shouldn't hide in the little house all day. Fresh air and exercise, plus a few fun activities that didn't involve nudity, would make her feel better. I was sure of it. So I made us lunch in the big kitchen in the guest house and trotted over to the little house, setting my picnic basket and guitar case on the ground beside me. I knocked on the door to avoid scaring Mara again.

When she opened the door, she smiled. "Hi, Ollie."

This girl had the most beautiful smile in the history of smiling. I had no idea how long ago people first started making that expression, but it didn't matter. To me, her smile was the best.

"Hey, Mara," I said. "Made us a picnic lunch. Want to come out to the lake with me? All the other guests are in the big house, in the exercise room or the entertainment room, so we'll have the lake to ourselves."

"I've never walked in the woods before."

"You came here to commune with nature, right? And do some birdwatching?" When she nodded, I said, "I want to show you my favorite spot for seeing birds and other wildlife. It's also a nice place for a picnic."

She peered out the door at the lawn, where only a few guests still hung out. They were chilling on chaises and talking, not doing anything crazy.

I held my hand out to Mara. "Come on, it'll be good to get some fresh air. Trust me."

She bit her lip, but then slipped her hand into mine.

My gaze dropped to her feet and those sexy little pink toenails.

Veering my attention to her face, I cleared my throat. "You might want tennies instead of sandals. Better for a nature walk."

Mara hurried off to change her shoes and came back wearing pink tennies. She stepped outside and shut the door, saying, "Let's go."

I picked up the picnic basket and my guitar case. "Follow me."

We headed toward the nature trail, skimming the edge of the lawn maybe thirty feet from the naturists who were hanging out there. Mara glanced sideways at them but didn't even flinch. Maybe her immersion therapy was working. I hoped so, because I didn't want her to leave. I kind of liked her, neuroses and all.

"Want me to carry something for you?" she asked. "You've got your hands full."

"I'm cool. Don't worry about it."

But yeah, I had a feeling I did have my hands full with this girl.

Maybe that's what I needed in my life—something unpredictable.

Chapter Five

Mara

Ollie guided me down the wide dirt path, pointing out the trees and wildflowers while explaining what each one was. I'd never gone out in the woods before. City parks had been the extent of my nature communing. I hadn't needed to leave the city, except to fly somewhere for a vacation at a fancy resort, so I never had.

The trees were so big and beautiful here, and their branches formed a canopy above our heads. The sunlight filtered through them, creating a gentle glow. I heard birds tweeting and squirrels chattering. Ollie had to explain to me what that chattering noise was, since I'd never heard such a thing before. There must've been squirrels in Philadelphia, but I swore I'd never noticed them making noises.

Today I'd learned something. I loved the outdoors.

Once we got to the lake, Ollie set up our picnic by laying out a blanket for us to sit on and setting food items on it. We sat facing each other, so we could talk while enjoying our meal. Ollie had made sandwiches—the best I'd ever eaten. He also brought cupcakes like the ones I'd eaten earlier.

I munched on a potato chip before asking him the question I'd been wondering about all morning. "How did you wind up working at a nudist resort? And how long have you worked here?"

He seemed so normal, not like the kind of guy who would want to spend his days with naked people.

Ollie winced, though I couldn't understand why. He looked down at the picnic blanket for a couple seconds before aiming his gorgeous amber eyes at me. "How long? I, uh, started working here last fall. It just sort of…happened. They needed an assistant manager, and I'd gotten laid off from my job as a computer systems engineer, so it all worked out. To be honest, I was sick of my old job, anyway. Staring at a computer screen all day got really old really fast."

"That's quite a leap, from computers to a nudist resort."

"Maybe, but it made sense to me." He screwed up his mouth, looking away again. "But I'm boring. Tell me more about you. What do you do for a living?"

Oh, I hated that question. Whenever I told a man about my work, they wound up finding excuses to run away. Escape from the spoiled rich girl, that was all they wanted to do. Nobody understood that I took my job seriously. Maybe Ollie would understand, but I didn't want to chase him off before we really got to know each other.

So I played it safe. By sort of lying.

"Me?" I said as a lame delaying tactic while I considered my answer. "Well, I'm basically in real estate."

"Cool. Do you sell a lot?"

"No. I'm more into…management." I picked up a cupcake and bit off a big chunk, eating it as another delaying tactic. Then I swigged water from the bottle Ollie had given me and decided to offer him part of the truth. "I'm really good at the business side of real estate. I know that sounds arrogant, but I don't mean it that way. I love figuring out the best marketing strategies, testing them, refining them, all that stuff."

Ollie grinned. "I knew you were smart. I mean, I thought you were crazy at first, but I could still tell you had brains too."

"How could you possibly know that? I've been acting like a complete idiot since the moment we met."

"Nah. You had a big shock when you found out what this place really is, that's all."

Wow, he was absolutely the sweetest man on earth.

"If you don't mind me asking," he said, "how did your travel agent screw things up so bad? She must not have even looked at our website or read what's on the travel sites."

"Ugh, I'm so mad at that woman. She came highly recommended, but I have no idea why she thought this was a birdwatching retreat." I shook my head. "She'll be getting an earful from me, let me tell you."

"I'd love to listen in on that conversation." He leaned over to set a hand on his guitar case. "Mind if I play for you?"

"No, I'd love that. Do you sing too?"

"Sure." He opened the case and brought out his guitar, bracing it on his lap while he tuned it, plucking each string and adjusting the little knob doohickeys. "I do modern songs too, but my favorites are the classics. Stuff from, like, the fifties and sixties. Some even earlier."

"That sounds wonderful. I'd love to hear it."

He started to play a tune I recognized, but only when he began to sing did I realize it was "Bridge Over Troubled Water." He sang beautifully, with a natural voice that didn't seem like an affectation or an attempt to sound like popular singers. I found myself smiling and swaying to the gentle rhythm of the song.

"You can sing along," Ollie said, while performing an instrumental break in the song.

"Oh, I couldn't. My singing is awful."

"I doubt that. Maybe another time."

He started singing again, taking the song to its climax, then he strummed one last chord. "How about a little birdwatching now?"

"Will you sing for me more later?"

"Sure." He returned the guitar to its case, stood, and offered me his hand. "I know a great spot for birds."

I took his hand, letting him help me up.

He grabbed a pair of binoculars out of the picnic basket while still holding my hand, then led me down to the lake's shore. I heard a strange, fluttery call, and Ollie told me it was a loon. He handed me the binoculars so I could get a closer view of the birds that had just landed in the lake, further away from the shore.

"Look!" he said, pointing at the sky. "It's a bald eagle."

I swung the binoculars up, getting a fantastic view of the majestic bird as it soared over our heads. Jumping up and down, I pointed at the eagle. "It's so beautiful! I've never seen one before!"

Ollie grinned and laughed, watching me jump around and squeal like a goofball. He didn't look annoyed by my behavior. He seemed to think it was entertaining.

Something buzzed past me from behind, sounding like the Godzilla of bees. Before I could react, the thing buzzed right past my face, inches away from my nose. I shrieked and ducked, spinning around to find the monster that seemed bent on having me for lunch. My heart thudded. I didn't dare move, what with adrenaline burning through my veins.

A tiny bird hovered above my head, its wings beating so fast they became a blur.

It dived toward me.

"Help!" I shrieked, flinging myself at Ollie. "It's trying to kill me!"

Ollie caught me right as I tripped over my own stupid feet.

I wound up clinging to his body with my face in his crotch.

And I shrieked again. Honestly, I couldn't help it. A dive-bombing bird? Nobody warned me about that.

Ollie stared down at me, his mouth open, like he had no frigging idea what the crazy girl attached to his body was doing.

I shoved myself away from him, landing on my ass with elbows sunk into the sand and my legs over my head.

He kept staring at me for a couple more seconds, then he rushed forward to drag me up off the ground. While he brushed sand off my shoulders, he asked, "Are you okay? What happened?"

"Well—I—" I flapped my arms, rotating them like an insane windmill. "That bird tried to kill me."

The sweet man tried not to laugh, but he wound up sputtering and snorting. The spittle flying from his lips sprayed my face.

"Oh crap," he said, wiping my face with the hem of his shirt. "Mara, I'm so sorry. Didn't mean to laugh. I know you were scared by that bird, but it was just a hummer. He must've thought you're cute and came in for a closer look."

He smiled when he said that and tapped my chin.

"I'm the one who needs to apologize," I said. "Don't know why I keep freaking out. I mean, I've never seen a bird like that one before, but that's no excuse."

"You don't need to apologize. I get that all this nature stuff is new for you."

"What was that bird? I've never heard of a hummer. Is that some bizarre species of bomber birds only found in Oregon?"

"No, it's a hummingbird." He pushed my hair off my shoulders and combed his fingers through it, cleaning the sand out. "Hummers like to dive bomb people, but they're not dangerous. That one looked like a black-chinned hummingbird. You can tell by its black head and purple throat."

"I didn't get a good look at it." Because I'd been too busy screaming and hurling my body at him. When I remembered where my face had wound up… Oh God, it was humiliating. "I swear I'm not usually this much of a disaster."

"Everybody has a little accident now and then." He patted my arm. "Maybe you've had more than your fair share in one day, but don't be embarrassed."

"Hard not to be." I frisked my hands over myself to get rid of the rest of the sand. "At best, I'm a total klutz."

"You should've seen me last summer when a porcupine chased me. Now *that* was humiliating."

Ollie really was the sweetest man on earth.

"Ready for more birdwatching?" he asked. "Or would you rather go back to a nice, bird-free house?"

"Let's keep going. I'm okay, I promise."

I picked up the binoculars, which I'd managed to send flying so they landed a good fifteen feet away, and scanned the vicinity again.

"Look over there," Ollie said, pointing toward shore ahead of us. "See that bird with a rust-colored head and neck?"

I swerved the binoculars over there. The long-legged bird was wading in the shallow waters along the lake shore, lifting its skinny legs high with each step. The black and white wings made a striking contract to its rusty neck and head, and the bird had the longest, slenderest beak I'd ever seen. Not that I'd seen much more than pigeons until today.

"What is that?" I asked. "It's so pretty and so weird at the same time."

"It's an American avocet." He moved behind me, his body brushing against my backside, and placed his hands over mine on the binoculars, guiding me to shift it toward the trees. "If you look real close, you can see a golden-crowned kinglet."

Ollie lowered his hands but stayed close behind me, the heat and scent of him surrounding me.

I adjusted the focus on the binoculars and spotted a small, plump bird with a bright yellow head that was rimmed in black. Its wings had yellow and gray on them. "How did you see that without the binoculars? It's so little."

"Yeah, but I saw the kinglet flying toward that tree. The yellow crown is hard to miss."

He had bent his head to speak to me, his mouth so close to my ear that his breaths tickled my skin when he spoke.

I wanted to kiss him again.

Damn, what was wrong with me? He hadn't wanted to kiss me earlier, so I really shouldn't try it again now. But maybe he'd meant what he said before, when he told me he didn't want to take advantage of me when I was upset.

God, I loved having him so close, his body almost touching mine. I didn't know if he used aftershave or cologne, but he smelled incredible. I couldn't resist turning my head to look at him. With his cheek no more than an inch from my face, I got an up-close look at those beautiful eyes. The sun wasn't glaring on his glasses, so I had a clear view of them. I'd never seen irises that color before, a golden amber shade that seemed to glow in the sunshine.

"Ollie?" I said.

He turned his head toward me, and our lips brushed. It was the faintest touch, but that's all it took to make my lips tingle and my breaths shorten. We gazed into each other's eyes for several seconds while the most intimate parts of me awakened, growing warm and slick. I'd been attracted to men at first sight, but never in my life had I become so lustful that the thought of kissing a man got me this aroused.

Ollie cleared his throat and stepped back, checking his watch. "Oh shit. I have to get back to the guest house. We've got new people coming any minute." He met my gaze again, his tongue darting out to moisten his lips. "Sorry to cut this short."

"Don't worry. You can always show me more of the wildlife another time."

"We'll definitely do that."

He led me back to our picnic site. We gathered up the leftovers of our lunch, and this time I carried the picnic basket. Ollie let me do that because it weighed almost nothing now. He'd slung the strap of the binoculars over his shoulder and carried his guitar case in his hand. We got back to the resort just as a bunch of nudists swarmed the lawn.

I stopped at the end of the trail, at the edge of the woods. Could I handle being around these people yet? The ones I'd met seemed super nice, and I couldn't go on hiding inside the little house. I wanted to get used to their nakedness. I had to. Maybe I couldn't change all the dumb mistakes I'd made in the past, but I could get myself over the shock of hanging around with nudists.

"Will you be okay alone?" Ollie asked. "You can go back into Eve and Val's house if you'll be more comfortable there."

"No, I want to introduce myself to everybody. I need to do it."

"Okay." He glanced around, then pointed at the gray-haired woman I'd met earlier. "You know Ruth Norris, so start with her. She'll take good care of you."

"Thank you, Ollie. I really enjoyed our picnic and seeing the birds."

"You're welcome."

He trotted off toward the guest house.

And I marched straight onto the lawn full of naked people.

Chapter Six

Ollie

For the rest of the day, I alternated between doing my job and keeping an eye on Mara, without seeming like I was spying on her. Even though I kinda was. But not in a creepy way. I hoped. Talking her into wearing tennies instead of sandals had spared me from seeing her pink toenails, but I'd neglected to take into account the fact that she was damn sexy all over, not just her toes. Every time she smiled, I felt my dick trying to firm up. When I sidled up behind her on the lake shore, to show her the kinglet, the proximity of her body had turned me on big time. Leaving her alone for the rest of the day seemed like the smartest choice.

Late in the afternoon, I headed outside and spotted Mara sitting on a lawn chaise, perched on its edge with her hands clasped on her lap. Her eyes were large, but she didn't seem freaked out like before. Some of the guests were playing miniten again, and she followed the players' movements with her eyes, flicking them left, right, left, right, up, down, right, left. Her lips curled up the tiniest bit at the corners, carving out the sweetest little dimples.

The goofy girls who'd been trying to catch butterflies this morning were at it again. One of them bumped into her friend, and the two tumbled to the ground, shrieking with laughter.

Mara smiled. Really smiled. Her teeth showed a little bit.

She was beautiful.

And just like that, my dick started to swell. Mara would freak out if she saw the lump in my pants getting bigger. I probably should've gone over there to remind those butterfly girls about the resort rules—like no body contact—but I couldn't do that when my dick thought this was a good time to get hard. Those dopey girls had wandered off toward the guest house, so I decided to give them the etiquette speech later. But I wanted to talk to Mara. Needed to. It was dumb but true.

I ducked back into the guest house to get a clipboard from the exercise room. It was the sign-up list for buying yoga mats. Didn't matter. I needed something to hold in front of my groin, and this would do. Armed with my clipboard, holding it in front of myself, I marched straight to Mara.

She noticed me and smiled, waving at me.

I clutched the clipboard to my crotch like it was glued to my body. No, that didn't look weird or pervy at all.

"Hey, Mara," I said, sitting down on the chaise next to hers. I kept the clipboard on my lap. "Seems like you're feeling a lot better about being out here with the naturists."

"I am, thank you." Her smile softened into a curling-up, dimple-carving expression that made my heart stutter. "Thank you again for our nature walk. It was amazing. And for the bazillionth time, I'm soooo sorry about the way I acted earlier. Honestly, I'm not terrified of naked people. But I was raised a certain way and taught to believe public nudity isn't proper."

"This isn't a public place. It's a private resort way out in the boonies." I tried to focus on her face, because her body looked so damn good in those pants and that top, but even her smile made me get stiffer in the one place I didn't want to get stiffer right now. "But I get that it was a shock. Glad you're feeling better."

Her brows knit together over her sweet little nose, and her gaze shifted to my lap. "Do you need me to sign something?"

I glanced down. Duh. I was holding a clipboard that had papers clipped onto it.

"No," I said, pushing my glasses up with one finger, "nothing like that. This is the sign-up sheet for guests who want to buy yoga mats from us. Do you do yoga?"

She nodded. "Not in public, though."

Of course not. Uptight city girls didn't do yoga poses in front of strangers, I guessed. But she hadn't seemed uptight when we had our picnic by the lake. The way she'd gotten so excited about seeing birds had made me want to kiss her. For a moment there, when we'd looked at each and our faces had been a breath apart, I'd been tempted to do it.

Until I remembered I was lying to her. Well, not outright lying. I let her believe I wasn't a nudist and gave her an evasive answer to her question about how I wound up working here. How could I kiss her, much less sleep with her, when I wasn't being honest with her?

Not that I intended to sleep with her. That would've been wrong. I was the assistant manager, and she was one of the guests. Even kissing her probably violated my professional ethics. I ought to avoid her as much as possible.

How could I do that when we were sleeping in the same small house?

Mara's smile had turned shy. She bowed her head, pecking up at me through her lush eyelashes.

And damn, even that made me harder.

I coughed into my fist and asked, "Did you want to buy a mat?"

"That's okay. I brought my own."

"Oh. Cool." I got up, careful to keep the clipboard in position. "I'll see later, then."

"Wait," she said. "Can I ask you a nosy question? Feel free to say no."

"Uh, sure." I sat down again. "Ask away."

She caught her lip between her teeth, letting it go little by little. "What do your friends and family think of you working at a nudist resort?"

"My parents are fine with it. They want me to be happy, that's all. My little sister doesn't care either." I tapped my finger on the clipboard, which I still held over my lap. "I don't have many close friends. But my best friend, Damian, thinks it's really funny that I work at a naturist resort."

"Funny? Why?"

"Because he dragged me to one of those adults-only naturist resorts for spring break during our first year of college. He said we needed to cut loose and get wild." I shook my head, though I couldn't help smiling a little when I remembered that vacation. "I hated that place. It was too slick and risque for my taste. I prefer—" I cut myself off before I announced I liked homey naturist resorts like this one. Maybe Mara would be okay with finding out the truth about me, but I wasn't sure. Better not to risk it. "I prefer more subdued vacation spots."

"It's nice you have a best friend. Don't think I've ever had one."

"Damian and I have known each other forever. He's lots of fun, but he really likes to play on the stereotype of gypsies."

Mara's brows crinkled. "Why would he do that?"

"Oh, I didn't tell you, did I? Damian's family is of Rom heritage. Most people call them gypsies." I rolled my eyes when I thought about my best friend's favorite pastime. "Damian thinks it's fun to play like he's a real gypsy, with supernatural powers and everything. He does palm readings, but I don't know how accurate his fortune telling is. Women seem to think his Rom stuff is hot."

"Doesn't sound all that hot to me." Mara smiled again, and my dick twitched. "I like normal guys who are reliable and don't pretend to have superpowers."

"Good to know." I stood up again. "Now, I really have to get back to work."

Like a coward, I sprinted for the guest house.

And though I took dinner to Mara later on, I ate mine in the guest house office and sneaked into the little house only after the lights went out in her bedroom. I'd have to rethink my avoiding-Mara plan, since I was in charge here until Val and Eve came home. But for tonight, I'd stay away.

Only a hallway separated my room from hers.

Sleeping right across from her room didn't ease my problem south of the equator. Of course, I didn't actually get much rest. My brain had other ideas. It tormented me with hot dreams about Mara and her pink toenails and all the dirty things I wanted to do with her.

Chapter Seven

Mara

The next morning, while I showered and got dressed, my thoughts rewound to yesterday and how Ollie kept running away from me—literally. Only during our nature walk had he stayed with me and not acted weird about it. After that, he'd raced back to the guest house within minutes after every time he came over to check on me, and I wondered why he'd seemed so tense when he was talking to me. Duh. I'd acted like a complete freaking lunatic since the second we'd met. Screaming and fainting because I saw naked people? No wonder he had to run away from me.

Once I'd gotten over the initial shock, I had decided to face up to my fears. Peeking out the window at the nudists had served as phase one in my desensitization plan. Once I felt okay about that, I'd ventured outside, staying right by the house at first. Eventually, after my walk with Ollie, I got brave enough to march over to the grassy area where the other guests were hanging out.

Everyone must have seen and heard me when I'd screamed. Still, they all treated me kindly. Ruth Norris, who described herself as "the busybody who helps spread all the gossip, but only in a loving way," seemed to have made it her mission to get me acclimated. She took me around the lawn, introducing me to everyone and putting her arm around my shoulders anytime I got anxious.

She intuitively knew when I needed a little support. Despite their nakedness and my lack thereof, every single guest treated me like an old friend.

Ruth had suggested I sit on a chaise and observe the nudists to get acclimated.

"Maybe after that," she'd told me, "you won't want to leave anymore. We'd sure love to have you stay, Mara. And I know Ollie would like that too."

She'd winked at me when she said the part about Ollie.

Ugh. How could he possibly want me to stick around? I'd acted like such an idiot, and I'd kissed him—which he clearly hadn't appreciated.

So stupid, Mara.

This morning, I decided to hide out for a while in the little house where Ollie had generously let me stay. He had left a note on my door saying he went to the office in the guest house and I should help myself to the breakfast he'd left in the fridge for me. Sure, I'd gotten somewhat accustomed to hanging out with naked people, but I needed a break from my immersion therapy. A little alone time. To decompress.

Nothing helped me relax more than a nice warm bath.

Unfortunately, this house had a shower, not a bathtub.

Did the guest house have a tub? I really, really, seriously needed some relaxation time, preferably with bubbles.

I peered out the kitchen window and spotted Ruth Norris right when she looked in my direction. I waved until she noticed, smiling, then gestured for her to come here. She nodded and hustled to the door. When I opened it, she walked right in.

"What can I do for you, sweetie?" she asked.

"Um, well…" I hunched my shoulders, feeling weird about what I wanted to ask.

She put her arm around my shoulders and gave me a gentle squeeze. "Don't be shy, hon. Whatever it is, you can tell me."

"I was wondering if there's a bathtub in the guest house. I'd love a nice, relaxing soak."

"There is a soaking tub attached to the exercise room. It's a jacuzzi-type thing, so it's great for relaxing."

"Exercise room?" I bit the inside of my lip, imagining all the ways I could be humiliated by someone walking in while I was soaking. Even if I wore a swimsuit, I'd feel embarrassed. "That sounds kind of…public."

"No-no, sweetie, you can shut the door. Nobody will go in there without knocking first." She gave my bottom a little pat. "Go on. Enjoy yourself. I'll let the other guests know not to use the exercise room while you're enjoying jacuzzi therapy."

"Thank you, Ruth. You've been so nice to me, in spite of the way I acted yesterday."

"Never mind that. We all have bad days."

Ruth gave me directions for how to find the exercise room, then left to alert the other guests that the room was off limits for a while. She even suggested I put a scarf or something on the door handle so I could take it off when I left the exercise room. That way, everyone would be sure to steer clear until I was done.

God, I loved that woman. I wished she were my grandma.

My real grandmother was just like my mom. If the people here thought I was uptight, they should meet my family. I loved them, but Mom and Grandma had high standards I never quite met.

I grabbed my conservative black one-piece swimsuit—along with a towel, a bottle of bath oil, and a silver scarf—before I trotted to the guest house and found the exercise room on the first floor. Like Ruth had promised, the room was empty. I hooked my scarf around the knob and shut the door. Once I got into the jacuzzi room, I discovered the tub was already filled and hot, with the jets turned on, bubbling away.

After pouring a small amount of bath oil into the water, I climbed in.

Only then did I realize maybe I shouldn't have used bath oil. Would it mess up the jacuzzi? Since it was too late to worry about that, I put the worry out of my mind.

Oh God, the water felt incredible. It was just hot enough to soothe me, but not so hot I'd sweat like in a sauna. I hated those. Getting drowned in steam made me nauseous. But this jacuzzi... Wow, I could live in it. The bath oil released its soothing scents while I leaned back and let the bubbles tease my skin. A jet pounded into my back, easing the tension there, and I moaned because it felt so damn good. I'd been stressed for a long time, with no real means of alleviating it. Nothing I did was good enough for anyone, and heaven forbid if I tried something that wasn't on the approved list of activities for a socialite.

Last year, I'd wanted to go to Disneyland, and my parents had said it was "too gauche for a lady like you." Well, my mom had said that. Dad let her do all the talking when it was slap-Mara-on-the-wrist time. No actual slapping was involved, though. Purely the verbal kind. My mom never yelled at me or insulted me. She simply reminded me of the rules for people in our echelon of society.

Sometimes, I really, really wanted to do something crazy, something totally opposite of what everyone expected. Something naughty. Something that might actually feel good.

That jet felt damn good pulsing against my low back.

Maybe if I turned around and lifted my hips…

I grinned, feeling deliciously wicked just thinking about it. Maybe the nudist resort setting had affected me, but I had an urge I couldn't resist. So I spun around and knelt in front of the water jet, letting the bubbly power of it pulsate on my body, right at the juncture of my thighs. It didn't quite hit the right spot, the one that would send me straight to the land of happy endings. I wiggled around, trying to find the sweet spot, but none of the jets had the perfect angle.

Shit. I was getting hot, and not from the water temperature. The second I'd thought about using the water jet to get off, I'd gone so hot and slick I almost couldn't stand it. Feeling the jet pounding into my thighs and hips ratcheted up my arousal until my rigid nub throbbed.

I lay back in the tub and slipped my fingers inside my swimsuit, straining to reach my clitoris. I couldn't get there. The suit was too snug for my hand to fit. *Ugh.* I tried rubbing myself through the swimsuit, but that wasn't working either. I kept getting wetter and more anxious, craving that release, but I couldn't reach that hard, aching nub to push myself over the edge.

Fuck, I needed to come. Needed it so badly.

Well, if I took off my swimsuit…

No, I couldn't. What if somebody saw me?

Ruth had sworn no one would disturb me. They'd stay away until I took the scarf off the door to the exercise room. And besides, I was inside the jacuzzi room with that door closed too. Two doors separated me from the rest of the guest house.

Whimpering, I slumped in the tub. I'd never needed an orgasm so much in my life, like I'd go insane if I couldn't hit that peak.

I glanced around, like I expected to see someone hiding behind me or on the floor. Nobody around. Nobody but me and the bubbles tormenting my sensitized skin.

So I peeled off my swimsuit.

While I relaxed against the tub's rim, slipping my fingers between my folds, I tried to think of a good fantasy to help me get off faster. I rolled my clit between two fingers while I stretched out my longest finger to rub up and down my cleft, coating my fingers with the evidence of my horny state, making my them more slippery with every stroke. Oh God, that felt goooood. Shutting my eyes, I let a fantasy play out in my mind, a vision of Ollie with his head between my legs, lapping and teasing, his hands pinning my hips down while I thrashed and thrust my fingers into his hair.

I came so hard and so fast a sharp cry exploded out of me.

"Oh shit!"

That exclamation had not come from me. The intensity of my release had robbed me of breath, allowing only that one small, wordless cry.

My lids sprang open—and I screamed.

Ollie was standing in the open doorway, his eyes wide and his mouth open. He whirled around to face away from me, throwing one hand up. "Sorry, shit, I'm sorry. Should've knocked, but—Fuck, I'm sorry."

He ran away.

Oh. My. God. Had Ollie seen me... touching myself? He had definitely seen me naked. But somehow, the idea of that didn't freak me out like I would've expected. Instead, I got more aroused again thinking about.

But he was shocked and humiliated.

My cheeks heated up, burning like a bonfire of shame. How could I get turned on by a virtual stranger seeing me naked? While I was giving myself a happy ending?

I should've known the one time I cut loose and did something naughty, I'd get caught.

With my cheeks on fire and my stomach churning, I pulled on my swimsuit and left the jacuzzi room. The exercise room door hung open, my scarf still hanging on the knob. I snatched it up, shuffling across the threshold.

Ollie was there. Standing beside the door. He leaned against the wall, his arms crossed over his chest, his lips crushed into a sharp line. The light glinted on his glasses, making it hard to see his eyes.

"I'm sorry," I told him. "What I did was completely inappropriate. You must think I'm disgusting."

"Disgusting?" He pushed away from the wall, coming closer, so close the natural, masculine scent of him surrounded me. "You are so fucking beautiful, Mara. And the look on your face when you come… It's incredible."

Oh no, no, no. He *had* seen me and known what I was doing.

"I've never done anything like that before," I said, edging sideways to get a little distance from him. His proximity was making me horny again. That and the hungry look on his face. "I mean, I've done *that* before. Everybody has, right? But doing it in a public place and getting caught…" I shook my head, squeezing my eyes shut. "That's so not me."

A shuffling sound made me open my eyes.

Ollie advanced on me, forcing me to back up to the wall. His hands landed on the wall at either side of me, penning me there. "Nothing wrong with getting off the solo way. I do it too. But you weren't in a public place. This is a naturist resort. Everybody gets naked around here, except you."

"But I was… you know… where anyone could catch me." I wriggled against the wall, getting warmer and wetter down below, more and more every second that he stayed so close. "Ruth said she'd tell everyone to stay away from the exercise room, but still, I should've known better than to do…that."

"I didn't get the memo. Haven't seen Ruth this morning." He leaned in, bending his arms, bringing his face within an inch of mine. "Wish I could say I regret what just happened, but I can't. I loved seeing your body, all wet and slippery, and seeing that look on your face when you came. I want to be the one to make you look like that next time."

"But you were horrified when I kissed you."

"No, not horrified. Surprised. And you'd been so upset about all the naked people, I didn't want to take advantage of you." He grazed his lips over mine, making me suck in a sharp breath. "You're not freaked out anymore, and I want to kiss you."

"I want that too."

And God, did I want it. His lips. On mine. *Yes, please, yes.*

Ollie groaned, the sound resonating with hunger, and claimed my mouth. His warm lips pressed hard against mine, demanding a response, and I couldn't resist letting him in, loving the silken glide of his tongue on mine and the way he thrust it deeper, over and over, pumping it with movements similar to how he might thrust his cock into me. The rhythm of it drove me wild with need, and my nipples hardened. I flung my arms around his neck, plunging my tongue into his mouth, moaning at the taste of him and the feel of my nipples rubbing against his firm chest.

He pinned me to the wall with his entire body, bending his head to keep our lips locked. The swollen length of him pressed into my belly.

I hooked my leg around his, all but begging him to take me right here, right now. Never in my life had I wanted a man this much, and for once, I felt no shame about wanting all the dirty things that my mind conjured up for me.

He pulled his head back, breaking the kiss, though his body stayed plastered to mine. "That's how much I want you. Get it?"

Speechless, I could do nothing more than nod once.

"Good." He backed away, the bulge in his pants like a flashing neon sign announcing how turned on he was. "The next time I see you naked, I'll be the reason you get that look on your face. I'll be the one making you come."

He hurried off down the hall and up the stairs.

The next time? I wanted that to happen right now.

But being me, I couldn't summon the courage to run after Ollie and tell him that.

Chapter Eight

Naked Mara. *Fuck me.* She was beautiful and so damn desirable I wanted to jump in that jacuzzi and show her a much better way to get off. Instead, I kissed her and left. What kind of moron was I? Sure, my record with women wasn't exactly the stuff of legends—unless those legends centered on a loser who couldn't keep a girlfriend for more than six months. They all kicked me to the curb eventually, for a hotter guy who didn't wear glasses or work as a computer systems engineer.

These days, I was the assistant manager of a naturist resort. Didn't that make me cooler now? More attractive to girls?

Nope. Not one bit.

My last girlfriend, Heidi, had gone back to her ex to "give it one more try, just to be sure." I'd wanted to ask her why she'd dumped him in the first place if she wasn't sure about it. And why she'd hooked up with me before she made double sure. Christ, we hadn't even slept together, that's how brief our so-called relationship had been. I'd been the rebound guy, for probably the tenth time, the guy who cheered girls up after their dickwad exes broke their hearts. Once they felt better about themselves, they cut me loose. And how many times had I cringed while a girl gave me the heave-ho by saying I was like her gay best friend?

I guess they thought that was a compliment, but it sounded like an insult to both me and all the actual gay guys out there.

Behold the legend of the loser geek, see him on display at the Museum of Loser Geekdom. Buy your tickets today for half price.

At least I wouldn't have to see Heidi this summer. She and her friends usually vacationed here at least twice a year, but Heidi had stayed home last time and her friends said she wouldn't be with them when they arrived later this week.

I started to head for the office upstairs but stopped when I got to the second-floor landing. Why was I running away? Mara had seemed really into our kiss. I'd been so into it I had to walk bowlegged when I hustled away from her. Maybe I could still catch her.

Sure, I might be a loser in some ways, but I had total confidence in two of my skills. First, my computer creds. Second...

I vaulted down the stairs two at a time, sprinted for the exercise room, and froze in the open doorway, breathing so hard I had to slap my hands on my thighs for support.

Mara wasn't there.

Damn. Where did she go?

I waited a few seconds, until I caught my breath, then I took off down the hall and out the main door. Mara was just going into the little house, so I kicked it into high gear and barreled across the gravel driveway. Thankfully, I was still wearing shoes—and clothes, but I didn't thank anybody for the fact I was trapped in polyester—because if I'd run barefoot across the gravel, I'd have blisters the size of Texas later on.

"What's the rush, Ollie?" somebody shouted.

"Yeah," another somebody hollered, "where's the fire?"

"It's in Ollie's pants, that's where," the first voice shouted. "Guess Val's rubbing off on him."

I didn't bother to glance back or respond. Didn't give a shit who was razzing me or why. My mind focused exclusively on the vision of Mara naked and what I planned to do once I caught up to her.

At the door to Eve and Val's house, I had to stop. Bent over at the waist, hands on my thighs, I gasped for air like a ninety-year-old chain smoker. I exercised. I was in great shape these days, but now I could barely breathe. Well, I hadn't practiced barreling down a flight of stairs, through the guest house, and across the driveway. Never in my life had I literally chased after a girl.

What was up with me? This was not at all my style.

The one thing that had been up was now down. Way down.

I growled at my dick. "Wake the hell up, little buddy. We've got work to do."

Oh great. Now I was talking to my dick. Out loud. In public.

Shoving the door open, I hurried inside and stopped short of slamming the door shut. That might freak Mara out. So I eased the door closed and walked through the kitchen into the hallway that led to the bathroom, bedrooms, and Eve's photo studio. I should've announced myself. Really, I should have. It would've been the polite, not-a-creepy-stalker way to behave. My mouth still wouldn't work, though, what with my lungs insisting I wheeze.

In front of the bathroom door, I stopped to wait out the wheezing. Slow, steady breaths. Mara would scream again if I stumbled into her room sounding like a heavy breather on a sleazy phone call and looking like I might drop dead any second.

Soothing new age music came from her room.

Listening to the music, I closed my eyes and took those slow, steady breaths until I calmed down. Then I walked to Mara's door, which hung open—and my little buddy woke up fast.

She was doing yoga. Wheel pose. She lay on her back with her feet flat on the floor, knees bent, and her palms on the floor just above her shoulders. While I watched, paralyzed and speechless, she lifted her hips off the floor and held that position for a couple breaths. Slowly, she raised the rest of her body until only her palms and feet touched the floor. Her head hung down, her ponytail dangling. With her spine arched upward like that, her breasts jutted out, her stiff nipples obvious under her thin tank top.

Yeah, she'd changed clothes. No more capris or short-sleeve shirt. Now she wore snug yoga pants and a snug tank top.

She looked good enough to fuck. Right here. Right now.

My little buddy loved that idea, twitching like he was telling me to go get her.

Jeez, I really needed to stop calling it my "little buddy," even in my head.

I cleared my throat to let her know I was here.

Mara yelped and tumbled out of wheel pose into a heap on the floor.

"Are you okay?" I asked, rushing over to help her.

She was already helping herself, scrambling into a sitting position on her yoga mat. She laid a hand on her chest and blew out a breath. "Ollie, you scared me half to death."

"I know, I'm sorry." Why had I thought throat-clearing was a good way to announce my presence? Yeah, social skills weren't one of the two things I rocked at. I knelt beside her. "I hope you didn't sprain anything."

"No, I'm fine." She smiled at me in her shy way, which made me want to kiss her. "But you're so sweet for worrying."

Just once I wanted a girl to say, "Damn, Ollie, that was so freaking hot the way you scared the shit out of me." Okay, maybe I didn't want to hear that after all. It had sounded good when I thought it, but now I realized how stupid it was.

"Twice today I've surprised you," I said. "Swear I'm not stalking you or anything."

"I know that." She got up and stretched her entire body, making her tits jut out again. "I decided to do yoga to relax, but it wasn't really working anyway."

Somehow, I managed to get up without looking like a clumsy dweeb. "Are you still anxious about being around all the naturists?"

"No, it's not that. I mean, I still feel a little weird about it, but everybody's so nice here." She sat on the edge of the bed. "They're like a big, extended family."

"Yeah, we get the same people coming back every year." I settled onto the bed beside her, leaving a couple feet of space between us. "Some people come back several times a year."

"I can see why. It's beautiful here."

"You haven't seen the hot spring yet. It's amazing."

Mara caught her lip between her teeth and aimed those incredible jade eyes at me. "Would you show me?"

"Now?"

She nodded, still biting her lip.

I wanted to take that lip between my teeth and suck on it. Since I wouldn't tell her that, I said, "Sure. I can be your nature guide."

What the hell was I saying? I'd come here to show her the other thing I rocked at, but instead of seducing her, I was offering to be her tour guide.

"Maybe we could take the hike later," I said, leaning in closer. "I have something I want to show you first."

"What is it?"

I cupped her face in one hand, slanting in even more, brushing my lips over hers. "I want to make love to you, Mara."

Her breathing had become shaky, her eyes big and luminous. "You don't want to have sex with me, Ollie. I...get inappropriately excited about it."

I almost laughed but swallowed it. The look on her face convinced me she wasn't joking.

"Who told you that?" I asked, caressing her cheek with my thumb.

"My—my ex." She squeezed her eyes shut, scrunching up her face. "He said I need to temper my carnal urges because no man of good breeding wants a wife who gets too excited. Sex is for men, not for women. It's our marital duty."

"Why the fuck would he tell you that? Your ex sounds like an asshole."

"I'm sure my mom would agree with him if she knew about that part of my life. She very into what's proper, what society would approve of, stuff like that."

"No offense, but your mom sounds like an asshole too."

"She's not that bad, really. But my family, especially my mom, cares a lot about what's proper and what the rest of our peers think."

"Peers? Do you mean, like, royalty?"

"No." She opened her eyes to gaze into mine. "You're very sexy, Ollie, and I'd really like to be with you, but I couldn't stand it if you were disgusted with me."

"I won't be. But maybe we should talk a little first, so you'll feel more comfortable. I kind of sprang this on you." I pulled my hand away. "Or we could wait until later, or not do it at all. Your choice."

"Let's talk."

And then have sex, I hoped. Her family sounded pretty damn awful to me, but then, I came from a home where my mom and dad hugged us every morning and said, "Have a good day at school, sweetie, I love you." I would've bet good money that Mara's family didn't even shake hands without slathering on sanitizing gel first.

Maybe that explained why Mara had gotten so uptight.

"What did you mean when you said 'peers'?" I asked.

She bowed her head, gripping the mattress like it might fly up into the sky at any second. "My parents are wealthy. They circulate among the most prestigious social circles, they never say or do anything inappropriate, and they only kiss on the cheek in public. I've only seen them kiss on the lips three times in my entire life."

"But you love to kiss, don't you? And you're really good at it."

Her head came up, and those beautiful eyes focused on me again. "You think so? I do like it, a lot. I loved kissing you." She winced, then sighed. "And that's another thing that's not proper."

"Kissing me? Or liking it?"

"Both." She made a noise that was part growl, part whine, and covered her face with her hands. "I'm so sick of being proper."

"Then don't do it anymore."

She dropped her hands to her thighs, slumping her shoulders. "I'm already the family screw-up, so it probably doesn't matter what I do. Might as well go crazy, right?"

"I'm all for going crazy in moderation."

Mara stared at me like I'd gone totally insane. But when I winked and smiled, she seemed to get the idea I'd been kidding. Nobody went insane moderately. They went all the way or not at all. Or at least that's what I thought. I didn't have any experience with lunatics.

She almost smiled at my dumb joke, but the expression crumbled quickly.

"You're not a screw-up," I said. "Everybody makes mistakes. Even the uptight jerks who claim they never mess up."

"You don't get it." She made that noise again and flopped back onto the bed. "I can't even speak Japanese."

Okay, that was one thing I'd never heard on somebody's list of ways they'd screwed up.

I braced one hand on the bed beside her and leaned into it, gazing down at her face. "If that's the yardstick for being a screw-up, I'm just as bad as you are. I can't speak Japanese either."

"But nobody expects you to." She moaned pitifully, rolling her head side to side. "My mom is super proud of our Japanese heritage. So is my grandmother. My dad is half Dutch, half Welsh, but he doesn't expect me to speak Dutch or Welsh. My mom is so humiliated that I couldn't learn Japanese, even after years of lessons. I suck at it."

"It's a really hard language, huh?"

She moaned again, even more pitifully. "My mom learned it when she was a little girl. She's never been to Japan, doesn't know anybody in Japan, and the Kanda family has been American since my great-great-whatever grandparents moved here in eighteen eighty-three. But learning the language is like a badge of honor in our family." She pounded her fists on the bed. "And I can't speak Japanese."

"I won't hold that against you. I mean, I flunked out of high school Spanish and had to repeat it in summer school. Even then, I had to pay a girl in my class to tutor me so I could squeak by with a C minus."

"Are your parents Spanish? Do they think not speaking the language is shameful?"

"No, I can't say they do. And my family's part Scottish, part Italian, part French. That means we love plaid, we curse and spit at everybody, and we make awesome bread."

Her lips twitched like she might smile any second. "Thank you for trying to cheer me up. I'm sorry I went off on a rant about my family."

"Don't worry about it. Seemed like you really needed to get all that off your chest." I looked down at her chest, at those sexy tits barely hidden inside her tank top. "And I'd be happy to help you out by getting that shirt off your chest too."

She laughed, the sound completely feminine and melodic, like tiny bells tinkling.

First, I talked to my dick. Now, I was thinking about tinkling bells. Time to get off that track before my balls derailed for good and I turned into a girl.

It was also way past time I told her the truth about me.

"So," I began, in a not-at-all lame way, "are you really cool with the nudity? You can handle seeing more people in the buff?"

"Yes, I can handle it. You don't have to worry about me shrieking and fainting in your arms again." She crossed her heart with one finger. "Promise."

"Hey, I didn't mind the fainting in my arms part. But if you're really sure, there's something I need to tell you. Or maybe I should just show you."

"I'd love to see whatever it is you want to show me. I trust you, Ollie."

"You've known me for barely more than a day."

"Doesn't matter. I trust you."

"Well, uh…" I straightened, scratching the back of my head. "I kind of—Well, I didn't quite lie to you, but I wasn't completely upfront about something."

Mara sat up too, hitting me with a sweet smile. "Considering how much I freaked out when I first got here, I don't blame you for holding back anything."

"You really are the nicest girl I've ever met." I let my gaze travel down her body and back up again. "And the hottest girl I've ever met."

She waved her hands in a come-on gesture. "Tell me whatever it is. Or show me. Whichever."

"Okay." I got up and took off my shirt, trying not to smirk when her eyes widened and she bit her lip. When I ditched my pants and stood naked in front of her, I spread my arms wide. "I'm a naturist, Mara."

Her tongue slipped out to moisten her lips, and her gaze seemed to have stalled slightly south of my hips. "Oh. I see. No underwear? Whew, I *really* see."

"And you're okay with it?"

She nodded her head so vigorously her ponytail flopped around. "Absolutely."

I was so relieved my shoulders sagged.

Her tongue darted out again, and she looked up at me with her lips curled into the sexiest little smile I'd ever seen. "Can we get it on now?"

Chapter Nine

Mara

Ollie naked. Wow, wow, *wow*, he was hot. Maybe he didn't have an outrageously ripped physique all the movie stars did these days, but Ollie Jackson had more sex appeal than any of them. His chest offered enough muscles to make me want to run my fingertips over every single one of them, followed by my tongue. I wanted to taste his skin. Run my hands over those biceps, where they bulged a touch, enough to offer visual proof of how strong he'd be in bed. Strong and agile. A man who did yoga? Damn, that was the hottest thing ever—and he'd know all the best moves, the ones that required dexterity and agility. And those thighs. Powerful, but not overdone. I wanted to feel every sinew flexing while he thrust into me.

But I could not overlook the most incredible part of him.

His dick hung semi-hard, the shaft thick and long and sleek. No one would ever guess, seeing him with his clothes on, that he concealed one impressive package down there. The crown was reddening, the length swelling and rising.

"Your turn," Ollie said.

Sometimes, when a man wanted to have sex, I got embarrassed about undressing. Worried about what they'd think of my body. Not with Ollie. He'd already seen me au naturel, but even if he hadn't, I would never feel shame with him. He was sweet and sexy, strong and tender, all the best combinations of everything.

I stood and pulled my tank top off over my head, then stripped off my bra. Cool air teased my naked skin, but the way my nipples hardened had less to do with the air temperature than the gorgeous man standing proudly nude in front of me. I shimmied out of my yoga pants, dragging my panties down with them.

Ollie ran a hand over his mouth. "Mara, you're so damn beautiful."

"Thank you." I moved closer, splaying my palms on his chest. "You're the hottest man I've ever seen."

He slung an arm around my waist, tugging me into his body, his erection caught between us. "Time to show you the second thing I rock at."

"What's the first thing?"

"My tech skills."

I skated my palms across his chest in slow circles. "Wow. Hot and smart. I'm impressed."

"Wait till you see the second thing." He cradled my face in one hand and kissed me, slowly, deeply, with such erotic skill that I moaned. His eyes were hooded when he murmured in a sexy rumble, "Actually, it's more of a sensory experience than a visual one. An immersive sensory experience."

A tingle raced over my skin, and I couldn't breathe. The thought of having sex with Ollie got me more excited than I'd ever been before.

He ducked around me to pull the covers off the bed, then picked me up and laid me down on the soft mattress and the silky sheet.

I spread my fingers over the fabric, loving the smooth texture of it. "These sheets feel so good on my skin."

"*You* feel so good on *my* skin." Ollie grabbed his pants off the floor and dug a condom out of the pocket. He tossed it onto the table. "Can't wait till I'm inside you."

"Please, Ollie, hurry."

He straddled my body, his face hovering over mine.

A shimmering, sensual heat rippled through me, fanning out through my entire body like delicate waves on a sun-warmed pond.

"I've wanted to do this since I first saw you," he said, inching backward on all fours. "Can't wait anymore. Gotta eat you up."

He kept backing away until his head was above my hips, then he eased my thighs apart with one hand. When he lay down with his face inches above my mound, I sucked in a breath, knowing what he planned to do and craving it with a need so intense it made me a little lightheaded. He took off his glasses and tossed them onto the bedside table. I gripped my pillow with both hands, suddenly breathing hard, almost panting. Ollie smiled with a hunger that stole my breath as he lifted my legs to rest my knees on his shoulders.

The second his tongue touched my flesh, I gasped and jerked.

He nuzzled the hairs on my mound, darted his tongue out to tease my skin, and kept his gaze on mine the whole time. I clenched my pillow harder, my fingers punching into it. He thrust his tongue between my folds and circled it around my taut nub, his tongue so agile it encircled my clit, wrapping around it again and again, the silken warmth of it driving me wild.

"Oh, Ollie," I moaned.

"Call me Oliver."

"I thought…oh…you didn't like that."

"Now I do, while I'm feasting on you. I want to hear my full name when you come. Please do this for me."

"I will, Oliver."

He shoved his head as far between my thighs as possible and devoured me. His tongue lapped and swirled, his breaths blustered over my flesh, and his teeth scraped and nipped at me. I writhed wildly, panting and gasping and crying out, not giving a damn if anyone heard me. The pleasure mounted inside my body, a rigid coil winding tighter and tighter until my back bowed into the mattress and my head came up off the pillow. My knees drew up too, and I clutched his head while it bobbed as he tormented me with more and more demanding strokes of his tongue.

But when he stopped, I almost screamed—in frustration.

I gripped a handful of his hair and pulled his head up so I could see his eyes. "What are you doing? Don't stop. Make me come, dammit."

He chuckled. "You're so cute when you're sexually frustrated."

"Will you do it if I beg? Please, Oliver, please." It came out more throaty than pleading, but considering the way his eyes narrowed and he licked his lips, I didn't think he cared.

He drew in a ragged breath. "Fuck, that's so hot. Hearing you say my name that way."

"Oliver," I purred, letting go of his hair. "Make me come, please. Then I'll return the favor."

I swore his pupils blew right as I watched. His eyes became dark, shimmering pools of carnal need.

He pulled my clit into his mouth and rolled his tongue around it.

And I came, just like that. My fingers clenched his hair again, my entire body caved in, and the cry that exploded out of me echoed off the walls. The pleasure ripped through me in waves so powerful I lost my voice and my breath. He kept licking, kept tormenting me with the most wonderful blend of ecstasy and pain I'd ever experienced. My muscles spasmed with such intensity that I was sure I'd be sore later from the strength of this one unbelievable climax.

When it finally subsided, I collapsed onto the bed. "Oh. Wow. God. You weren't kidding. You absolutely do rock the sex."

"Glad you're satisfied." He sat back on his heels, kneeling near my feet. "But that was only phase one."

"Wait a minute so I can catch my breath and then it's my turn. I want to feast on you."

"Later. I'm on a mission right now."

I stretched my arms above my head, dancing my fingertips along the top of the headboard. "What mission is that?"

"To fuck you so long and so good that you'll never want to be with anyone else."

"Oh yes, please do that."

He rose onto hands and knees, crawling up my body, his expression one of pure hunger and determination. He wanted me that badly. I wanted him just as much, maybe more, so much that my pulse raced and my breaths came fast and short.

Growling softly, he skimmed a hand over my belly and up between my breasts, his fingers grazing them, setting off a flurry of excitement that tingled over my skin and made my clit pulsate. My skin grew so sensitized to his touch that I choked back a whimper, every brush of his fingers a beautiful torment. No one had ever touched me the way he did or made me feel the way he did. I'd known him for such a short time, yet I couldn't deny that I felt more comfortable with him than I ever had with anyone else.

Sex with a virtual stranger? Never, not me.

Except today. With him.

He dipped his fingers into his mouth one by one, moistening their tips until they glistened. When he swirled his damp fingertips around my nipple, not touching it, I wanted him so much I almost whimpered again. He circled his forefinger around and around, moving ever closer to my rigid peak, his focus intently on the task, until at last he brushed that finger over my nipple.

I gasped, my back arching.

"You like that," he murmured, his gaze shifting to my face. "You want me to take this"—he raked his thumb across my nipple—"into my mouth and make you squirm because it feels so damn good."

"Unh. Yes. Please."

He laved the peak with his hot tongue, leaving it aching and moist, the air chilling my skin, the sensation even more arousing. "You taste incredible, from your lips and your skin to your cream."

I could manage nothing more useful than a desperate grunt, since he'd latched his mouth onto my nipple again, suckling and swiping his tongue over it, nipping gently, all the while cupping my other breast in his hand. He massaged it and flicked his thumb over the peak, back and forth, on and on.

"Oh God, Oliver," I moaned. My voice grew strained and more desperate while his hand and mouth drove me to the edge of bliss. "Yes, oh God, yes, Oliver, I'm about to—"

He removed his hand from my breast and pulled his mouth away from the other one. A sexy smirk tightened his mouth. "Not yet, Mara."

I writhed, fisting my hands in my pillow, the pain of not quite coming so frustrating and yet so electrifying. "I can't take any more, please. Fuck me, Oliver."

"Damn, you just had to go and say that, with your voice all hot and sexy and needy."

"You sound hot and sexy and *hungry*." I glanced down at his cock, hanging between our bodies, and licked my lips. "Mm, I want your dick, Oliver. It's beautiful and big, and I'm sure it tastes even better than dark chocolate filled with caramel that melts on your tongue."

"I am hungry, but not for food." He hoisted my leg up, hooking it over his shoulder, and bracketed my body with his hands on the bed. "For you, Mara. I'll lose my mind if I don't do this right away."

"Do it." I set my palms on his chest. "Now, Oliver."

He thrust into me, filling my body, and began a sure, measured rhythm of strokes. I gripped his shoulders, hanging on while he pushed inside me and withdrew, over and over, every thrust a hot, silky glide of his flesh against mine, my body molding to his rigid length while I grew slicker and more sensitive. I experienced his every movement with a powerful surge of pleasure, not quite a climax, but getting closer every second. Never had anything felt as good as this. I clutched him with my hands and my body, and he lowered onto his elbows, bending my knee even further and giving him deeper access. I couldn't stop the words that tumbled out of me—desperate, greedy, lustful, wild cries.

"Ohmygodyes, Oliver! Please, yes. I love this, I love your cock, it's incredible, I love your body too. Oh God, you're the hottest man on the planet, please don't stop, don't stop, I'm about to—oh! God! Yes!"

My release struck so fast, and with such intensity, that I couldn't scream any more stupid words. I couldn't breathe, couldn't think, couldn't stop from sinking my nails into his shoulders and locking my free leg around his hip, needing him even deeper inside me while the waves of my climax thundered through me, shredding my self-control.

He came inside me while my body was still gripping him. I felt the pulsating rhythm of his release, even while I spiraled down from the heights of pleasure, dazed and beyond satisfied.

The mattress bounced, and I realized he'd collapsed onto it beside me. I had my eyes squeezed shut, tears trickling down my cheeks.

"Did I hurt you?" he asked, his tender voice close to my ear.

I shook my head, unable to do anything more.

"Can you open your eyes?" he asked, his tone becoming slightly amused. "I know I'm good, but I didn't think I was good enough to leave a girl paralyzed. Not sure that would be a good thing."

Pulling in a deep breath, I let it out gradually and forced my lids to open. My heart still pounded, but I managed to smile, as much as anyone could while stunned by the most amazing sex ever.

Lying on his side, he brushed sweat-dampened hair away from my cheek. "You are gorgeous when you come, especially the way you just did, like it was the first time and a sex bomb went off inside you."

"I think it did." I rolled onto my side, snuggling up to him, my head tucked under his chin. His skin was damp, and he smelled like sweat, but I loved it. "I said a bunch of stupid things a minute ago. Sorry."

"Don't be. I loved all the goofy things you screamed, especially the part about how I'm the hottest guy on the planet."

"What about when I said I love your incredible cock?"

"That was awesome too." He kissed the top of my head. "Everything you said got me going even more. I've never fucked a woman like the world was about to explode and it was my last chance to have sex. But damn, Mara, you made me that hot."

I looped an arm around him, skating my hand up and down his back. "Why don't you have a girlfriend? You're amazing."

"We met yesterday, so I'm not sure you have the info to make that announcement yet. But I appreciate." He sighed into my hair, his hands wandering over my body. "Truth is, I'm not that popular with girls. You wouldn't believe how many of them dump my ass by saying, 'You're like my gay best friend.' I mean, what the fuck? That's not what they screamed the night before."

Lifting my head, I gazed into his amber eyes. "I will never, ever call you my gay best friend."

His lips quirked into a crooked smile. "Thanks."

I studied him for a moment until I worked up the courage to ask. "What did those insanely stupid girls scream the night before?"

"Kind of what you did, but they weren't as good at it."

I was better than those silly girls. Maybe it was weird, but hearing him say that made me feel even better than I already did. My body had become deliciously relaxed, still warmed by our fantastic sex. I cuddled up to him again, but my tummy was starting to rumble.

"Hungry?" he asked.

"Mm-hm. But I don't want to move."

"I'll go into the kitchen and make us lunch." He wriggled away from my body, kissed me, and hopped off the bed. "Gotta call to check on lunch for the guests, but we've got great cooks. I shouldn't need to go over there." He leaned over the bed to run a hand along my thigh, sending an electric shiver down my skin. "That means I can focus on you."

Ollie walked out the door, stark naked.

And I lay on the bed, stretched out like a Roman empress. That man had given me the best sex of my entire life while making me feel sexy and powerful, not at all like a screw-up who couldn't keep a man.

Thank you, Ollie.

Chapter Ten

Ollie

I went into the kitchen and called to check on things at the guest house, then I gathered ingredients from the fridge to make lunch for Mara and me. While I whipped up my culinary creations, I thought about how this day had changed so completely from what I could've ever expected. I had sex with Mara. Holy shit, that happened. She'd freaked out when she first saw the naturists in the buff, but when she'd stepped out of that taxi I'd been dumbstruck by how beautiful and sexy she was. Mara had calmed down pretty fast after her freak-out. Though she swore was okay with naturism, I figured she must still have had some issues with it. She wanted to get past them. I knew that.

Not that I expected she'd ever become a naturist.

But damn, she had the body for it.

While I sliced cucumbers for a salad, I considered the problem of Mara. She had hangups, for sure. Her parents seemed to have done a bang-up job of convincing her she wasn't good enough—for anything. I'd never met them, but I already didn't like them. Mara seemed like such a sweet girl, and smart too. Not to mention amazing in bed.

I had fucked a woman I'd known for less than two days.

Yeah, I still had trouble wrapping my head around that one. I was a computer nerd who struggled to get dates and couldn't keep a girlfriend. As for one-nighters… Yeah, that never happened to me. How did I get so lucky today?

Mara wandered into the kitchen while I was finishing up. She'd put on the same outfit she wore earlier, with the capri pants and sandals.

"Sit down," I told her, pointing at the stools on her side of the island. "Lunch is almost ready."

She perched on a stool, folding her hands atop the island. "Thank you for making me lunch."

"It's the least I can do after the workout we just had." I couldn't help smirking when I remembered our time in the bedroom. "I've never had sex with a girl I barely know, but it was incredible."

Mara blushed a little. "It was wonderful. And I've never had sex with someone I barely know either."

"We're both first-timers, eh?" I slid two plates across the island, one for Mara and one for me, then I slid two glasses of lemonade over there too. The salads were on the plates, beside double-decker sandwiches. "Here you go. Figured we both needed a big lunch to catch up on the calories we burned in bed."

"I am starving." She pulled her plate closer and licked her lips. "It looks delicious."

"Dig in." I walked around to her side of the island and sat on the stool next to hers. "The sandwich is ham, turkey, and bacon with vinaigrette dressing and provolone cheese. I made the lemonade from scratch. The salad has thousand island dressing, but Eve made that. She always whips up a big batch of the dressing and puts it in glass jars herself so we can use them as needed."

"Wow, you don't get homemade dressing at a regular resort." She picked up her fork and ate a mouthful of salad. "Mm, yummy."

"Glad you like it."

She took her double-decker sandwich in both hands, biting off a sizable chunk. While she chewed, she closed her eyes and moaned.

My dick started waking up again.

"Uh, I'll go put on some clothes," I told her, sliding off my stool. "You're still getting used to the naturist thing, and I don't want you to feel weird about me sitting her in the nude eating a sandwich."

"That's okay. You don't need to do that on my account."

"It's no trouble."

Running back to my room gave me a chance to get a grip on myself. If I got hard every time I saw Mara, we were in trouble.

After putting on jeans and a T-shirt, I went back to the kitchen and to Mara. Her plate had the same amount of food on it as when I'd left.

"Don't you like it?" I asked, nodding at her plate. "You haven't eaten much."

"I was waiting for you."

She smiled shyly, which for some reason always got my dick excited, so I jumped onto my stool and started eating as a way to avoid looking at her. The food did taste pretty good. Maybe I couldn't keep a girlfriend, but I had three things I rocked at—computers, sex, and now food. Serving as Eve's sous chef, in the days before we hired actual kitchen staff, had taught me a lot about cooking.

Not that sandwiches and salad counted as cooking.

Mara moaned again while devouring her sandwich.

I shifted uncomfortably on my stool and focused on my own plate. Never in my life had I eaten as fast as I did now.

"Really hungry, huh?" Mara said.

"Kinda," I mumbled through the food I'd stuffed into my mouth. Swallowing, I said, "Tell me more about you. I know your family's rich, but what about you? Do you work?"

"Yes." She swigged her lemonade. "Mm, this is delicious too. I do have a business. Kind of. Like I said before, I'm basically in real estate."

"Right, I forgot you said that. What exactly do you do?"

She hunched her shoulders, staring down at her almost-empty plate while picking at the crumbs on it. "I sort of, um, own a building."

"You own a building?" I probably gaped at her like a moron, but jeez, I'd never met anyone who owned anything that big. "What kind of building is it?"

She winced. "An apartment complex."

I gaped some more. A minute, maybe longer, ticked by while I tried to cobble together words, any words, in the hopes I wouldn't come off as a total idiot.

"That's amazing," I finally said. "Do you run the place or just own it?"

"Everyone and everything in the building is my responsibility." She shut her eyes for a moment, then sighed and looked at me. "When I was twenty-two, fresh out of college, my parents bought the building and gave it to me as a graduation present. They said I needed to grow up and take responsibility for something, so I could prove to them I'm a mature adult."

"How did that go?"

"The building was empty, had been for a few months. My first job was to get the place in shape for tenants—the high-end kind, not the riffraff—and then attract those tenants."

"Sounds like a big project." I watched her face, though she'd turned it away from me to gaze toward the window above the sink. "You seem really smart, so I'm guessing you pulled it off."

Her gaze swerved to me, her eyes wide. "You assume I did a good job? That's not how anybody else felt. My parents were sure I'd screw up. They didn't say it outright, but I figured they must feel that way. I screw up all the time."

"Did you mess up with your building?"

She hugged herself, scratching her arms. "It wasn't easy. I hired contractors and decorators to fix up the place, always mindful of the fact I had to pay back the loans my parents had helped me get. Once the building was ready for occupancy, I came up with a marketing campaign to attract tenants. The complex was at full occupancy within two weeks after it opened."

"Your folks must've been proud."

She laughed, though it didn't sound cheerful. "My mom said she was glad I hadn't gone bankrupt yet, but that it would take several years to know whether I'd made the business successful. It's been years, and still she acts like it's a work-in-progress. Like I'm a work-in-progress."

"They never say they're proud of you, do they?"

"My dad does."

I studied her for a moment, trying to figure out why her Mom treated her like she was a mess. Mara was so sweet, not to mention funny and sexy and awesome at business stuff. I wished I had her skills at that. "I don't get it. You made your building a success, so why does your mom think you're a screw-up?"

"For all the reasons I told you earlier."

"Because you can't speak Japanese." I leaned over the gap between our stools, grasped her hands, and looked her square in the eye. "That's bullshit, Mara. I've known you for a day and a half, and already I can tell you're an incredible woman."

"It's more than not speaking Japanese." She glanced down at our hands. "I drove my husband away."

That sounded like bullshit too, especially considering what she'd told me earlier about her ex complaining she got too excited about sex. What kind of asshole was that guy? Mara was hot. More than that, she was a good person. She deserved praise, not insults from sniveling turds.

"I lied to you," she said, still staring down at our hands. "Well, maybe not outright lied. I let you believe I can't afford to buy another plane ticket to go home. The truth is, I don't want to go home because I'll get another lecture about how I screwed up yet again. Accidentally booking a vacation at a nudist resort? I'll never hear the end of it."

"Then stay." I lifted one hand away from hers to cup her cheek. "Hang out here with the crazy naturists. Chill out, enjoy the sunshine, go on nature hikes, whatever. I guarantee you nobody here will ridicule you or say you're not good enough. The guests are good people, like a big family, and they'll make you feel welcome."

And I'd never met anyone who needed a vacation more than Mara Severins.

She chewed on her lip, finally looking at me again. "I'd love to stay here. Is forever too long to book a room for?"

"I think we can arrange that."

"Thank you, Ollie." She gave me a tentative smile. "You're the nicest man I've ever met."

"Just doing my job." Now who was full of shit? I didn't say all that stuff to Mara because it was my job. I liked her, that's why I said it. "You can call me Oliver if you want. I usually don't like it when people use my whole name, but I love the way you say it. Especially when we're having sex."

Her cheeks dimpled with the cutest smile. "Okay, Oliver. I like your name, by the way. It's sexy."

My manly parts were about to get active again, so I had to make up a dumb excuse to get away from her for a few minutes. Just until I cooled down. Her smile, and her statement that my name was sexy, had way too much of an effect on me.

"Excuse me for a minute," I said, sliding off my stool. "Gotta hit the head."

The best I could hope for was that some time alone would let me figure out how to survive being around Mara, indefinitely, without walking around with a giant hard-on twenty-four seven.

Was that a pig flying past the window?

I returned to the kitchen a few minutes later, with my problem mostly under control, and found Mara standing at the sink. She was gazing out the window. I came up beside her to see what had caught her attention.

The guests were playing miniten.

Mara glanced at me, then returned her attention to the game going on outside. "What are they doing? I saw people playing that game yesterday, but I don't know what it is. Looks kind of like tennis or badminton, but they have bizarre boxes on their hands."

"It's called miniten. Naturists invented the game. Miniten is short for mini tennis." I pointed with my finger while I explained, "See, most naturist retreats don't have a lot of room for tennis courts, so they had to adjust the game to suit the space they had. Those wedge-shaped boxes are called thugs. Each player has a thug on one hand, which they use like a racket. Miniten is popular because it's more relaxed than tennis, so there's no need for jock straps or sports bras."

Mara leaned sideways toward me to whisper, "I think some of those people could use a little…support."

I chuckled. "Yeah, you're right. I'm sure the balls they're hitting aren't the only ones flying around out there."

"Not to mention the tits."

Her statement shocked me for about two seconds, then I grinned. "Mara, I love your sense of humor."

"Thanks." She grinned too. "You make me feel so comfortable that I can say all the things I would never say at home."

I slung an arm around her shoulders, tugging her close. "I'm sorry you feel that way at home. But here, you can be whoever you want to be."

The house phone rang.

Reluctantly, I gave up having Mara tucked under my arm and answered the phone. "What's up?"

"You're late," Ruth Norris said. "Yoga time was ten minutes ago, and the natives are getting restless. We might have an uprising if you don't get out there and lead them to serenity. And you know how Sylvester loves your yoga sessions."

Yeah, a seventy-two-year-old naturist did yoga. Why not? Sylvester was in better shape than he looked like he was. Having some flab didn't mean he had no strength or agility.

Just watching Sly play miniten proved that point.

"If they're dying for yoga," I said, "why is the miniten net still up? We need the space, unless everybody wants indoor yoga this time."

My outdoor yoga classes had become popular. I'd done the first one last summer when I was a guest, just for fun, but once I became assistant manager everybody begged me to make yoga a regular thing here.

"We'll take care of the net," Ruth said, "and you get yourself out here, cutie-pie."

"Be right out." I hung up the phone and faced Mara. "Sorry, I forgot about a yoga class I'm supposed to teach. Gotta go."

"I'll be fine, don't worry."

"Yeah, I know you will." I started for the door but stopped. "Do you want to come out with me? You can watch the class, and after, we can go for a walk down the nature trails."

"I'd like that."

"Cool." I swung the door open, waving for her to exit. "Beautiful, sexy ladies first."

She walked out, flashing me another shy smile.

And damn, my dick loved that.

Chapter Eleven

Mara

I felt hot all over, like I was in a sauna with the steam going full blast and those hot coals sizzling away. The coals were inside me, though. Red-hot, smoldering lumps of lust. It was completely Ollie's fault that I couldn't cool down. When he taught a nude yoga class, he should've handed out flyers with a big warning written on them in bright-red letters: "ALERT: You will get hot and bothered watching your gorgeous instructor move his sexy body into all those poses."

Never had I thought of yoga as salacious. Today, I did.

And I wasn't even paying attention to the other attractive young men in attendance. No one else interested me, only Ollie.

I might've thought that was because we'd had sex a little while ago, but something told me it was more than that. I felt comfortable with him, even when he was naked. Talking to him, I didn't feel like a loser who had let her family down over and over and over, or like the girl who couldn't keep a husband. Honestly, I hadn't wanted to keep Nico. Not at the end.

My phone chimed, indicating a new text.

When I checked it, I groaned. Nico. Did my ex-husband have psychic powers? Or had he bugged my phone so he could tap into the camera and spy on me? Neither, I knew, but he sure did have perfect timing.

Perfect for ruining my day. Yeah, he'd always been great at that. The text said, "Can we talk?"

I started to type a response but stopped. Why was I indulging him? He wanted to make me feel like shit, but I did not have to let him. So I deleted his text and slipped the phone back into the little purse-like bag for it that hung from a belt loop on my pants. The hem of my shirt hid it, not that I was worried somebody might steal my phone. Nobody here seemed like the type. Ollie had been right when he said everybody here acted like one big family.

Ollie was currently in standing splits pose, with one foot on the ground and the other leg raised almost vertical. Both his hands lay flat on the ground, his arms were bent, and his head hung upside down. Before we came outside, he'd taken his glasses off and asked me to keep them in my shirt pocket. Since I sat on a chaise facing sideways to him, he could see me if he glanced this way.

He did, and he smiled and winked.

I smiled and waved.

"Okay," Ollie said to his class, "let's kick this up a notch and move into a headstand. Slowly straighten your arms. Then we're going to push up with the foot that's on the ground and ease into the headstand."

"Jeez, Ollie," one young man said, "that's way too advanced for me."

"Then skip it. Nobody will think you're a wuss if you don't do this one."

Ollie eased into the headstand pose with grace and agility, having no trouble achieving it.

Another young man tried to do the headstand but tumbled out of it, muttering a curse.

"You okay?" Ollie asked.

The guy sat up and gave Ollie the thumbs-up sign. "Totally good, man."

Ollie's ability to do a headstand impressed me, but the part that got me really hot for him came a little later when they all got into downward dog pose. The basic version of it wasn't super sexy. The pose involved planting the hands and feet flat on the ground and straightening the arms and legs to get into a kind of inverted V position. I could do that pose. It was pretty basic, not an advanced move.

But when Ollie raised one leg straight up, I got a great view of his manly parts. Oh wow, the sight of his dick and his balls made me flash back to earlier, in my room, when we'd gotten hot and heavy—and I'd come like a supernova. God, he was fantastic in bed.

What would it be like to have sex with him outdoors?

I froze, stunned by own thought. Holy shit. I wanted to have sex outdoors.

But only with Oliver Jackson.

No, I couldn't do that. It wasn't proper. And what if someone caught us? What if my family found out I'd not only done the deed with a virtual stranger, but I'd done it outdoors?

I let my head fall back against the chair and expelled a long sigh. Why did I still care what my parents thought? I'd always done what they wanted, what they expected, and it had gotten me exactly nowhere. Sure, I'd done okay with the apartment complex. But I was divorced. Another failure.

My phone rang.

The noise made me jump, and I fumbled to get my phone out of its little case. I twisted around, trying to dig the phone out, but my fingers slipped. I lost my balance, since I'd apparently been leaning too far over, and flopped onto the ground with a yelp.

Crunch.

I'd landed on my stomach. My phone stopped ringing just as my chest collided with the ground—and crushed Ollie's glasses in my pocket.

Pushing up onto my knees, I winced as I pulled his glasses out. The lenses were broken.

"Are you all right?" Ollie asked, rushing over to kneel beside me.

"Yeah, I'm fine," I said, kind of whining when I spoke the words. I squeezed my eyes shut and offered him his glasses. "I'll pay for replacing them. It's my fault, I'm sorry."

He took the glasses. "It's okay, Mara. I have a backup pair."

"I'm such a klutz. A walking disaster."

"Come on, it's not like you shoved that iceberg into the Titanic." He laid a palm on my cheek, his thumb brushing over my skin. "Relax. Everybody has accidents."

I moaned miserably.

"Open your eyes," he said. "It's okay. Look at me, Mara."

Though I didn't want to, I looked at him.

He smiled and kissed me. It was soft and brief, but the feel of his lips made my tummy flutter.

"See?" he said, waving his other hand to indicate our surroundings. "You didn't destroy the world. I'd call that a win."

I couldn't help smiling. How did he know exactly what to do and say to make me feel better?

Ollie set his broken glasses on the chaise and helped me up. "I'll get my backup glasses and then we can take that hike. Would you be more comfortable if I got dressed?"

"No, that's okay. I'm getting used to being around naked people."

He kissed me again, then grabbed his glasses and headed for the little house.

I slumped onto my chaise, frowning down at the ground.

My phone rang again.

This time, I carefully pulled it out of its case. The screen told me who was calling—Nico. Oh great, that's exactly who I wanted to talk to right now. I didn't want to talk to him ever again, but I knew he wouldn't give up until I did.

So I answered. "What do you want, Nico?"

"I miss you, Mar-Mar. When are you coming home?"

"When I feel like it. And my name is Mara, not Mar-Mar. You know I hate that nickname."

"But you used to love it when I called Mar-Mar while we were making love."

I huffed. "No, I hated it then too. You ignored me when I told you so."

"We were good together. Let's not throw that away."

Good together? Was he on drugs? And he had filed for divorce, so he had no right to imply I'd thrown our relationship away. He did that all on his own. I knew my ditsy behavior had pushed him away, but he hadn't even tried to work things out. Even when I'd learned about his infidelity, I tried to work it out with him. What an idiot. I was better off without him.

"You and I are divorced," I told him. "That's the definition of 'over.' Stop calling and texting me, Nico, or I'll get a restraining order."

I hung up on him. And I had no idea if I could get a restraining order because my ex-husband was annoying the hell out of me. I hoped the threat would convince him to go away.

A throat-clearing behind me made me jump and squeak.

"Sorry," Ollie said, coming around in front of me. He wore his backup glasses, which looked just like his wrecked ones. "Didn't mean to scare you, but I kind of thought you hadn't noticed me there. Guess I could've done something more smooth to let you know."

"It's fine." I got up. "Let's go for that hike."

He screwed up his mouth and hummed like he was trying to decide whether to tell me something.

"What is it?" I asked, sounding a touch more…touchy than I'd intended.

"I sort of accidentally overheard the last part of that phone call. Your end of it, anyway."

"Oh." My shoulders slumped. "I suppose you figured out I was talking to my ex-husband."

"Yeah." He took my hand. "Let's talk while we walk."

I let him lead me down the nature trail into the woods. Birds twittered and sang. The breeze ruffled the trees. Above us, the sunlight filtered down to the ground, muted by the foliage, and its warmth seemed muted too. The heat I'd experienced while watching Ollie do yoga had given way to a slight chill.

Ollie led me down the path until we reached a spot where a downed tree lay alongside the trail. He motioned for me to sit on it.

I settled my bottom onto the tree. It was surprisingly comfortable to use as a bench.

He sat right next to me and clasped my hand again. "You don't have to tell me anything."

"But I want to. Not sure why, but I feel like I should tell you."

"We hardly know each other. You don't owe me anything." He clasped my other hand too. "But I'm here if you need to talk."

"It's my ex. Our divorce was finalized six months ago, and I haven't heard from him since. Until the day I arrived here, and he texted me to say he wants me back." I turned my face toward Ollie. "Nico called me today to say he misses me and wants to give it another try."

"What do you want?"

"Not him." I moaned again, even more miserably this time. "He cheated on me. I mean, he used to tell me all the time how I don't behave like a proper lady, then he goes and screws the checkout girl at the grocery store." I gritted my teeth. "At the store."

"He sounds like a real prick." Ollie gave my hands a little squeeze. "And he's obviously a moron. He had an incredible woman like you, and he went and fucked some checkout girl? If I ever meet him, I'll punch his lights out."

Maybe his anger should have shocked me, possibly even disgusted me, but it didn't. I got a funny warmth in my chest when he threatened to deck my ex. Nobody had ever taken my side when they found out Nico had cheated, and definitely not when we got divorced.

"You're so sweet, Ollie," I said. "But how can you be sure he's the idiot? Maybe I messed things up."

"No way. I get that you've got this complex about thinking you're a mess and screw everything up, but I don't see that at all. You're amazing."

"I feel so good when I'm with you. The sex was incredible, and I really want to do that again, but maybe we should spend some time getting to know each other first." I hunched my shoulders, afraid he might say no to the next part. "Like maybe a week with no sex?"

"Sure. Let's do that."

Relief sagged my shoulders. "I'm so glad you said yes."

He got up and held out his hand. "Time for me to show you more of my world."

I took his hand and let him lead me away.

Chapter Twelve

Ollie

Mara was so much fun to be with, which would've surprised me if we hadn't screwed each other's brains out earlier. She put on an uptight front most of the time, but when given the chance and some encouragement, she could cut loose like nobody's business. When we got to the hot spring, I made a joke about jumping in with our clothes on and how she was scared of nudity. She knew I was kidding.

"Is that a challenge?" she asked teasingly. "Because I'm not freaking out anymore, in case you haven't noticed."

"Oh, I noticed. But I'll bet you a free massage that you won't get in the hot spring even if you keep your clothes on."

"You're on."

She kicked her sandals off and took a running leap at the hot spring, splashing down with so much energy that the water sprayed up around her and splattered me where I stood six feet from the pool. She surfaced a couple seconds later, grinning and laughing.

I jumped in too, with my clothes on.

We got into a splash fight, both of us laughing so hard we had to stop to catch our breath. She was so fucking amazing. Anyone who met her for the first time would never realize she had so much joy inside her, just waiting to come out and play. I got to see it. She trusted me enough to show me the real Mara, the one she'd been afraid to show to anyone. I loved that. I liked her, a lot.

And I'd known her for less than two days.

Once I managed to drag Mara out of the hot spring, we headed down some of my favorite trails where we could see the birds and the wildlife, places I hadn't shown her yesterday. She got so excited when a deer trotted past us. The girl had never seen one in person. Never.

"How is that possible?" I asked.

We sat in a small clearing filled with wildflowers, their blossoms in full bloom—just like Mara, who had spread her petals today.

"I lived in the city, in Philadelphia, and never drove anywhere," she said, picking a small flower and studying it. "The few vacations I took were at big resorts. I've seen the beach in Tahiti, but not the woods in America."

"You never, ever left the city. Not even for a day."

"Well, I've driven through rural areas. But I never got out to do more than use the bathroom at a rest stop."

"Uh-huh." I was still struggling to wrap my head around that. Never seeing the woods? Or a freaking deer? "Guess I can't imagine living that way, but everybody's different. The city is your home. I found out a rural naturist retreat is where I belong."

She ran her fingers over the petals on the flower she'd picked, still focused on it. "Not sure the city is my home. It's all I know, but…" She dropped the flower and looked at me. "Being here, with you, I'm starting to wonder if I've missed out on what really matters." She sucked in a deep breath, her eyes fluttering shut. "I love the way it smells here, so fresh and clean and sweet. And the grass feels soft on my toes. It's wonderful."

I loved watching her face while she enjoyed all of those things and so much more. She seemed younger, and definitely freer.

We stayed in that clearing for a while, kissing and talking and kissing some more. I could've kissed Mara all day. Her lips were soft, and she tasted better than any woman I'd ever kissed before. Maybe I was kind of smitten. Maybe she didn't actually taste different from other girls. I didn't care, because I'd never felt this good in my life.

We went to the lake again too. Mara waded out into the water up to her knees, giggling when she realized how cold this water was compared to the hot spring. She waved for me to join her, so of course I did. At first, we held hands and splashed our feet in the water. Then, she slipped her arms around me, and I put mine around her, and we just stood there like that for a while. Eventually, we started kissing. Mara didn't seem to care anymore if someone stumbled onto us doing whatever the heck we wanted. Well, no tourists other than the resort guests could come here, since the lake lay on private land owned by Eve and Val.

While I gazed down at Mara, at her gorgeous green eyes and the cute smile on her lips, I found myself thinking about Eve and Val. They had seemed like complete opposites, and I supposed they still were, but their relationship worked despite that—or maybe because of it. They were business partners and partners in life. Spending every day with Eve and Val, seeing how their partnership encompassed every aspect of their lives and how they made each other stronger and better, it made me want that too. I wanted to find the right girl and share a life with her. I didn't know if Mara could be that woman, but I intended to find out.

A week of getting to know her. Yeah, that sounded perfect.

Except that I still had this little problem of getting turned on every time she smiled. When she'd jumped into the hot spring and emerged completely soaked, her shirt had gone almost transparent, and I could see her nipples. Oh yeah, hard-on alert.

I was an adult. I could handle this.

Probably.

We were relaxing on the beach, watching the gentle waves lap on the shore, when Mara asked me a question.

"Do you get along with your family?" she asked.

"Sure. My parents are good people, and they've always supported me in whatever I wanted to do." I winced, realizing how that might sound to Mara. "Not that I'm bragging or something. I'm sorry your family isn't like that."

"It's okay. You don't need to apologize for having good parents." She smiled shyly. "They certainly raised an amazing son."

Her compliment made me feel a little weird, or maybe I was embarrassed. Hard to say for sure. But I knew without any doubts that I liked the way she made me feel.

"My family isn't as bad as you think," she said. "My mom is always there for me when I need her. When I was growing up, anytime I got sick she would make me soup or get ice cream for me, and she'd sit by my bed reading stories to me. She and my dad would take turns doing that."

"Then what's up with the 'you have to be proper' garbage?"

She shrugged. "My mom and grandma worry about stuff like

that. We have to fit into the level of society we're in, where people care about appearances more than anything else."

"No offense, but that's dumb."

"Yeah, I know. But I'm stuck in that world, so I have to try to be what people expect. A proper lady."

I couldn't imagine how stressful that must've been. Constantly worrying about how other people viewed me and whether I'd lived up to their expectations sounded like the definition of hell.

No wonder Mara had been so uptight.

"Do you have any brothers or sisters?" she asked. "I don't. Only child here. But I always wished I had a brother or sister."

"I've got one sister, Bailey. She's fourteen and likes to call me Liver."

Mara laughed. "Liver?"

"Yeah, it's short for Oliver." I shook my head but felt my mouth tightening into a closed-mouth smile. "She's a brat, but I love her anyway. You have to cut teenagers some slack, because their brains haven't grown any common sense yet."

"When I was a teenager, I never did anything I wasn't supposed to do. I was the shy girl nobody wanted to be friends with."

"I would've been your friend. As the nerd with glasses who loved computers, I didn't fit in either."

"But now you do." She glanced around, her lips curving into a soft smile. "You found where you belong, didn't you? I can tell how much you love this place."

"I do love it. But it's more than the trees and the hot spring. I love the people too."

She aimed her smile at me. "I can see why. They're really nice people."

After our visit to the lake, we headed back to the main resort area. Nobody was using the lawn where the miniten net had been set up earlier, but I knew why. It was time for the weekly bingo competition. Everyone would be in the dining hall for that.

Mara and I joined the game. She won twice, earning two snack-size bags of candy. Afterward, we relaxed on the lawn watching one of the guests lead an impromptu tai chi session—nude tai chi, of course. Mara seemed fascinated by the slow, precise movements.

She tore open one of her candy packets and dropped one of the chocolate-covered peanuts onto her tongue. Sealing her lips, she smiled faintly while she let the chocolate melt in her mouth and hummed with satisfaction. Then she chewed the peanut, slowly, almost sensually.

I wanted to drag her down onto the grass, strip her naked, and give her a different reason to hum like that.

"Want one?" she asked, holding a peanut to my lips. "They're so yummy."

She said that like a chocolate-covered peanut was the most succulent, delicious thing on earth, like she wanted to devour the entire bag while writhing on the ground in ecstasy.

Okay, maybe that was my fantasy, not what she actually wanted to do. Licking melted chocolate off her body... Yeah, I wanted that.

"Are you allergic?" she asked. "To peanuts, I mean."

"No, not allergic." I closed my mouth around the candy and her fingers, lapping up every molecule of chocolate before I chewed and swallowed the peanut. "Mm, you're right. That's really good."

But it didn't taste as good as Mara.

We had sex this morning, but I wanted her. Right now.

I'd told her we should get to know each other better before we got naked again, so I had to keep to my own word. For the rest of the day, we talked and hung out with the other guests and fed each other peanuts until both of the bags she'd won were empty.

At the end of the evening, I kissed her cheek to say good night at the door to her room.

Did I sleep? Sort of. But I dreamed about Mara—that smile, that body, the way she felt wrapped around me.

A week without feeling that again. I might just go insane.

Chapter Thirteen

I'd learned a lot about Ollie in one day, but the next three days taught me even more about him. Not only did he teach yoga, but he also entertained the guests with music, singing and playing the guitar like he had for me on that first day. On the second evening of my stay here, everyone gathered around the fire pit behind the guest house to toast marshmallows and have a good time.

I'd never seen a fire pit like that one, but it was a nice way to have a small bonfire without worrying about how to contain it. A circular brick enclosure surrounded the pit itself, which looked like a large metal bowl. A mesh screen formed a dome over the fire, but Ollie took that off so everyone could toast their marshmallows.

The newest guests, who'd shown up the day after I'd come here, had brought their children with them. Those boys put on a hilarious play about a dragon and dueling knights, with the bonfire as their backdrop.

After that, Ollie took center stage.

Well, he took center lawn. Ollie sat on the grass, cross-legged, and played his guitar so beautifully that he ought to have been a musician, not a computer systems engineer. But when he started to sing, he enthralled me. I'd heard him sing before, but his talent still amazed me. His voice wasn't polished like he'd taken years of lessons. He sang in a natural voice that suited the low-key pop songs he'd chosen to perform. I loved listening to him. His voice made me feel warm in a very different way from the warmth he gave me the rest of the time. This wasn't lust. His singing gave me a good feeling deep inside, one that morphed into a glow in my chest.

After every song, the crowd clapped and whistled. A few people whooped. I was one of them. God, Ollie was incredible. I wanted to see him perform his musical act in the nude, but he still insisted on wearing clothes for my sake.

Though I had gotten used to the nudists, once in a while they surprised me.

On the afternoon of the third day, Ollie had to do some assistant manager work, so I headed down the nature trail on my own. Ollie and I had taken several walks together, and I knew the way. I'd asked him to meet me at the hot spring when he got done with his work, but on the way there, I decided to detour down one of the side trails where he'd shown me a meadow full of wildflowers that attracted lots of butterflies.

I loved that meadow. On this day, the sky was pure blue, and the sun beamed down on me to toast my skin. I spent some time there, enjoying nature, but I didn't keep track of the time. What did it matter? I'd wanted to escape from my structured life in the city, so here I was ignoring the clock and reveling in the beauty of nature.

After a blessedly indeterminate length of time, I returned to the main path and followed it until I reached the junction with the hot spring trail. I turned down that path, but only got a little ways before it happened.

I had just rounded a curve in the trail and when I saw a gray-haired man standing alongside the trail, maybe twenty feet away. He faced sideways to me and had his head down, focused on his hand that cupped his penis.

And he was urinating. Right there. In full view of anyone who walked down the trail.

In full view of me.

"Oh!" I said, slapping a hand over my eyes. Realizing how dumb that was—I'd been around nudists all day every day for the past several days—I lowered my hand and focused on his face.

The man smiled and shrugged. "Sorry. I didn't think anybody would be on this trail. Everybody's playing badminton or watching the games. Everyone except you."

Since this man was clearly in his seventies, maybe even eighties, I decided he wasn't a pervert. He just needed to pee.

I was very proud of myself for not screaming or fainting.

"Don't worry about it," I told the man. "Sometimes you can't fight the call of nature."

My new friend ambled back to the trail and approached me. He offered me his hand to shake—the hand he hadn't used to hold his dick while he relieved himself. "I'm Carl Weatherman. And no, I never worked as an actual weatherman."

He smiled when he said that.

I shook his hand. "Mara Severins. You just got here this morning, right?"

"Yeah, me and my wife got here today."

That meant he probably hadn't heard about me, the idiot who screamed and fainted when she got her first glimpse of nudists. He must've wondered why I wore clothes, but he didn't say anything about that.

Carl wanted to go back to the guest house, so I walked back to the junction with the main trail with him to keep him company. We chatted about how beautiful it was here and how all the other nudists were so nice. He finally asked the obvious question when we stopped at the trail junction.

"It's none of my business," he said, "but I'm wondering why you wear clothes. This is a naturist resort, after all."

"Yeah, I wondered when you'd ask me that." I bit my lip while I considered how best to answer. Well, he'd probably hear about my freak-out sooner or later. Might as well get it out there now. "My travel agent made a mistake and thought naturist meant birdwatching and observing wildlife. So when I got here, I wasn't prepared for all the nudists. I shrieked and passed out. I've gotten used to all the naked people, but I still don't feel comfortable going au naturel."

"This is a clothes-optional resort, so keeping your duds on is acceptable. Maybe one day you'll try it our way." He patted my arm. "Never know, kid, you might enjoy it."

Carl and I said goodbye, and I went back down the trail to the hot spring. Ollie wasn't here yet, so I kicked off my sandals and sat down on the rocky ledge that surrounded the pool, letting my feet dangle in the water. I swung my legs, splashing my feet in the blue water, loving the silky warmth of the hot spring. It felt so nice, but I wanted to experience it all around me like I had the first time, when Ollie brought me here. I'd dived into the spring with my clothes on, but today, I wanted to feel the steamy water on my skin.

I couldn't. I mean, I was the girl who went wacko when I saw naked people eating lunch in a cafeteria.

But things had changed since then. I had changed. Ollie had shown me how to relax and take pleasure in the simple things without worrying about whether other people thought I was an idiot. He'd helped me loosen up in record time, but I knew I still had a ways to go before I'd shed that part of me for good. Eventually, I'd have to go home—to my family and to the disapproval of those high-society idiots who turned their noses up at my sometimes ditsy behavior. Would this new version of me, the one I really liked, disappear when I left the resort?

God, I hoped not. But just in case, I wanted to revel in my newfound freedom as much as possible before I had to leave this magical place.

I got up, glancing around to make sure nobody was around, then I stripped off my clothes. A breeze tickled my skin, and my nipples went rigid from the cool kiss of the air. I walked to the very edge of the rock ledge that encompassed the spring, my toes curled over its rim, and gazed down at the beautiful blue water and the steam wafting up from it.

Then I dived in, cannonball style.

Water plumed up around me.

I sank beneath the surface, bobbing up out of it. Laughter bubbled out of me, and I dived under the surface again, springing up out of the water, laughing even more, squealing when a wavelet lapped against my face. I couldn't remember the last time I had this much fun. Well, fun that didn't involve Ollie naked on top of me.

And I had never felt this free, except with him.

Paddling around the pool, I flipped over to do the backstroke and then moved into the center of the spring to float on my back. The sun shined down through an opening in the trees, casting its glow on the water around me and on my face. I shut my eyes while I swirled my fingers in the water, letting the rest of the world drift away until nothing remained except the sound of the breeze rustling the trees and the birds twittering.

"Mara?"

Ollie's voice pulled me out of my meditation. He stood near the edge of the spring, looking down at me with a confused expression.

I swam to him, folding my arms on the ledge. "There you are. I thought you'd forgotten about me."

"That won't ever happen." He knelt to get closer to me. "You're swimming. Naked. In the outdoors."

"Mm-hm. It feels wonderful." I splashed my hand in the water, some of the spray landing on his face. "Have you ever made love in the hot spring?"

He swallowed hard enough I could see it, and his voice dropped to a husky register. "No, I've never done that. Everybody knows Eve and Val did that once. Probably more than once, but nobody's caught them since that first time. I wouldn't want to be a copycat."

"But I want you, Ollie. Want you so bad."

"I, uh…" He blinked several times and shook his head, like he was trying to clear his thoughts. "I want you too, Mara, but there's been a complication."

"What's wrong?"

"Your parents are here."

Everything inside me froze, mutating into solid ice. My parents? Here? At a nudist resort? *Oh shit, shit, shit, shit, shit.*

I scrambled out of the hot spring, pushing Ollie over in the process, and struggled to get my clothes on. Taking them off had been so easy, but now I couldn't seem to get them back on the right way. Words tumbled out of me while I fought with my clothes.

"They can't see me like this, they can't. Naked? In public? Oh God, they'll have me committed or arrested or—"

"Stop." Ollie grasped my shoulders, turning me toward him. "Take a deep breath and exhale out all that anxiety and panic. Come on, Mara, you can do it."

I drew in one shaky breath, letting it out slowly.

"Again," Ollie said, his voice so calm and soothing that I believed I could shake off the panic as long as he stayed with me.

I pulled in a less shaky breath, blew it out, and inhaled a good, deep lungful of clean air. No quivering breath this time when I exhaled. I released the air in my lungs little by little, feeling the anxiety melt away.

Ollie smiled tenderly and brushed hair away from my eyes. "There. See? You did it."

"Yeah, thanks to you." I moaned pitifully. "But my parents…"

He kissed me, hard and quick. "You are an adult, Mara. You don't need anyone's permission or approval. If your parents are dicks about it when they realize this is a naturist resort, that's their problem."

Easy to say... Not so easy to believe.

Dammit, girl, you can do this.

I squared my shoulders, lifted my chin, and nodded once with conviction. "Yes, I can do this. Once I get my clothes on the right way."

Ollie grinned. "I can help you with that."

He did help me, and I loved feeling his hands on my body again, even it was purely to get my clothes on right. He kissed me again, slower and hotter, giving me the boost I needed to face my judgment day.

Ollie took my hand, leading me back toward the guest house—and my parents.

Chapter Fourteen

Ollie

Nothing had prepared me for walking in on Mara swimming in the hot spring in the nude. Sure, I'd seen her naked before. Once. We'd done the deed, but somehow, seeing her frolicking in the hot spring without a stitch of clothing on had hit me harder than the first time I'd seen her naked. Surrounded by the blue waters, she looked so peaceful and so damn sexy.

But her tranquility evaporated when I told Mara her parents were here. Still, she was handling the news better than I'd expected.

The closer we got to the main resort area, the more we could hear the badminton game unfolding out on the lawn. Some of the younger guests, who were in their twenties like me, had wanted to make badminton a contact sport. The guys kept bumping chests and whooping, and the girls hopped up and down while giggling.

I told them to please calm down, but I guessed as soon as I'd left the vicinity, they'd gone wild again. Their screams and whoops echoed through the open area beyond the last bit of trees at the end of the nature trail.

Mara stopped us within sight of the trailhead. She chewed on her lip, staring at the vague shapes of human beings we could see through the trees.

"You okay?" I asked. "It's cool to take a minute before we go out there."

She sucked in a breath, rolled her shoulders back, and gave me a tight smile. "It's okay. I can do this. About time I stood up to my mom, anyway."

"I know you can do it. You're one amazing woman, Mara. Don't forget that."

"Thank you, Oliver."

Every time she called me Oliver, I wanted to tear her clothes off and make her scream my name. Since I couldn't do that right now, I settled for kissing her.

More whoops and shrieks erupted beyond the trees.

I led Mara out of the woods.

Some guy shouted, "Go for it, Tad! All the way!"

Just as Mara and I reached the edge of the lawn, maybe fifteen feet from the edge of the makeshift badminton court, it happened.

"Go for it for real, dude!" someone hollered.

Everything seemed to unfold in slow motion. I saw the shuttlecock, that comet-shaped ball, fly through the air. And I saw a muscular guy with buzz-cut hair leap high off the ground, his racket outstretched, determined to whack that shuttlecock. He missed and kept sailing, sailing, sailing through the air...

The guy slammed into Mara.

My hand was torn from hers. I tripped and hit the ground rolling.

And Mara screamed.

I came to a stop facedown on the dirt and lifted my head to see what had happened to Mara.

She lay on her back on the ground.

The shuttlecock guy had landed smack on top of Mara, but in the opposite direction. His face was between her thighs, and his dick was crushed to her face.

Mara screamed again, flailing her arms in an attempt to shove the guy off her.

I scrambled to my feet and rushed to her. "Get off her, you dickwad."

The guy seemed stunned, and he didn't move.

So I thrust my hands under him and pushed the shuttlecock ass off Mara. He ended up on his back beside her, laughing so hard his eyes watered.

"Are you okay?" I asked Mara, kneeling beside her. "Did that jerk hurt you?"

She shook her head, but her lips were trembling.

I picked her up and cradled her to me, kissing the top of her head.

And I glared at the dickwad.

He was still laughing.

"Shut up," I snarled at him. "Get your shit and get the fuck out of here. You're banned from Au Naturel Naturist Resort for life."

The idiot stopped laughing. "What? You can't do that, man, it was an accident."

"I told you to calm things down and behave like grown-ups. You and your pals think it's funny to act like lunatics, but we do not condone that kind of behavior here. Your broke all the rules." I hugged Mara tighter. "Get out of here. Right now."

The guy stared at me for a moment, then got up and slunk back to the guest house. His friends followed him.

Every single one of the remaining guests started clapping and cheering.

"Way to go, Ollie!" someone shouted.

Ruth Norris gave me an appreciative nod.

Mara, snug in my arms, was gazing up at me like I'd just defeated Godzilla single-handed. "Thank you, Oliver. You're my hero."

I opened my mouth but couldn't think of a damn thing to say.

Two people, a man and a woman, stood separate from the crowd, doing their damnedest not to look at all the naked guests. The woman lifted her chin and marched straight up to me and Mara. The man trailed after her. He had auburn hair and green eyes like Mara, and the woman had Mara's golden skin coloring and almond-shaped eyes. I'd met these people earlier, so I knew who they were—Peter Severins and Sheryl Kanda Severins.

They were Mara's parents. If I hadn't met them already, I would've guessed who they were based on their clothes. Mrs. Severins wore a navy pantsuit that I figured was designer, not that I knew squat about women's clothing, and her husband wore a gray suit and tie.

It was eighty degrees today.

Mrs. Severins puckered her lips, narrowing her gaze on me. "What have you done to our daughter?"

"Uh, I was just helping her—"

"She's filthy. And wet."

Yeah, Mara's dip in the hot spring had gotten her clothes wet when she put them back on, and her hair was still drenched. Since she'd gotten knocked down by that asshat, she now had dirt on her backside.

Mara wriggled in my arms like she was trying to get free.

I set her down.

She straightened her clothes and patted her hair, but apparently realized there was no hope of fixing that without at least a hairbrush.

"Ollie didn't do anything," she told her mother. "That jerk rammed into me, and Ollie dealt with the situation. That's all."

Mrs. Severins squinted at Mara. "Why are you wet? You're a mess. What's happened to my proper, ladylike daughter?"

"I..." Mara's expression fell, and her shoulders drooped. She spoke in a small voice when she said, "I was just having fun in the hot spring."

The word proper seemed to have been the trigger for Mara's change in attitude. I wanted to butt my nose into the conversation and tell Mrs. Severins to go jump in the hot spring headfirst, but it wasn't my place to do that. Mara needed to stand up to her parents on her own. I knew she *could* do it, but I had no idea if she *would* do it. She'd only just gotten used to being around people who played sports in the buff.

Mara slumped more and gnawed on her lip.

Sheryl Kanda Severins grasped her daughter's arm. "You're coming home with us this instant."

For a second, I thought Mara would leave with her parents.

But then she lifted her chin, straightened, and said, "No."

"No?" her mother repeated. "Mara Tamiko Severins—"

"I said no, Mom." Mara crossed her arms over her chest. "I'm staying here. With Ollie." She grabbed my hand, tugging me closer. "This is Oliver Jackson—my boyfriend."

This was news to me. Boyfriend? Sure, we'd had sex once and had been hanging out a lot since then. But she never told me I was her boyfriend. Not that I minded. Actually, I kind of loved the idea.

Mrs. Severins launched into a tirade that I couldn't understand, so I guessed it was in Japanese. Mara seemed equally confused, which confirmed my suspicion about the language her mom was speaking. That day when we'd gotten it on in her bedroom, Mara had moaned, "I can't even speak Japanese." That had been the cutest thing ever, until I realized she wasn't kidding. She felt like a failure because she'd never mastered that language.

Her mom knew Mara couldn't understand Japanese. So why was she barraging her daughter with words that made no sense to her?

"Stop it, Mom," Mara said. "I know you love to babble in Japanese when you're ticked at me, but you know I have no clue what you're saying."

Mrs. Severins shut up, though she still looked pissed.

Her husband cleared his throat. "Your mother is saying a lot of things that I won't translate. Honestly, Sheryl, I've never heard you curse so much. Mara is an adult, and we need to respect her decisions even when we don't agree with them."

Okay, I liked her dad a lot more now. Definitely more than her mom. But I supposed I shouldn't condemn Mrs. Severins right off the bat since she might've been in shock from finding out her daughter had been staying at a naturist resort.

Mr. Severins offered his hand to me. "I'm Peter Severins. It's nice to meet you, Oliver."

I shook his hand. "Nice to meet you too. You can call me Ollie."

"Thank you, Ollie. You can call me Peter." He glanced at his wife. "Don't be rude, Sheryl. Say hello to the man our daughter is dating."

Mrs. Severins shuffled closer to me and held out her hand, limply. "I am Sheryl Kanda Severins, Mr. Jackson."

"It's Ollie." I shook her hand, but she didn't clasp mine at all. "Mara's told me a lot about you guys. It's good to finally meet you."

"I'm sure."

Peter threw his wife a long-suffering look.

She rolled her eyes at him, then sighed, squared her shoulders, and aimed a polite smile at me. "Please call me Sheryl."

"Thanks."

I wasn't sure I wanted to call her Sheryl, considering her husband had goaded her into saying that.

Sylvester Norris walked up beside Mara's mom—completely nude, of course. All his manly bits were swinging free when he patted Sheryl's shoulder and announced, "It's a real pleasure to meet Mara's folks. She's such a sweet kid, and smart too. You must be proud of her."

Mara's mom turned her face toward Sly and forced a polite smile. But then she made the mistake of glancing down—a lot of newcomers who aren't already naturists make that mistake, it's like a reflex action or something—and her eyes bulged bigger than I'd ever seen anyone's eyes do. Her mouth gaped open, and a strangled gasp burst out of her. Her jaw flapped.

I swore she looked like a fish that got yanked out of the water. All she needed was a hook jammed into her cheek.

And I kind of felt sorry for her. She wasn't used to this sort of thing. I also finally understood where Mara got her fear of naked people. It wasn't proper, after all.

Sly, oblivious as usual, grabbed Sheryl's hand and shook it. "I'm Sylvester Norris. That's my wife, Ruth, over there." He nodded toward Ruth, who stood several feet away. "We're so dang pleased to welcome you to our home away from home, Au Naturel Naturist Resort."

Peter slung an arm around Sheryl and gently pulled her away from the naked man who was smiling at her. Sheryl's face had gone pale, and she looked like she was on the verge of fainting or throwing up. Jeez, it wasn't like a porcupine had jumped her. Having experienced that myself, I would've sympathized a lot more if Mara's mom had gotten chased by one of those buggers. But this was just an old fart who let everything hang out.

What was it with the Severins women and nudity?

"Calm down," Peter told his wife in a patient, soothing tone. "That nice man is naked, but he's not going to hurt you. He wants to say hi, that's all."

Another senior citizen nudist, Ralph Edwards, trotted up to Sheryl and offered her a bottle of whiskey. "One swig of this and you'll feel all better. Trust me."

Sheryl stared at Ralph's face for a few seconds, then swerved her attention down to his equipment. Her cheeks turned pink, which seemed like a step up from her pale-and-about-to-barf expression.

Finally, she took the bottle. "Thank you."

She sounded a little hoarse, but at least she was speaking a language everyone here understood.

"No problem," Ralph said, smiling. "A shot of Jack Daniels always makes me feel better."

Ralph moseyed off, disappearing into the crowd.

Sheryl took the cap off the bottle and downed one huge swig of whiskey. She ran the back of her hand across her mouth and gave her husband the bottle. "I would like to speak to my daughter in private, please."

"We can talk," Mara said, "but with Ollie there too."

Mara's mom pursed her lips, lifting her chin.

Peter waved the whiskey bottle in her face. "Maybe a few more gulps of this will loosen you up, Sher."

His wife flashed him a frown, then smiled politely at me. "Of course, Ollie. You may join us, if that's what Mara wants."

"It is," Mara said. "Thank you, Mom."

Sheryl tugged her suit jacket down and smoothed the lapels. "Where may we speak in private?"

"In the caretaker's house." Yeah, I'd just made up that name for the place, since I figured Mara's parents wouldn't understand if I called it Eve and Val's house. "Follow me."

Mara clinched my hand tighter as we led her parents away from the congregation of nudists.

Mara

Ollie and I sat on the stools at the kitchen island while my parents stood on the other side. My mom had refused to sit even when Ollie invited her to take the other stool. After that, Ollie had suggested we go into the living room, since it had plenty of comfy places to sit.

My mother said no. Curtly.

Dad threw her a chastising look, but she ignored it.

So here we were, Ollie and I on this side of the island and my parents on the other side. Dad leaned back against the sink counter, but Mom kept her spine straight and her backside away from the counter.

"Explain yourself, Mara," Mom said. "Why on earth would you want to vacation at a nudist camp?"

"I didn't know that's what it was."

"And you didn't even tell us," she went on, completely ignoring the fact I'd spoken. "If you want to sow wild oats, at least have the courtesy to inform us."

"Like I just said, I didn't know this was a nudist resort. The travel agent screwed up. She told me 'naturist' meant birdwatching."

"How could I have raised such a naïve daughter?" Before I could respond, she barreled straight ahead. "And why didn't you tell us once you found out what sort of…resort you were staying at?"

Only my mom could make "resort" sound like this place was Sodom, Gomorrah, and Caligula's palace all rolled up together.

Apparently, I said that out loud—probably mumbled it, but Mom heard.

She huffed. "You know I don't understand all that young person slang."

"That's not young person slang, Mom. Sodom and Gomorrah are from the Bible, so as a devout Methodist, you really ought to know what I'm saying." I sat up straighter, because finally standing up to my mother made me feel emboldened and strangely energized. "And Caligula was the most depraved emperor in the entire history of the Roman Empire."

Her cheeks turned slightly pink. "Of course I know about Sodom and Gomorrah. But I thought Caligula was a reference to—I don't know. That's not the point, Mara. You have a lot of explaining to do."

"No, I don't." Wow, was that me saying those words? I sounded so…confident. Hanging around with nudists was good for me. "I'm happy to tell you all the fun things I've done since I came here, but I'm not going to justify myself to you. I didn't call to let you know about the mix-up because I knew you'd go crazy over it. And really, it's none of your business. I'm an adult."

"Then act like one."

Dad laid a hand on her arm. "Calm down, Sher. Mara is a strong, capable woman. It's about time we let her know we appreciate that and stop treating her like a child."

My father had never, ever contradicted my mother. She seemed as stunned as I was.

He took hold of her arms and turned her toward him. "I love you, Sheryl, but you can be a bit of a dictator. I've never spoken up about it because you never went this far before. Cut Mara some slack. She's a good girl, and she deserves better than a dressing-down from her mother."

Dad was right. Mom never had behaved like this before, so overtly hostile to my life decisions or my mistakes. She would primly inform me of what I should have done, but she did not get angry.

"Relax," my dad said to my mom. He kissed her forehead and smiled gently. "Let's have a normal, adult conversation with our daughter."

Mom let her head fall back and moaned, the way I often did. I'd never seen or heard my mother do that, though.

"All right," she said. "Let's go into the living room and have an adult conversation."

Ollie led us into the living room, where Mom and Dad settled onto the sofa side by side. I took the smaller of the two armchairs in the room, leaving Ollie with the bigger, much puffier one. He looked kind of silly sitting in that oversize chair, like a kid in a furniture store trying out all the big recliners. Though he looked outwardly silly, his demeanor and posture made him all man. His clothes clung to his body just enough to provide hints of the muscles underneath, muscles I had vivid memories of feeling pressed against me.

What I wouldn't have given to sneak off to the bedroom with him.

Instead, I sat there in an armchair with my feet on the floor and my hands clasped on my lap. I looked at my parents, not Ollie. My gaze did keep gravitating back to him, but I forced myself to focus on my parents.

Mom stayed ramrod straight, her hands on her lap, though she clasped hers much more primly than I clasped mine. She threw Ollie a sideways look before aiming her disapproving gaze at me. "How long have you known this young man? A few days?"

"Yes. We met on the day I arrived here." The day I'd freaked out and fainted in Ollie's arms. Yeah, I didn't plan on telling my parents about that.

"Days?" Mom's eyes widened, but to her credit, she calmed down within seconds. "Mara, I'm trying to understand this, I honestly am. But it's difficult to reconcile my obedient daughter with the woman I see before me today. You have been keeping company with…nudists."

"Naturists," Ollie said. "Some of us prefer to be called naturists."

Mom veered her squinty gaze to him. "Some of *us*?"

Oh crap. If my mom figured out Ollie was a nudist, she would shanghai me back to Philly.

At the same moment I realized what he'd let slip, Ollie seemed to realize it too. He froze, not even blinking while he stared at me. After a couple seconds, he shook his head the tiniest bit and mouthed, "Sorry."

I shrugged, pretending to not panic about this even while my heart raced like an Olympic sprinter on speed.

And of course, Mom understood what was going on. She'd always had the uncanny ability to root out my secrets. Or in this case, Ollie's secret that had become mine too. We had kept the truth from only my parents.

Mom stared at Ollie. "You are a nudist. My daughter has been doing who knows what with a pervert who wears no clothes in public."

"This isn't a public place," Ollie said calmly. "It's a private resort. I wear clothes when I go into town, and also when I greet new guests."

"I see." Mom looked at me. "You are coming home with us, and that's that."

"No, I am not," I told her. "Ollie is a good man, not a pervert, and the fact he prefers to be naked has nothing to do with why you're mad at me. I screwed up again, didn't I? That's what you think. Stupid little Mara made another fuck-up."

She sat up even straighter. "Watch your language, Mara."

"No, I don't think I will." I jumped out of the chair. "And I am not going anywhere. I like Ollie, and I want to stay here with him to find out if we could have something together. He's helped me overcome some of my fears already. I plan to keep on doing that, getting past the things that used to make me a frazzled mess. I'm stronger than you think, Mom, and I don't need you to tell me how to live my life anymore."

Never had I spoken to my mom like that. I'd always cringed at the idea of telling my mom what I really wanted, what I needed. Standing up to her both invigorated and terrified me.

She opened her mouth, about to speak.

I held up a hand. "I'm not done yet."

My mother shut her mouth.

Dad's lips slid into a closed-mouth smile. He winked at me.

I rolled my shoulders back and forged ahead. "Mom, I know you love me. I know you're trying to look out for me, but you tend to forget I'm an adult now. I'm twenty-nine years old, and I can take care of myself. Please trust me to do that."

She wasn't staring at me anymore in that mother-knows-best way. Instead, she looked down at her hands and sighed. "I worry about you, Mara. You're my only child."

"Haven't I proved I can handle things on my own? You gave me an abandoned apartment building, and I made it a success. Doesn't that show I'm capable of running my own life?"

Mom fiddled with the cuff of her shirt, tugging it out from under her jacket sleeve.

Dad got up and hugged me. "Mara, I'm so proud of you."

"For what?" I asked.

"Everything. Standing up to your mother, turning the apartment complex into a real business, making your own decisions." He kissed my forehead. "You're a fine woman. And I already like Ollie Jackson more than I ever liked Nico."

"Really?"

"Yes. I never cared for Nico, actually." He rolled his eyes to indicate my mom. "I let your mother have her way most of the time, and she thought Nico was a catch. He acted like a decent guy, but something about him always bothered me. Maybe I should've spoken up about that. I'm sorry."

"Not your fault. I'm the one who married him."

I glanced at Ollie, maybe expecting him to look annoyed or disgusted or something, but he just smiled at me.

Mom cleared her throat. "It's possible I've been wrong about a few things."

"A few?" Dad said with a slight smile and a twinkle in his eyes.

"Possibly more than a few." Mom slumped into the sofa. "What do you think we should do, Peter?"

My father stared at my mother blankly for several seconds, then a broad smile broke across his face. "You know, Sher, I think that's the first time you've ever asked me that."

"I always ask for your opinion."

"No, I always give you my opinion. But then we do whatever you want." He settled onto the sofa again, taking Mom's hands in his. "I'm proud of you too. Mara's a grown woman, and we need to stop treating her like she can't do things herself. It's time we show her that we do trust her judgment."

"How do you suggest we do that?"

"It's simple." He lifted her hand to his mouth and kissed it. "We stay here with Mara for a while."

"What?" Mom gaped at Dad like he'd suggested she sign up for a nude mud wrestling contest. "You expect me to stay here with all those…nude people?"

"That's right. Maybe it'll be good for you to be exposed to a different way of life." Dad glanced at me. "It's sure been good for Mara."

Mom moaned and dropped her head onto Dad's shoulder. "Our daughter is a nudist."

"No, Mom, I'm not." Though I had jumped into the hot spring naked. She didn't need to hear about that. "I don't know if I'll ever want to be a nudist like Ollie and the others here, but I like these people. They're nice. Everyone here has accepted me as-is, and that's a new experience for me."

Though I'd kept my clothes on the whole time, staying here had turned into the most liberating experience of my life.

Dad murmured things to my mom that I couldn't hear, but it seemed to relax her a bit. She raised her head to look at me.

"All right," she said. "We'll stay here. Could someone please get my bags? I need Xanax."

I couldn't blame her for that. Maybe I needed some too. This conversation with my parents had been more stressful than when I'd gotten my first glimpse of nudists. The whole thing had left me on edge, and I needed to decompress soon, maybe by doing yoga—or doing Ollie.

Glancing at him, I couldn't help wetting my lips.

He caught me watching him and smiled in a sexy, yet oddly supportive, way.

I exhaled the breath I hadn't realized I'd been holding.

Ollie set his hands on his chair's arms, about to get up. "I'll grab your bags."

"No," I said, "let me. I know which one Mom keeps her Xanax in, so I can bring it to her faster. We can get the rest of their stuff later, once they're settled in somewhere."

"I'll stay in the guest house. Your parents can have the room here."

"Are you sure your bosses won't mind? It's their room, after all."

"Yeah, but Eve and Val are cool. They won't care." Ollie flicked his gaze to my mom and back to me. "Besides, I think your mother will be happier here than in the guest house."

With all the naked people. Yeah, he had a point.

"Thank you, Ollie," my dad said. "I appreciate that."

"No problem."

I marched into the kitchen, straight to the door to the outside, and swung it open.

An enormous naked man with wild hair and the most enormous penis I'd ever seen filled the doorway.

Every ounce of blood in my body seemed to evaporate. My heart pounded so hard and fast I couldn't catch my breath.

And I screamed.

Chapter Sixteen

Ollie

Mara's scream echoed through the house. She didn't just scream once, though. She did over and over, with only a little gap between each outburst, probably to pull in more air so she could shriek again. What the heck was going on out there?

The shock of her screams kept me frozen for a moment, but then I leaped up and bolted into the kitchen.

Mara stood at the door that led outside, one hand on the open door, her body stiff.

Val Silva hunkered at the threshold, completely naked, his lips moving. He seemed to be trying to calm Mara down, though her screaming drowned out his words. He moved his hands like he wanted to grasp her shoulders but seemed to nix that idea. Instead, he held his hands up like he was in a bank during a holdup and Mara was the robber pointing a gun at him.

I raced up to them, inserting myself between her and Val. "Mara, it's okay."

Her last scream wound down into silence, the only noise her ragged breaths. Her chest heaved, and her lips quivered.

"Take it easy," I said, bracketing her face with my hands. "It's okay. This is Val Silva. I told you about him, remember? He and Eve own the resort. This is their house."

Over Mara's shoulder, I spotted her parents in the living room doorway. Sheryl had her hand over her mouth while she stared wide-eyed at Val. Peter watched everything with a slightly bemused expression. When Val shifted a little to the side, Sheryl got her first good look at his dick, and her eyes went even wider. Her husband, now smirking, slapped his hand over his wife's eyes.

"I'm sorry," Val said. "I didn't mean to scare her. Eve and I just came from the airport, and I couldn't wait to get rid of my clothes. I had no idea you were hosting guests in our house."

Val didn't mean "our house" as chastisement. He was stating a fact, that's all. And I hadn't called Eve or Val since I decided to let Mara stay here with me. So this was my fault.

I could explain that to Val later.

"Take a slow, deep breath," I told Mara, rubbing her arms. "Val usually has a strong effect on women, but you're the first one who's screamed at him."

She took my advice, hauling in slow, deep breaths until she calmed down enough to speak. "I'm okay. I promise."

Val snaked a hand around me to offer it to Mara. "It's a pleasure to meet you, Mara. I'm Val Silva, and I don't make a habit of terrifying women. I hope you can forgive me."

She shook his hand. "It's okay. At least I didn't faint this time."

"I'll get some clothes from the truck and get dressed."

Val left.

Mara's shoulders sagged, and she leaned her forehead on my chest. "That was so embarrassing."

"Nah, that was nothing. You should've been there when Val got attacked by no-see-ums."

She lifted her head to look at me, her lips kinking into an almost-smile. "I'd love to hear that story."

"Tell you later. When your parents aren't watching."

Mara glanced over her shoulder and smiled sheepishly at her parents. "I'm okay. He surprised me, that's all."

Sheryl still had her hand over her mouth, but her husband lowered his hand from her eyes. Mara's dad looked tickled pink by the commotion. Well, at least he was having a good time.

Peter took his wife's hand. "Why don't we go outside and let Ollie and Mara have a moment alone."

Sheryl's eyes flared so big this time that the whites seemed to glow in the sunlight that came in through the window. She said in an indignant tone, "I am not going out there with all those perverts. And with that…man who has…" She fake shivered and made a disgusted noise. "Walking around with no clothing on is not proper."

Yeah, I decided she must've thought Val was hot—jeez, what woman didn't?—and now she was embarrassed by that fact. Even Ruth Norris, a seventy-something grandmother, made no attempt to conceal her appreciation for Val's body. Val had been a model after he retired from football, so yeah, nobody could deny he had the looks women loved. He was also smart and a nice guy, but that was never the first thing anybody noticed about him.

He worked out. A lot. I worked out too, but not like he did. Compared to Val Silva, I looked like a puny geek.

Peter Severins all but dragged his wife outside, winking at me and Mara as they passed by us. "I trust you to take care of my daughter."

"Yes, sir, I will."

He closed the door behind himself and his wife.

Mara sucked in a big breath and blew it out. "Wow, that was totally not fun in any sense of the word."

I shrugged one shoulder, trying not to laugh. "I don't know. That was kinda fun for me."

She slugged my shoulder. "Hey! My boyfriend isn't supposed to laugh at me."

"Come on, I wouldn't do that." I grinned. "Now your mom's reaction is another story. I think she was drooling. Definitely devouring Val with her eyes, even while they seemed like they might pop out of her skull any second."

Mara's lips puckered like she was trying really hard not to smile. "Yeah, Mom was ogling him for sure. I don't think she's ever seen a naked man before. I always kind of assumed she and Dad have sex in total darkness. I wouldn't be surprised if she has no idea what a man's penis looks like."

"Well, she does now."

Mara held a hand to her mouth while half-suppressed laughter snorted out of her. "I shouldn't be laughing. Mom was horrified."

"Yeah, but your dad thought it was hilarious."

"He knows how to handle Mom, but today is the first time I've ever heard him disagree with her."

I cupped her face in my hands and kissed her forehead. "Maybe he's finally realizing how much your mom's 'this is not proper' stuff has affected you. I bet things will change a lot after this."

"Don't hold your breath for the day when Mom becomes a nudist."

"Yeah, that'll never happen." I chuckled. "But your mom might not mind being around naturists now that Val has come home."

"He is hot. Can't say I blame Mom for being flustered by him."

God, I hoped she wasn't about to call me her gay best friend. I knew Mara liked me, but she hadn't met Val until today. The guy was a god, according to every straight woman on the planet. Okay, maybe Eve was the only one I'd actually heard say that. I inferred the rest.

"What's wrong?" Mara asked. "You're scrunching up your face."

Shit. I didn't realize I'd been doing that.

"It's nothing," I said, totally lying to her.

Mara set her hands on her hips. "That's baloney. What's bothering you, Ollie?"

This time I knew I scrunched up my face, and I bowed my head to scratch the back of it. "It's dumb. And it's doesn't matter."

"Anything that bothers you matters to me." She rested her palms on my chest. "You matter to me."

I raised my head, stunned by her statement, though it really shouldn't have surprised me. Other good-looking men had visited the resort while she'd been here, and she had never paid much attention to them. She liked me, not them. So why was I worried she might get turned on by Val's ripped body?

Letting out a long sigh, I told her the truth. "Val is a sex god. He works out like crazy, and he used to be a model, had his picture in magazines and on billboards. Before that, he was an international football star. That means soccer, by the way. His team won the freaking Olympics, mostly because of him. He also made a sex tape that everybody saw."

"Not me. I never saw it. And I've never heard of Val Silva, never laid eyes on him before today, not even in a magazine."

"But he's to die for, according to Eve."

Mara laughed, the sound soft and gentle. "Eve is in love with him. Of course she thinks he's the hottest thing since the ghost pepper."

"What's a ghost pepper?"

She laughed again, and her delight tickled my senses. "It's the hottest chili pepper on the planet. At least it used to be. Not sure if it still is."

"Oh." I tried to grumble, but it came out a little whiny. "Well then, every woman who sees Val thinks he's a ghost pepper. Even the senior citizens drool over him."

"Are you jealous of Val? I thought he was your friend."

"He is. Val's an awesome friend and a great boss." I scrubbed my face with both hands, groaning. "I swear I'm not jealous of him. Not until today." I hunched my shoulders. "Not until you met him."

A radiant smile carved out dimples in her cheeks. "You are so incredibly adorable. How can you not realize how ghost-pepper hot you are? I'd much rather ogle your naked body than Val's."

"Seriously? You claim his ginormous muscles don't do anything for you."

"Of course I think he's gorgeous, but I don't want to sleep with him. Or go hiking with him. Or swim naked in the hot spring with him."

"We haven't done that yet. You did it by yourself."

She snuggled up to me, sliding her arms around my waist. "We could do that right now."

"Your parents are waiting outside."

"Dad can take care of Mom." She nuzzled my neck. "Take me to the hot spring, Oliver."

"You know how I get when you call me that."

She nibbled on my chin. "Yes, I know. Oliver."

I swept her up in my arms. "Let's sneak out the back way."

Mara grinned.

Damn, I was one lucky geek.

<h1 style="text-align:center">Chapter Seventeen</h1>

Mara

We snuck out the back door, which I hadn't noticed before. Ollie told me Eve and Val had installed a secondary door only this year, so they'd have a back entrance for receiving deliveries of supplies. The door blended into the wall and had no knob on it, another thing Eve had wanted because she thought a regular door wouldn't look good there.

Ollie pushed a button on the thermostat to open the door.

I asked him why the button was there, instead of on the wall.

"To be sneaky," he said with a crooked smile. "Eve and Val are the horniest people on the planet. They need a secret escape route so nobody will bother them when they run off into the woods to get it on."

"Can we do that?"

"What? Sneak off? I thought that was the plan before you saw this door."

"It is the plan." I bit my lip, trying to look sexy but not at all sure I pulled it off. "But I was talking about the getting-it-on-out-doors part."

"Oh." His smile turned into a grin. "Love to do that. And I've got all your favorite foods to feed you after."

He had packed a picnic lunch for us and held the basket in one hand, by its handle.

We ran out the back door, heading for a side path to avoid the main nature trail. Other guests might be using that path, and besides, my parents might see us if we went that way. I needed time alone with Ollie. Lots of time. Completely alone. After a stressful talk with my parents and the scare Val Silva gave me, I needed to do something wild and hot.

Didn't a girl deserve hot sex in the outdoors once in a while?

Nico would never believe I was capable of doing anything so brazen. Hell, he wouldn't believe I could do anything he or my mother disapproved of, including eating a hamburger with the works on it. That was too messy, and naturally, a lady didn't get mustard smeared on her face. Besides, it might make me gain weight.

I didn't hate my mother. I loved her, and I didn't even blame her for my hang-ups. But I'd realized lately that I didn't want to be like her anymore. Maybe she loved dressing just so and behaving just so and speaking just so. I didn't. Ollie Jackson had shown me how wonderful it could be to stop worrying what other people thought and follow my true desires. It was about more than sex. I'd been rethinking my whole life.

Ollie led me deeper into the woods than I'd been before, into a new area with a less-groomed trail. This path led into real woods, not the semi-manicured version of it. Birds chirped all around us, and only the occasional ray of sunshine penetrated the canopy of trees. The peacefulness of this area helped me shake off the remnants of the stress that had gripped me earlier. Ollie's hand in mine helped even more. I loved the feel of his palm on mine, his fingers curled around my hand.

He stopped us in front of a huge tree that had big branches high up. Lower down, a single thinner branch stretched out from the trunk. It hung a few feet higher than my head.

Ollie patted the branch. "Take your clothes off and grab onto this."

"What?"

"You heard me. Do what I said."

His bossy tone should've annoyed me, but instead, it made me shiver in the most delicious way.

I stripped off my clothes and moved under the branch, stretching my arms to grasp it.

Ollie removed his clothes and sauntered up to me. He settled his hands on my hips, gazing into my eyes with a lustful look in his. "I love that you did what I said without asking why. Girls don't usually do that."

"I trust you, Oliver."

"Damn, it's even hotter when you say my name right after saying you trust me." He skimmed his hands up my sides, then back down to my hips. He shifted them behind me, cupping my ass. "I trust you too. All the way. I've got an idea for something I've never tried before, but I had a feeling you'd go for it."

"Anything you want to do, I want to do too." I rocked my hips forward, grazing his erection. "*You* are the sex god, Oliver. Val Silva has nothing on you."

"I love that you mean that."

He kissed me, slowly, decadently, groaning his pleasure while I moaned into his mouth. Our tongues coiled around each other, slick and hot and hungry, while I hooked my leg around his and he skated his hands up and down my back. The sensation of his fingers dancing over my skin heightened my arousal until my flesh felt electrified, sensitized to his touch. And God, he tasted so good, like magical things I couldn't describe, things that made me want him even more. Maybe he had cast a spell over me so I would bend to his will, or maybe I just loved being with him. I'd do anything he wanted, because I craved the same things he did.

I craved him, period.

Ollie kissed his way down my neck, his tongue teasing my skin, while he traced his hands over my shoulders and along my arms. His lips traveled down my chest, between my breasts, until he reached my nipples, where he paused to lick and nip and suckle them, cranking my lust up a few more notches with every swipe of his tongue. I moaned and thrust my hips, but I couldn't reach his amazing dick, the part of him I hungered for most of all. God, I remembered how fantastic it felt to have him pushing inside me, filling me up, touching parts of me I'd never known existed until he found them.

He bent his knees as he kissed and licked a path down my tummy, inching closer and closer to where my body ached and throbbed for him, to where I was already drenched and ready for anything he might do to me.

"Oliver," I whispered, reaching down to tunnel my fingers into his hair.

Millimeters from my mound, he stopped and looked up at me. "Uh-uh-uh. Keep those hands on the branch."

I grasped it with both hands again.

And now I was completely on fire for him. If he didn't make me come soon, I'd lose my mind.

Before I could voice my need, he seemed to recognize it. He dropped to his knees and laid a hand on my inner thigh, pushing gently, urging me to spread my legs.

"Yes, Oliver, please."

He shoved his head between my thighs, latching onto my clitoris.

The first tug of his teeth on my flesh made me buck my hips and cry out. It felt incredible, so fantastic beyond words, and he'd barely touched me. When he began to swirl his tongue around my taut nub, I gripped the branch even harder and threw my head back. He pushed his hand between my folds, rubbing in an irregular rhythm, driving me so wild that I thrashed and cried out again.

Just when I thought I couldn't get more turned on, he thrust a finger inside me, then another, and another. He fucked me with his fingers while tormenting my nub, his own breathing ragged and labored, just like mine.

"Ollie! Yes, please, yes, yes, yes!"

He nipped my clit, and I erupted.

My scream reverberated through the forest.

But Ollie didn't stop until he'd teased every last spasm of pleasure out of me, until my arms quivered from the strain of holding me up and he'd robbed me of breath.

He rose in front of me, his expression the embodiment of sheer, unbridled lust. His voice sounded deeper and rougher when he said, "Breathe, Mara. Can't have you passing out before we get to the best part."

I did what he said, taking slow breaths until my heart stopped pounding like a jackhammer. I let go of the branch and stumbled a little, still weak from the power of what he'd done to me.

Ollie slung an arm around my waist and hugged me to him. "Let me know when you're ready for more. I can't wait to be inside you again."

"I want that too, and I'm okay now." I walked my fingers up his chest. "But I'd like to give you something special first."

"Just being with you is special enough for me."

"You're so sweet, Ollie. But I've been fantasizing about this all week." I wriggled free of his embrace and knelt in front of him. His cock curved up in front of me, making my mouth water. "I want this."

"Oh… uh… You don't have to…"

He blushed.

I couldn't help grinning and laughing. His embarrassment was the cutest thing I'd ever seen, and it made me want to do this even more.

"Relax, Ollie," I said, "I've done this before. My husband thought my enthusiasm for sex was unseemly, but he loved it when I gave him a blow job. Apparently, it wasn't unseemly to enjoy doing that for him. But I'll love doing this for you so much more."

He combed his fingers through my hair, gazing down at me with a tender smile curving his lips. "You're the sexiest woman in the world, Mara. I'd love for you to do that."

"Maybe you should hold on to the branch. I plan to make you come so hard your knees will buckle."

"Damn, that sounds incredible."

He moved to stand directly under the branch, clasping it with both hands.

I knelt in front of him and took his erection in my hand, closing my fingers around its girth, loving the heat and firmness of him. A drop of moisture formed on the head of his cock. I licked it away, making him shudder and suck in a breath.

"Are you ready, Oliver?"

"Fuck yes."

I pumped his length in a leisurely rhythm while I began to massage his inner thigh with my other hand, easing it upward inch by inch, moving closer and closer to his groin. His head fell back, the look on his face the epitome of pleasure. He groaned softly when I cupped his sac and gasped when I fondled the skin behind it.

"Mara," he said through gritted teeth. "You're so—uh. So hot."

"Can't wait to taste you." I rasped my tongue over the crown of his cock, flicking it out to taste the slit. His breathing turned rough and labored, and I grew even slicker than he'd made me when he put his mouth on me. "Oh Oliver, I'm going to eat you up."

Knowing he loved giving me oral sex as much as he loved receiving it from me made this even hotter, even more perfect. I took him in my mouth, sliding his length in as far as I could before I pulled away.

"Fuck, Mara, you better hurry." His face had become pinched even while it took on a look of sheer ecstasy. "I don't think I'll last long, not with you doing this to me."

"Look at me, Oliver. I want you to watch me feast on you and swallow everything you give me."

Chest heaving, he bowed his head to watch me. His gaze drilled into mine, and he licked his lips. "I definitely won't last long if I'm looking at you."

"Doesn't matter how long it takes, as long as your eyes roll back in your head."

I swallowed him, drawing his cock deep inside my mouth while I massaged his sac. He tasted so good, though I couldn't describe the flavor of his skin. No words on earth seemed right, but giving him this gift seemed like the most right thing I'd ever done with a man. Nico might've loved blow jobs, but only because of the pleasure it gave him. He'd always kept his eyes closed, focused solely on how what I did affected him. He never said anything until after he'd come, then he would tell me, "I really needed that."

Ollie called me sexy and wanted to watch me do this to him. I had no doubts that afterward he would compliment me in the sweetest way. He was that kind of man.

His breathing grew even heavier, and his lids drifted half shut, but he kept looking at me. Our gazes were tied to each other with an invisible thread, a link between us that I'd felt since the moment I'd met him.

I worked his cock with my mouth, my lips covering my teeth, while I stroked the skin behind his balls. He groaned and grunted and murmured my name, his voice rough and almost hoarse. I dragged my tongue over the tip of his erection, and he hissed in a breath. His entire face scrunched up with blissful agony when I began to slide my mouth up and down his length, sucking and laving him with my tongue even as I grasped the base of his cock and pumped there too.

"Shit, Mara," he growled. "God, I'm about to—"

With a shout, he came. His whole body jerked. The salty flavor of him filled my mouth, making me hum with pleasure. I kept going until he was done, completely done, and so spent he dangled from the tree branch with his head limp, his chin almost touching his chest. The most adorable look of dazed rapture came over his face.

He managed a lopsided smile. "You rock the blow jobs, Mara. Any guy who couldn't see what a hot, amazing woman you are is a total idiot and a complete dick. I've never been with a sexier, more exciting woman in my life."

I couldn't help smiling. "Anytime you want this again, let me know. I loved doing that to you, and watching your face while you came. It got me so turned on."

He peeled his hands away from the branch to kneel in front of me. Gliding his hands up and down my arms, he leaned in to kiss me.

I expected a lips-only kiss. I mean, what man wanted to taste himself in my mouth? But Ollie didn't care. He sealed his mouth to mine and thrust his tongue deep, letting out a groan of pure carnal delight. We kissed with languor, like we had all day to sit here on our knees, in the woods, enjoying each other's mouths until the sun set and the moon rose, and then we could make love by moonlight.

We didn't get the chance. A phone rang.

Ollie kept kissing me, wrapping his arms around me and crushing my breasts to his chest, crushing my entire body to him.

The phone rang again, and I pushed his face away with my palms on his cheeks. "Is that your phone or mine?"

"Don't know. Don't care."

He claimed my mouth again, devouring me so deeply and hotly that I forgot about everything else in the world.

But that damn phone rang again.

Ollie broke the kiss and huffed. "Can't anybody get along without us for one frigging hour?"

"I think it's only been, like, fifteen minutes."

"But I was planning to make love to you for another forty-five minutes, at the very least."

I grinned.

He scowled as he scrambled around on his knees to find our clothes, then dug in various pockets until he found the ringing phone. He handed it to me. "It's yours. Says 'Mom' on the caller ID."

"Oh." I took the phone and answered it. "Mom?"

"Mara, where on earth are you? Eve and Val let us into the house, but you're not here. We were getting worried."

"Ollie and I went for a walk. We'll be back in a little while."

"Mara…" Her voice took on a sheepish tone I'd never heard before. "There's something I meant to tell you, but after that naked man frightened you, I forgot."

"What is it?"

The silence that followed my question dragged on for several seconds. I knew we hadn't been disconnected thanks to the background noises of men's voices. I couldn't make out what they were saying.

"Mara," Mom began, still sounding slightly embarrassed, "it's about Nico. Before your father and I left Philadelphia, I called him."

"Nico? Why would you do that?"

"I was convinced you were in some sort of trouble, and I knew he wanted you back. So I thought he might be able to talk you into coming home." She hesitated, sighing. "Nico just got here. He's with us in the caretaker's house."

"What?" I almost shrieked that word. My skin went cold, and I was pretty sure my blood froze to solid ice. "You invited my ex-husband to come here? Like it's some kind of intervention for your crazy daughter?"

"Yes. I'm sorry. But you'd better get back here before Nico takes off into the woods to look for you."

Shit. He would do that, for sure. Nico was exactly the kind of jackass who believed he knew what was best for me, and finding out I'd come to a nudist resort would set him off for sure.

"Okay, I'm coming."

I hung up on my mom and rushed to get my clothes on.

"What's wrong?" Ollie asked.

"My—" I paused in yanking my clothes on and tried to calm my racing heart, but I failed. "My ex-husband is here. I have to get back to the house before he calls the state police or who knows what to come search for me."

I didn't wait for Ollie. Once I was dressed, I took off down the trail, headed for the house.

Nico. Here. Could things get any worse?

Chapter Eighteen

Mara took off at a dead run. I scrambled to get my clothes on and gave up on tucking my shirt in, determined to keep up with her. I had longer legs, so I caught up to Mara in a few seconds, despite the time it had taken to get dressed. Only when we reached the trailhead, behind the little house, did I realize I'd forgotten my shoes.

She slid to a stop, almost falling over in the process.

I grabbed her arms to keep her from tumbling to the ground.

Gasping for air, she laid a hand on her chest. Her eyes were big, her mouth hung open, and she stared at the house like it might turn into a giant monster and squash her with its foot.

"You okay?" I asked.

"Uh-huh, sure," she said, sounding sarcastic even while she fought to calm her breathing. "My mom invited my ex-husband to an intervention at a nudist resort, so they can set me straight. But sure, everything's peachy."

I grasped her shoulders and turned her to face me, though her gaze stayed trained on the house. "Look at me, Mara. Come on, look at me."

She rotated her wide eyes toward me.

"Take slow, deep breaths," I told her. "That's right. Keep breathing. Take it easy and keep looking at me. You don't need to panic because I'm here with you, and I won't leave you alone with any-body unless you tell me it's okay. Got it?"

Mara nodded, clamping her teeth over her lips. She kept taking deep breaths and exhaling them gradually, and the panic on her face relaxed into something more like mild anxiety mixed with a hint of annoyance. I was pretty sure she wasn't annoyed with me. Her ex-husband and her mom seemed like the most likely targets.

"Thank you, Ollie," Mara said once she'd calmed down. "You're better than Xanax."

I chuckled. "That's the strangest compliment I've ever gotten, but coming from you, it's also the nicest one." I thought about what she'd said and asked, "Do you take Xanax? Or Prozac? Any-thing like that?"

"Never took Prozac, or any antidepressant. But my mom in-sisted I get a prescription for Xanax." She squared her shoulders and stood up straighter. "I haven't taken one since I came here. Not even after the dining hall incident that first day."

"Good." I pecked a quick kiss on her lips. "I'm proud of you, Mara. Your parents showed up, and you didn't freak out. You stood up to your mom. Now your ex is here, and I know you can handle that too."

The start of tears glistened in her eyes. "You're the first person who ever really believed in me."

"Oh, I think your parents believe in you. Your dad for sure. But I think even your mom does, deep down, and maybe she'll tell you that sometime and explain why she told you all that shit about be-ing proper."

"Maybe." She lifted her chin and cleared her throat. "Right now, I have to face my ex."

"I'll be right here with you, all the way."

She touched my cheek. "I know, Ollie, and that means more to me than you could possibly know."

I took her hand in mine and turned toward the trailhead. "Ready?"

She nodded.

We marched out of the woods and walked into the house via the back door, stepping into the kitchen.

Five people swiveled their gazes toward us.

Eve and Val smiled.

Peter Severins smiled too.

Sheryl glanced at her daughter but quickly averted her gaze, hugging herself.

The fifth person—Mara's ex, I assumed—glared at me for a couple seconds, then he rushed up to Mara. He pulled her into a hug and, like I wasn't standing right there next to her still holding her hand, he planted a big old kiss on her.

A long kiss. Like, loooong long.

I gritted my teeth and tried to be the understanding boyfriend, but honestly, how long would she let him keep doing that? The creep had treated her like dirt. She couldn't want him back. So why was she standing there while he kissed her?

Oh no, he couldn't have done what I thought he just did. He could not have shoved his tongue into her mouth.

Yeah, the asswipe had.

I was pretty sure I growled. My free hand clenched into a fist, and I had an almost overpowering urge to slug this creep.

Finally, after what seemed like an hour, he pulled his mouth away from hers. Giving Mara the smarmiest smile I'd ever seen, he said, "I was so worried about you, baby. Glad to see you're okay."

She gaped at him. Not moving. Not speaking. Her cheeks had turned pink.

I still held her hand even while my other one stayed balled into a tight fist.

Her ex glared at me again but quickly pulled on a cloak of civility, smiling politely and offering me his hand. "I'm Nico Marshall, Mara's husband. You must be one of her new friends."

Did this asshole really think I wanted to shake his hand? He couldn't be that stupid.

Mara was still standing beside me gaping at her ex. Was that stunned look because she couldn't believe he'd had the gall to show up here? Or was that a stunned "I want to get back with my douchebag ex-husband" expression?

"It was nice of you to take my Mara for a walk," Nico said. "She's always been afraid of the woods. You must be a great wilderness counselor."

Wilderness counselor? What the fuck was that? Maybe they had those in the big city, where people thought "wilderness" meant a patch of grass with a scraggly bush on it.

"Mara doesn't need counseling," I said. "There's nothing wrong with her."

The prick patted my shoulder. "You don't know her the way I do."

Okay, so he *was* as stupid as I'd thought. Only a moron would say that to me when I was holding his ex-wife's hand.

A breath blustered out of Mara, like she'd been holding it in and finally let it all out. Her stunned expression evaporated, blown away by her big sigh.

"Nico," she snapped. Once he looked at her, she rolled her shoulders back and said, "I do not need or want you here. Go home."

Okay, not an "I want my asswipe ex back" expression after all. I tried to keep my mouth from forming a smirk, but it happened anyway. Who cared what Nico thought? I had Mara, he didn't, and he could go jump into a volcano for all I cared.

"I can't leave," Nico said, "until we talk about what's going on with you. A nudie resort? That's the craziest mess you've ever gotten yourself into, and I've seen you do a lot of crazy things."

She puckered her lips, and I swore a little bit of steam erupted from her nostrils.

"Listen up, Nico," she said. "You don't know me at all, because you never bothered to ask me anything. That was the problem with our marriage. It was all about you, when it should have been about us. A shared life. But that's something you can't even comprehend."

He opened his mouth, but she held up a hand, her expression stern and determined.

That look was sexy as hell. Everything about her in this moment made me want to fuck her right here in front of everybody.

"I never did a single crazy thing in my life," she said, "and that's the problem. I always did what was expected of me, living by rules you and Mom and other people made up for me. Of course I turned into a neurotic mess. I never had any fun."

Nico eyed her like she might kick him in the balls any second.

I would've loved to see that.

Mara jerked her hand free of mine, spreading her arms. "Look at me. Do I seem anxious or neurotic? No, I don't. Know why? Because I stopped caring about those stupid rules and started listening to my heart. I love being here at this 'nudie' resort. I'm not leaving, but you need to go. Right away."

"Mara—"

"No. I'm not listening to you anymore." She made a shooing motion with her hands. "Go. Get out."

He stared at her for a moment, his mouth open, then got a sneakily determined look on his face. "You can't make me leave. I paid for a room here. For a week-long stay."

"What?"

I glanced at Eve and Val. Eve shrugged and shook her head. Val bowed his head, scratching it.

"Why don't I show Nico to his room," Eve said, "and give everyone a little time to decompress."

Nico didn't look like he wanted to go anywhere, but Eve knew how to graciously force someone to get the hell out. She and Nico left.

"I'm sorry," Val said to me and Mara. "He made the reservation online, and we didn't know—"

"Don't worry," Mara said. "I know it's not your fault. Let him stick around. He'll realize eventually that I'm not going home with him."

"If he harasses you, let us know. We will evict him and ban him from the resort for life."

"Thank you, Val. I appreciate that."

He left too, no doubt heading for the guest house to help Eve.

Mara's parents stayed put. Sheryl still hugged herself, her head down.

Peter smiled at his daughter. "Good for you, Mara."

High-pitched squeals erupted outside the house.

What on earth?

I stayed confused for about thirty seconds, until the house phone rang and I picked it up.

Before I could speak, Ruth Norris said, "Dear, the Kitten Brigade is here. And they're swarming Val with even more enthusiasm than usual. Maybe you should get out there and save the poor boy."

Val didn't need saving, but with Eve escorting Nico to his room in the guest house, I was the only other employee available to greet the Kittens. Val preferred not to get involved in guest intake. His forte was organizing sporting events.

I looked at Mara. "Will you be okay if I go? The Kitten Brigade is here, and I really need to get them settled in. Val isn't good at that, since those girls think he's a walking lollipop."

Sheryl's head popped up, her eyes wide. "Lollipop? Kittens? What kind of perverted resort is this?"

Peter hooked an arm around his wife's shoulders. "Relax, Sher, I'm sure it's nothing like that."

"No," I said, "it's really not. The Kitten Brigade is our name for a group of women in their twenties who come here at least twice a year. They all have serious, stable jobs, but visiting the resort gives them a chance to cut loose. And I was joking about Val being a lollipop. The Kittens think he's the cat's pajamas."

Mara snickered at my bad joke, and Peter smiled, but Sheryl kept gaping at me.

Yeah, she'd need more time to adjust to the naturist thing.

"Go on," Mara said, "I'll be fine. Sounds like Val needs a little help."

More screams echoed outside, confirming her statement.

"Why don't you go with Ollie?" Peter asked Mara. "I'll take care of Mom. Honestly, I think she just needs to lie down for a while. We had a long plane ride to get here, and a long drive from the airport."

"Okay, if you're sure."

"I am. Go." He glanced at me, then Mara. "It's nice to see you having a good time, honey."

Mara smiled shyly, and I led her out of the house.

Chapter Nineteen

Mara

A throng of lovely women frolicked in the area between Eve and Val's little home and the guest house. Well, frolicking wasn't the right word for it. They jumped and danced and chest-bumped and spun around and around. Every single one of them wore a pale-blue T-shirt dress and sandals, though each had her own version of the footwear. Some wore sandals with sparkly decorations on them, while others donned platform sandals or flip-flops.

They shrieked and hooted too.

My goodness, those ladies had powerful lungs.

In the middle of the throng, Val Silva stood there seeming quite calm and somewhat amused by the antics of the ladies around him. None of them touched him, but they danced around the man like they'd never seen a hot guy before—or like they were performing a bizarre ritual.

Suddenly, they all looked at each other and tore their dresses off over their heads. They hurled the garments high in the air, letting them flutter down to the ground.

The Kitten Brigade pumped their fists in the air and whooped.

Ollie shoved two fingers from each hand into his mouth and blew hard, emitting the loudest, most piercing whistle I'd ever heard.

I slapped my hands over my ears until he finished.

The entire Kitten Brigade froze. They swung their heads in our direction, all gazes zeroing in on Ollie.

A blonde girl broke off from the crowd and approached him. "Hey, Ollie, it's been a while."

He stared at her, not blinking and apparently not breathing either. His jaw fell open, then clapped shut. His eyes rotated toward me only to veer back to the blonde. "Heidi, hey. Wow. I, uh, didn't expect you to be here."

"I wasn't going to come, but then I realized it's silly not to. We're both adults. We can handle seeing each other again, can't we?"

Her innocent expression didn't seem fake, but Ollie eyed her like she'd suggested he drink that funny-smelling fruit punch she was offering him.

"Yeah, sure," Ollie said, "it's cool."

"So glad you feel that way."

Heidi flung her arms around Ollie and mashed her mouth to his, shutting her eyes, holding that position for several long seconds. Ollie kept his eyes open. His brows knit together over his nose, and he held his arms out like he was afraid to touch Heidi. When he glanced at me, he lifted his shoulders in the best version of a shrug he could manage with a beautiful blonde attached to him.

Finally, he pushed her away.

Wiping his mouth, he gave a nervous laugh. "Whoa, Heidi, we're not dating anymore. Remember?"

Heidi bit down on her bottom lip. "I missed you, Ollie. Maybe we could talk alone?"

"Talk?" His jaw fell open again, but this time it didn't clap shut for so long I started to wonder if bugs would fly into his mouth. Then he shook his head vigorously and swallowed hard. "Heidi, I have a new girlfriend. This is Mara." He slung his arm around me and pulled me tight against him. "Mara, this is Heidi Mackenzie. We dated for about thirty seconds last year."

Ollie's ex froze. Only her eyes moved when she looked at me. "New girlfriend? So soon?"

"I haven't seen you in almost a year," he said. "You went back to your ex. Was I supposed to wait around wishing you'd change your mind and come back? I moved on, and so should you."

Heidi gnawed on her lip, newly formed tears shimmering in her blue eyes. "Oh. I get it, sure."

It was totally bizarre to stand here with Ollie, both of us fully clothed, while his nude ex-girlfriend seemed on the verge of crying. Had Ollie hoped one day Heidi would come back and want to reconcile? He'd seemed shocked to see her, but that could mean one of two things. Maybe he was over her and hadn't expected to see her again, so he was caught off guard by her appearance. Or maybe he secretly wanted to get back with her, but he felt trapped by his involvement with me.

Which was it? I didn't know, and I couldn't ask him in front of his ex.

"Should I leave?" Heidi asked. "I mean, this is awkward, right?"

Ollie scrunched up his mouth, moving his lips like he couldn't quite figure out what to do in this situation. "You paid to be here, so you should stay. It'll be fine."

He looked at me, a question on his face.

What else could I say? "Sure, Heidi ought to stay."

"For real?" Heidi said. "You don't have to say that."

"It's all good," I said. "Don't worry about it."

"Yay!" Heidi flung her arms around me, squeezing me tight. "Thank you, Mara, you're awesome."

Why was she thanking me? I didn't own the resort, so my permission didn't mean much. When I glanced at Ollie, who'd been shoved away when Heidi hugged me, he shook his head and shrugged, a slight smile on his lips.

"Sure, yeah," I said. "You're welcome."

Heidi let go of me and rushed back into the crowd.

They had all remained silent during Ollie and Heidi's reunion, and they stayed like that after she rejoined them, waiting for whatever Ollie had been about to say after he whistled.

He raised his arms, spreading them wide. "Welcome back, Kittens. Get your tents set up and let's meet on the lawn for a game of miniten, okay?"

They shrieked.

All those beautiful, naked women split off in smaller groups and started gathering stuff from inside their big, neon-pink motor home.

"Wanna help me set up the miniten net?" Ollie asked me.

"Sure."

He kept a hand on the small of my back while he headed into the guest house to retrieve the net and the other equipment that went with it, like the thugs and the tennis balls. Ollie carried the rolled-up net while I lugged a bag full of thugs and balls, though he tried to convince me to carry just the balls and leave the thugs for him to get later.

"That's sweet," I said, "but I can handle it. They're not that heavy."

When I lifted the big canvas bag and hooked its straps over my shoulder, Ollie's brows rose.

"You're no wimpy girlie-girl, are you?" he said, smiling. "My Mara's a tough chick in disguise."

I loved it when he called me "his Mara." It gave me a warm, fuzzy feeling in my tummy.

After we set up the net, I lounged on a chaise at the periphery of the lawn. Ollie gathered the guests who wanted to play miniten and split them into two teams—the Kittens and the Silver Foxes, which meant the older guests. Val opted out, despite the Kittens begging him to play for their side, saying he and Eve needed to rest and recover from jet lag. They'd only just gotten back from Brazil.

As the two of them retreated into their house, Ollie leaned in to whisper in my ear, "Eve and Val have a different idea about what resting means. I hope your mom won't freak out if she hears them having a good time in their room. It's right across the hall from where I put them."

"It might be good for Mom to be exposed to inappropriate behavior."

He chuckled. "You're the best, Mara."

With Eve and Val home again, Ollie and I had to take rooms in the guest house. Val had moved my stuff there while Ollie and I got the miniten court ready, so I didn't need to do a thing except watch my hot boyfriend referee the game. Ollie had kept his clothes on, partly for my sake, I was sure. But I also suspected he did it so my mom wouldn't go ballistic.

My parents emerged from the main house not long after the miniten game started and took seats on the chaises next to mine. Mom sat right beside me, with Dad on the other side of her.

And Mom tried really, really hard not to look at the naked people knocking tennis balls around with wedge-shaped boxes on their hands.

I still had a little trouble with nudism. Whenever these people played sports, parts of them flapped that I didn't really need to see flapping. Sometimes they wore jockstraps or sports bras. Other times, they didn't. Ollie had told me, and my experience over the past few days had confirmed it, that naturists liked miniten because it was less strenuous than tennis and therefore didn't, um, flap their flappable parts as much.

The Kittens didn't seem to have gotten that memo. They played miniten with a vengeance, like they were competing for the Olympic gold medal in naturist sports. All but one of them had put on a sports bra. All but Heidi Mackenzie.

Her boobs bounced like crazy every time she leaped up to slam her thug into the ball. Good thing she had modest-size breasts instead of big jugs. I couldn't imagine how painful it would be to play so roughly with a huge set of tits.

My mom sat sideways on her chaise, hands on her lap, studiously avoiding glancing at the nudists frolicking off to her right.

"Dear lord, Mara," she said. "How can you stand to be around these…people?"

"You mean how can I stand being around super nice, friendly people who make me feel like I belong here? Who don't treat me like a screw-up who can't do anything right?"

"It's not proper, running around with no clothing on, where anyone can see you."

"Not anyone." I folded my arms over my chest. "This is a private resort in a secluded section of the woods. The only people who can see the nudists are the other nudists."

She rolled her gaze up to the sky. "What about satellites? Your father showed me Google Earth once. Did you know you can see into people's backyards with that website or software or whatever it is? It was horrifying."

"Oh come on, Sher," Dad said from where he reclined on his chaise, his baseball cap over his eyes. "You once sunbathed in the nude. And I remember that time at the lake when you suggested we skinny dip."

My eyes flew so wide the air dried them up. "Mom! You skinny dipped? And sunbathed naked?"

She threw Dad a chastising look. "Peter, you promised never to tell anyone."

He sighed and sat up, plopping the cap onto his head. "Mara's not anyone. She's our daughter, and I think it's about time she learned the truth about her mother."

"But—"

Dad tipped his head down to peer at her with an expression I'd never seen before. He seemed to be…almost scolding her with that look. "We both know why you've force-fed Mara all this nonsense about being a proper lady. You were humiliated once, and that's all it took. You stopped being the adventurous woman I'd married and turned into a prude." He winked and smirked. "At least in front of other people. You still love sex, don't you, Sher?"

My mom's mouth dropped open so far her chin might've touched her chest.

Okay, maybe not quite that far, but still really far. I watched for insects so I could warn her if any of them tried to fly into her mouth.

Dad moved onto Mom's chaise and clasped her hand in both of his. "Relax, honey. It's time we told her the truth. I let you instill your fears into our daughter, and today I realized how wrong that was. I should've made you stop. I should've helped you get over your fears before you ever started in on Mara. I love you, Sheryl, but things have to change."

Mom shut her eyes, exhaled a long breath, and leaned against Dad. "Maybe you're right. But what will Mara think of me?"

"She'll understand."

"I will," I said. "You can tell me whatever it is. I can handle it. Believe it or not, being here with all these nudists has helped me realize how silly all my fears were. If I can get over it, so can you, Mom."

She opened her eyes, fixing her uncertain gaze on me. "But I've done things you would never have done."

"You'd be surprised what I might do."

Nico strolled up to my chaise. "Hey Mara, let's go for a walk."

"I'm having a conversation with my parents. You're being rude, and I don't want to go anywhere with you." I faced my parents, blatantly ignoring him. "Take yourself for a walk, Nico."

Out the corner of my eye, I could see him watching me.

"Go," I said, waving a hand to dismiss him.

Nico headed for the nature trail.

Mom cleared her throat and said, "About the skinny dipping…"

Chapter Twenty

Ollie

I was keeping an eye on the miniten game—okay, mostly I watched Mara—when I saw Nico Marshall traipsing down the nature trail. Had that guy ever been in the woods before? I kind of doubted it. He seemed like the urban type, not the vacay-in-the-wilderness type. Maybe I ought to go check on him, to make sure he knew to stay on the trails and not wander off into who-knew-where. The last thing I wanted to do was talk to Mara's ex, but it was my job to look after the guests.

With Eve and Val "recuperating" from their big trip south of the equator, I was the only one who could stop Nico from getting himself into trouble. Not that I cared if he got bitten by velvety tree ants or quilled by a porcupine. In my opinion, he totally deserved that. But we had these annoying things called laws that required us to keep our guests safe. Letting Nico wander into a bear's den might be fun, but it would get us shut down for sure.

So, I tramped toward the nature trail.

I passed Mara and her parents, but they were too involved in their conversation to notice, and I didn't want to interrupt just to let Mara know I was stalking her douchebag ex.

By the time I got into the woods, Nico had disappeared down the trail.

Where had the moron gone? He clearly knew nothing about the

woods. If I were an arrogant ass who'd never left the city before, where would I go?

Nope. I had nothing.

When I got to the fork in the trail, where one branch led to the hot spring and the other toward the lake, I hesitated. Two signs announced where each trail went, but I had no idea which one Nico might've chosen. Was he a hot spring guy? Or did he prefer a lake? Maybe he didn't like water, in which case he could take one of the offshoot trails after he picked left or right at this junction. Which did not help me find him.

Damn. What would I tell Mara if her ex disappeared in the woods? Or got mauled by a wild animal?

"Help!"

The cry echoed in the distance. It sounded like a man's voice.

Oh great. What had Nico done now?

"Help me!"

I decided the cry was coming from the hot spring trail and hustled down that path. Not far in, I found Nico.

He huddled in a tree, clinging to a slender branch with his ass pushed into the trunk and his arms lashed around the branch. His eyes were big, and his lips quivered.

"Oh thank God," he said, almost whimpering, when he saw me standing a few dozen yards away. "I'm gonna die. You have to do something."

"Come on, man, you got yourself up there. I'm sure you can get your sorry butt back down again." I waved at the branch he clung to, then at the ground. "It's not that far. Jump."

He flapped his head. "I can't. It'll get me."

I glanced around but couldn't see any dangers. "What will get you?"

"That." He jabbed a finger toward the ground, pointing to the other side of the tree. In a hushed but hoarse voice, he said, "It's waiting to eat me."

Maybe I should've brought a can of bear spray. I hadn't, though, so I crept around the tree, keeping a good twenty feet between me and it at all times. As I rounded the backside, I saw the vicious wild beast that had treed Nico.

The raccoon sat up on its hind legs, holding its cute little paws up.

I looked at Nico and chuckled. "It's a raccoon."

He jabbed his finger toward the animal again. "That thing chased me. It bared its teeth, and now that monster wants to eat me alive. Do something, will you? Save me."

I stifled a laugh, which turned it into a snort. "You probably scared the little guy, so he bared his teeth. Raccoons don't eat people." I glanced at the critter, who was watching Nico with what I took for curiosity. "I think your yelling and fussing caught his attention. He's curious, that's all."

"Do something," Nico snarled. "It's your job to take care of guests, isn't it? That means you work for me. So kill that monster right now."

"Kill it? No way, man. It's a harmless animal." I rushed toward the raccoon, stomping my feet and clapping my hands. "Shoo, little man. Shoo."

The raccoon scampered off, out of sight.

"See?" I said to Nico. "It's gone."

He whimpered again, injecting a slight whine into it too.

"It's okay," I said, trying to sound encouraging. I wanted to tell him to man up and get his own dumb ass down here. Instead, I told him, "You can do it. Just slide off the branch, keeping your arms around it until you're ready to drop."

"Drop?" He almost shrieked the word. "I'll break my neck. You have to call the fire department and get them to bring their truck out here."

"A fire truck?" I tried not to laugh, but come on, the guy was acting like more of a scaredy-cat than my little sister had been when she saw a big old wolf spider for the first time. Bailey had been six, so I cut her some slack. The jerk in the tree didn't deserve any of that. "You can jump down. It's only, like, six feet to the ground."

"No way. It's at least twenty feet."

Oh jeez. Nico was freaking out more than Mara had when she walked into the dining hall and saw all the nudists for the first time.

Nico whimpered again.

"Are you afraid of heights?" I asked.

He glared at me. "No, I am not."

"Okay then, get some cojones and slide off that branch."

"Could you at least pile up some leaves to break my fall?"

I spread my arms, indicating our surroundings "It's spring. There are no dead leaves, and I'm not denuding the frigging forest to make you feel better. Oh look, there's some moss down here. Aim for that. Time to suck it up, princess, and get your own ass out of the tree."

He scowled at me for a few seconds, then slid his body off the branch with all the lightning speed of a sloth. Which meant he did it so damn slow that I probably developed gray hairs watching it. Seriously. It took him at least a minute to get one leg off the branch. Finally, he was hanging by his arms. Which were wrapped around it like he was dangling over the open jaws of a great white shark. He gaped at the ground like it *was* a man-eating beast.

"Jump," I said. "Take a breath and just do it."

Nico squeezed his eyes shut, whined like a freaking dog, and let go of the branch. The second his feet touched the ground, his knees buckled. He fell into a heap on the grass.

And he started whimpering again.

"What's wrong with you now?" I asked.

He bent his leg toward his chest, bent his knee, and hugged it while whimpering some more. "I broke my ankle."

Yeah, right. Mr. Whiny-Ass broke his ankle.

"Let me have a look," I said, kneeling beside him. "You have to let go of your leg if you want me to check out your ankle."

He eyed me with deep suspicion, like I might rip his ankle clean off his leg. "Are you a registered nurse?"

I rolled my eyes. "No, princess, I'm not a nurse. But I've taken first aid classes, so I'm qualified to look at her your ankle without killing you."

Even though I'd kind of like to do that. Never in my life had I fantasized about murdering someone, but I did now. And the more time I spent around Nico, the more gruesome those fantasies got. The one that went through my head while I palpated his ankle involved a chainsaw.

He squealed. Seriously. Like a little pink piggy.

"Calm down," I said in my patient, professional voice, the one Eve had taught me. She'd told me everyone needed to have a voice like that for dealing with annoying people. Damn, she was right. I told Nico, "I'm barely touching you, so just try to relax while I gently feel your ankle to check for injuries. Okay?"

He nodded, his bottom lip quivering.

And yeah, he had tears forming in his eyes.

I focused on his ankle. Once I'd finished checking it out, I said, "No broken bones. But if it keeps hurting"—I held up a hand to stop him when he opened his mouth, to complain, no doubt—"I'll take you to the hospital. But only if it's super painful. Got it?"

"Yeah," he mumbled.

A squirrel chattered from high above us.

Nico screamed.

My ears hurt. I was kneeling right beside him, a few feet from his big mouth.

"That's a squirrel," I told him when he stopped screaming. "It won't hurt you."

"Are you sure?"

"Positive." I sighed. "I'll help you get up, and you can lean on me while we walk back to the guest house. If you can't manage that, I'll go get somebody to help me carry you. Okay?"

"Yeah. Thanks."

Nico was being polite. I'd known the guy for maybe an hour, but he'd acted like a jerk the whole time. I guessed getting injured while fleeing from a raccoon had made him humbler. At least for now.

I shoved my arms under his and hefted him up, careful not to bump his ankle or get it bent wrong. He threw an arm around me, and I kept my arm around him. Oh yeah, this was how I'd imagined spending my afternoon. Hugging Mara's ex-husband.

We started down the trail. It was slow going, with Nico limping, but we made gradual progress toward the trailhead. Nico got winded twice, and we stopped so he could rest. Maybe his ankle really did hurt a lot. I had to assume it did and give him the benefit of the doubt. When we trudged out of the woods, Val saw us. He'd been standing at the edge of the lawn, at this end, so he ran over to help me get Nico into the main house. It was closer than the guest house.

Nico didn't even bitch about a naked guy assisting him.

After a lot of wrangling, we got Nico on the sofa in the living room, lying lengthwise on it with his ankle propped up on pillows.

"We have Tylenol and Advil," Val said to Nico. "Would you like either of those?"

"Advil," he said. "Thanks."

I sat down on an armchair across from Nico. "How's your ankle?"

"Kind of better. Still hurts like a son of a bitch, though."

"Maybe I should get you some ice."

"That might help. Thanks."

By the time I got the ice, Val had given Nico the Advil, and Mara and Eve had come to see what was happening. We finally decided Nico didn't need a doctor—and he actually agreed. His room in the guest house was upstairs, so Eve and Val offered to stay there instead so he could sleep in their room here.

Mara's parents seemed kind of annoyed by Nico's needy, whiny behavior. Because yeah, the guy kept complaining and demanding everybody get him things, like water "not from the tap but with electrolytes" and "organic gluten-free crackers with sea salt." Luckily, we had bottled water and those funky crackers, though not organic ones, thanks to Eve's insistence we try to accommodate anything our guests might want. Some people genuinely needed gluten-free foods, but Nico just wanted that because it was trendy. I knew because I asked if he had any food allergies, and he said no.

When Mara and I finally got to our rooms in the guest house, we were so tired, mentally and physically, that we kissed each other good night and went to bed.

Man, what a day. Mara's parents. Her ex. My ex. Jeez, what would happen tomorrow?

Chapter Twenty-One

The next day passed in a blur, with Ollie too busy to spend much time with me and Nico constantly texting me to ask for food or a drink or whatever thing he decided he had to have at the moment. I didn't see my parents much either, since I felt like I had to take care of Nico so Ollie, Eve, and Val could do their jobs instead of catering to the needs of my annoying ex. By the end of the day, I needed a break from all of it.

Nico tried to get me to sit at his bedside all night to "watch over" him, but I said no. He had dumped me. I'd given up my day for him. Why should I tend to his needs all night? It wasn't like he was dying. He didn't need a twenty-four-hour nurse for a twisted ankle. Once I'd explained that to him, Nico pouted but stopped demanding I stay with him.

I met up with Ollie in the guest house, and we walked upstairs hand in hand.

At the door to my room, we stopped. I pushed the door open and leaned against the jamb while Ollie slanted in to kiss me. It started out sweet and soft but swiftly intensified as I thrust my tongue between his lips and slid my hands up his neck to link them at his nape, tugging him closer. He groaned and responded with increased hunger, but despite the need growing inside us both, he kept the kiss heated but slow, taking his time while we both savored the taste and feel of each other.

He pressed his body into mine, the rigid line of erection prodding my belly.

God, I wanted him. Naked. In my bed. Right now.

I moaned and wrapped my leg around his.

Without severing the kiss, he picked me up and carried me into the room. I heard the door slam shut—he must've kicked it closed—and the next thing I knew, I was sprawled on the bed with him on top of me. The weight of him felt so good. I moaned again, tunneling my fingers into his hair, wishing he would strip my clothes off and make love to me right now. We kissed and kissed and kissed, with Ollie driving me wild with the need to have him inside me, and the velvety heat of his tongue making me so crazed my moans turned into greedy little grunts.

He pulled his head back to look at me, breathing hard. "Mara, damn, can you kiss."

"Mm, I love kissing you. It's so much more fun than it was with any other guys." I trailed my fingers down his back and up again, cradling his nape. "Especially Nico. He thinks he's a great kisser, but ugh, he really is not. I'm so grateful I found you—or fainted in your arms is more like it."

"I'm glad too." He brushed his lips over mine. "You're the best thing that's ever happened to me."

The best thing that ever happened to him? Me? My throat grew tight and dry. No man I'd ever dated described me that way. Hearing Ollie say it gave me a warm feeling in my chest that bloomed outward, intensifying into a delicious, liquid sizzle.

"Make love to me, Ollie."

He kissed me again, and this time it didn't stop there. We shed our clothes without disentangling our bodies, which required quite a bit of twisting and pulling, but we got it done. He made love to me slowly, with a languid intensity that turned sex into more than physical pleasure. It became a joining of our bodies, our hearts, our everything, in a way I'd never experienced in my life. I'd known Ollie for less than a week, but I felt like we'd always known each other, like all the failed relationships and heartbreaks had been preparation for this moment, in this time, with each other.

We fell asleep together.

And we woke up together too. Ollie roused me with feathery kisses on my neck, moving lower and touching his lips to my skin more firmly when he realized I'd woken up. I lay there with my eyes closed, reveling in the decadent sensation of his mouth exploring my body, his tongue flicking out to taste me, his fingers following the same trail down my skin. By the time he got to my feet, I was wet and aching for him.

"Yes, Oliver," I moaned. "Please, yes."

He drew my little toe into his mouth and suckled it.

I gasped at the strangely exciting sensation. Nobody had ever done that to me before. It felt… "Ohhh, yes. Do more of that, Oliver."

Releasing my toe, he chuckled. "You like toe sucking. Who knew? I learn more things about you all the time, and every single of those things makes me hot for you."

"So fuck me, Oliver." I did my damnedest to mold his name into an erotic come-on.

And it worked, because he let out a soft growl and pounced on me. With his face an inch from mine, he said, in the sexiest voice ever, "Your wish is my command, baby."

Oh God, I loved the way he called me baby.

Someone banged on the door. "Ollie, are you in there?"

It sounded like Eve Holt.

Ollie rolled off me and groaned, but not in a sexy way this time. "Yeah, what is it, Eve?"

"Your friend is here. Damian Petrescu?"

"Damian?" Ollie sprang upright. "What's he doing here?"

"I don't know, sweetie, but he swears it's urgent."

"Okay, I'm coming."

"He's in the office."

Jumping off the bed, Ollie scrambled to find his clothes. "Tell him I'll be right there."

"Who's Damian Petrescu?" I asked, sitting up.

"My old high school buddy. I mentioned him before, remember?" Ollie yanked his pants on and began the hunt for his shirt. "We went to college together too, but we haven't seen each other as much since we graduated. I got a job in Arizona, and he got one on the other side of the country, in South Carolina. We keep in touch mostly by text and email, though Damian insists on at least one phone call a month."

"It's nice that you have a friend like that. I've never had that kind of person in my life."

Ollie paused in pulling on his shirt to look at me. "Never? You said that before, but it's still hard to believe."

"Most people think I'm weird."

"What's wrong with that? Weird can be awesome." He finished getting his shirt on, tucking it into his pants. "I love your weird hang-ups, your weird…everything. I'm not exactly normal either." He points at himself with both hands. "Naturist here. That's way weirder to most people than screaming when you see nudists in the buff."

"But I don't scream when I see you naked."

His lips eased into a smoldering smile. "Sure you do. But it's a different kind of scream, and it only happens when I'm fucking you."

I bit my lip, my cheeks turning slightly warm. "That's true. I don't mind screaming then."

Ollie leaned over the bed to kiss me. "I gotta go. Have a shower if you want, then meet me in the dining hall, okay?"

"Sure."

He hurried out of the room.

I lounged in bed for another few minutes, reminiscing about last night with Ollie. I hadn't screamed that time, but it had been the most incredible sex of my life. Everything with Ollie was a revelation. I'd learned things about myself I'd never realized before, like that I love getting it on in the woods. Being here, with Ollie and the other nudists, had forced me to face my hang-ups and figure out the root cause. I couldn't blame my mother for all of it. I had gotten more and more uptight over the years, because I kept listening to people like Nico who told me I wasn't good enough.

Ollie showed me every day how much he appreciated me, just the way I was.

After a quick shower, I got dressed and left my room, heading down the hall toward the resort office at the end. When I turned into the doorway, I froze.

He stood by the desk with a gorgeous, nude blonde leaning so close to him that her breasts nudged his chest.

The blonde was Heidi Mackenzie. His ex-girlfriend.

"Please, Ollie," she said, "can't you give me one more chance? I screwed up. I'm sorry, and I miss you, and I—"

"Stop, Heidi. You dumped me, remember?"

Neither of them had noticed me yet, since they stood at an angle to me, turned slightly away. I should've announced my presence, but I couldn't make my voice function. My muscles decided to stop working too, leaving me trapped on the threshold.

"That was such a huge mistake," Heidi said. She placed a hand on Ollie's cheek. "Can't we try again?"

"I'm with Mara now."

"But we have history."

She tried to kiss him, but he turned his head away.

And saw me.

"Mara," Ollie said, shoving Heidi away. "This isn't what it looks like."

Heidi stumbled and grabbed the desk to stop her fall.

I stepped into the room. "She's trying to seduce you, right? It's not that hard to figure that one out."

Ollie frowned at Heidi. "She might've been trying, but it was not working."

"Sorry," Heidi mumbled, then she raced past me, out into the hall, her bare feet slapping on the wood floor.

"I'm not into Heidi anymore," Ollie said, coming up to me, grasping my upper arms. "I'm with you, Mara. Only you. That's all I want or need."

I glanced around the office. "Where's your friend? I thought he was waiting for you here."

"Damian was here. I gave him the room I was going to sleep in, which actually works out great since I'd much rather bunk with you." He scrunched up his nose. "We shared a dorm room in college, and Damian farts while he's asleep. Really stinky ones."

"Ew. I didn't need to know that."

Ollie laughed, pulling me into his arms. He kissed the top of my head. "Sleeping with you is way more fun. Are you okay with sharing a room?"

"We'd better be sharing more than a room. I want you in my bed every night."

"Yes, ma'am." He skimmed a hand down my back, gliding it over my bottom. "It's my job to ensure guests get everything need."

"In that case, I need you twenty-four seven. Can you be my personal concierge?"

"Not sure Eve and Val would go for that, but you can always text me if you get...needy."

"Mm, good." I snuggled into him, my arms around his waist. "Why is your friend Damian here? I mean, if it's a super personal thing, you don't have to tell me."

"It's nothing like that. He wanted to get away from the city, and he knows how much I love it here, so he decided on a surprise visit."

"You must be glad to see him."

"Sure. It's always good to see him." Ollie crooked a finger under my chin and lifted it until I met his gaze. "Damian is my top guy friend. You're my number one best friend."

"That's the sweetest thing anyone's ever said to me." I hunched my shoulders and wanted to avert my gaze, but I made myself keep looking at him. "You're my best friend too. I've never had one before."

"About time, then." He cupped my ass in both hands, lifting so my heels came up off the floor and our eyes aligned. "Mind if I kiss you? I'm having a Mara craving, real bad."

I grinned. "Please kiss me. I'm having a serious Ollie craving."

He gripped my ass more firmly, and our mouths collided. Just when things started heating up, someone coughed from the doorway.

Ollie and I turned our heads at the same time.

A man stood there. A man about Ollie's age.

"Damian," Ollie said, not letting go of my tush. "Settled in already?"

"I didn't bring much luggage," Damian said. His attention settled on me, and the corners of hi mouth ticked upward. "Who's the sexy girl glued to you?"

While Damian swept his gaze over me, I did the same to him. He had a physique somewhere between Val's enormous muscles and Ollie's more subdued buffness. His skin had an olive undertone, accentuated by his dark eyes and hair. That hair flowed down to his shoulders in wavy locks.

Damn. Were all of Ollie's friends as hot as he and Damian were?

Ollie rolled his eyes at his friend and let go of me. He took my hand, clasping it in both of his. "This is Mara Severins. She's my girlfriend."

"Yeah, I figured. Good going, Ollie. She's bodacious."

"She's also sweet and smart and amazing."

Damian grinned. "Not trying to steal your girl. She seems one hundred percent attached to you. Physically. I'm surprised you didn't need a laser to separate your bodies, the way you two were going at it a minute ago."

My cheeks flamed.

"Sorry," Damian said to me. "I didn't mean to embarrass you. That was just guy talk. We can be real asses, you know?"

"Hey!" Ollie said. "Speak for yourself. I'm sensitive and charming. You're the douche who bangs women and never calls them back."

Damian strode up to me and claimed my free hand, raising it to his lips. He kissed my hand. "It's a pleasure to meet you, Mara. I'm Damian Petrescu, a Ludar prince."

"A what?"

Ollie sighed and planted a hand on Damian's chest, pushing him away from me. "Damian's family emigrated from Romania a way long time ago, when the Ludar people fled. They still like to call themselves Rom, but most people call them gypsies."

"Don't be so culturally insensitive," Damian said. "Do I call you a nerd?"

"No, but we nerds own the title. That means it's no longer an insult. It's sexy."

I giggled. Seriously, I did. I must've sounded like an idiot, but I didn't care.

"Ollie is definitely one sexy nerd," I said. "And so unbelievably hot in bed."

Damian's brows shot up. He slung an arm around my shoulders and tugged me away from Ollie, leaning in to speak in a pseudo-whisper. "Now, Mara, you'll need to tell me all about that. Tell me everything he does to you."

Ollie seized my arm and hauled me away from Damian. "Leave my girl alone. Haven't you got a dozen of them waiting for you to go home? Maybe you should do that."

I might've thought they were arguing, if not for their smirks and the humor in their voices. These two had a strange friend dynamic, but I could go with the flow. A week ago, I would've freaked. To-day, I could take it.

And give it.

Hugging Ollie, I said, "Maybe we should tape ourselves having sex. Then Damian can see for himself how wicked hot you are."

"Oh no," Ollie said, "Damian does not get to see you naked."

"What if I become a naturist like you?"

"You can't do that until after Damian goes home." Ollie shook his head. "No sex tapes. Haven't you heard how that turned out for Val?"

"Oh yeah, Eve told me. It got leaked on the internet."

"Fantastic!" Damian said. "I'll wait for yours to come up on Cinemax."

"Let's go outside," Ollie said, towing me toward the door. "Lots of girls for you to sexually harass out there, Damian. Maybe you'll get arrested, and I won't have to look at your ugly face anymore."

I let him take me outside, with Damian following.

Today might turn out to be even more exciting than yesterday.

Chapter Twenty-Two

Damian Petrescu was an awesome friend. I would never have called it a bromance, because that term was so lame, but we were absolutely best friends. So I was glad to have him here, especially since he'd never visited the resort before. Now he got to see where I worked and why I'd quit being a computer systems engineer—well, after I got laid off I decided to quit that line of work—and took a job at a naturist resort. He seemed cool with the idea.

And of course, he loved watching the Kitten Brigade play volleyball. All but Heidi wore sports bras. Damian paid the most attention to her, tracking her every movement with his gaze.

Fine by me. If he slept with Heidi, maybe she'd stop pestering me to take her back.

Heidi was a nice girl, but I didn't want her anymore. She chucked me overboard. Why would I want to crawl back onto that boat?

Mara and I sat on a chaise together, with her on my lap. Nude guests weren't allowed to do this, since it was a violation of the resort rules, but Mara and I were both wearing clothes. We could totally paste ourselves to each other in public.

Damian reclined on the chaise next to us. He'd ditched his clothes.

Mara's jaw had dropped when he did that.

I did not get jealous. She still hadn't gotten completely comfortable with naked people, and Damian worked out a lot, so I expected her to be surprised by her first look at his physique. But she only stared at him for a few seconds, then she went back to adoring me, her lips curled up in a sweet smile.

Yeah, that worked for me.

Mara tickled my lips with her fingertips. "You don't have to keep your clothes on for my sake. I know you'd rather be nude, and I don't mind."

"You sure? I'm cool with staying covered up. You've had a lot of surprises lately, and I don't want to add more stress."

She grinned. "Seeing you naked is the antithesis of stressful. I love ogling you."

"Good. But getting naked would mean I have to move you off my lap, and I'm not ready to do that yet."

Eve and Val had ordered me to take the day off to spend time with my girl and my best friend. How could I say no to that? I hadn't seen Damian in almost a year, and I wanted lots more time with Mara. Catching up with Damian and hanging with Mara seemed like the best day ever.

Except Nico decided to butt his nose into things.

The volleyball game had just ended when the jerk approached us. Mara was still on my lap, her arms around my neck. Damian was still distracted by watching Heidi.

"Could we talk?" Nico asked Mara, completely ignoring me and the fact she was sprawled over my lap.

"No," Mara said, without even looking at him.

She didn't sound annoyed, or even vaguely interested. With her focus on me, she just seemed happy and not the least curious about why Nico wanted to talk.

"Please, Mara," the jerk said. "It's important."

With a sigh, Mara turned to look at him. "Maybe it's important to you, but it's not even a teeny bit important to me. I don't care what you want. I've moved on, and you should do the same."

She focused on me again.

Yeah, I liked this. Mara on my lap, Mara smiling at me, Mara giving her dick of an ex the big brush-off.

Nico hunched his shoulders, shoving his hands into his pants pockets. "Mara, please. You have every reason to tell me to buzz off, but I just want to talk. That's all. I swear."

He sounded contrite and maybe a little sad.

Aw, hell. Being a total sap, I felt bad for the guy. He had gotten scared shitless by a raccoon, and though I hadn't told anyone about that, I still felt for the guy. Maybe he'd realized, after his humiliating tree-hugging incident, that he needed to change his ways.

Mara sighed and asked me, "Would you mind?"

"If you talk to Nico? It's none of my business."

She chewed on her lip. "But we're together now."

"We met this week. You don't owe me any explanations, and you sure don't need my permission." I patted her leg. "Go on, it's okay."

Mara slid off my lap. "All right, Nico, let's talk."

I watched them wander off toward the little house. Once they'd gone inside, I got up and stretched, trying to think of what I should do while Mara was gone.

Damian raised his brows at me. "You're one brave guy, Ollie. Don't think I would've let my new girlfriend run off with her ex."

"They didn't run off. They went into the house for privacy."

"How much history do they have? Did they date for a long time?"

I hesitated, not sure why, before I answered. "They were married for two years. Knew each other since college, though."

Damian's brows hiked up even more. "Damn, that's… Are you sure you're okay? I like Mara, but if she still wants to hear what her ex has to say, I'm thinking it's not as over as you might want to believe."

"You met Mara a couple hours ago. I know her better."

"Uh-huh." He sat up, straddling the chaise. "Look, man, I'm your best friend. It's my job to make sure you're not jumping head-first into an empty pool."

"Mara is the most amazing girl I've ever met."

"Yeah, but is she really over her ex?" He held up his hands when I started to protest. "Hey, just doing my best friend job here."

"I know you mean well, but stay out of it. Okay?"

"Sure. Whatever you want. Keep your eyes open, that's all I'm saying. My Ludar lidar is pinging like crazy."

"Your Ludar lidar thought Trina was the perfect woman for me. But she dumped me for another girl."

"It's not a foolproof system."

Yeah, Damian loved to talk about Ludar lidar. He was a Ludar by heritage, but they didn't have lidar back when his ancestors fled Romania. That was a modern technology, like radar but with lasers instead of microwaves. Whenever Damian thought I was making a mistake, or stepping into iffy territory, he would tell me his Ludar lidar was pinging.

"You said your piece," I told him. "Let's drop the subject, okay? Help me figure out what to do to distract myself while Mara's having a heart-to-heart with her ex-husband."

Damian glanced at the Kittens, who were gathered at the other end of the lawn, laughing and making big hand gestures. "I wonder what those luscious ladies are up to."

"No frigging idea."

He got up, smiled, and slapped my arm. "Let's go find out."

Sure, I wanted to go hang out with my ex while Mara had a private meeting with her ex. Which meant I didn't want to do it at all. This day had started out so good, with my girl and my best friend. Now it seemed primed for getting flushed down the toilet, with all my good luck swirling and swirling until it dropped into the septic tank of life.

Yeah, that was my luck. A rotten shithole buried under my feet.

I could tell from Damian's expression that he really wanted to meet the Kitten Brigade.

"Sure," I said, "let's go see what they're up to."

Chapter Twenty-Three

Mara

Why was I inside Eve and Val's house talking to Nico when I'd rather be outside with Ollie? I felt sorry for Nico, I guessed. Which was ridiculous. He filed for divorce. He made me feel unworthy, like a total screw-up who didn't deserve to be with him. Sure, he never said those exact words. But I heard them between the lines.

Our marriage had started out good. I couldn't deny that.

But he trashed it, not me.

Nico sat on a stool at the kitchen island, while I stood on the opposite side of it. I wanted distance between us, to let him know I was not ready and willing to leap into his arms at the first chance.

He fidgeted, scratching his neck. "Look, I know I messed up big time. I had a great girl. I had you, and I threw it all away. It was the worst mistake of my life."

"You wanted a divorce, Nico. I gave it to you."

"Thought that's what I wanted, but I realize now I was just scared."

"Of what?"

He glanced down at his lap, then back up at me. "I love you so much, and I didn't think I deserved a woman as special and incredible as you. Kept thinking you'd leave me. So I, uh, decided leaving you first was the best way to keep from getting hurt later on."

"You said I was stifling you. That my neurotic behavior drove you crazy, and you couldn't stand being with such a screw-up."

"I know. I said that." He rested his arms on the island, keeping his head bowed. "That was my fear talking. Took me a long time to realize it, but I made a huge mistake that I need to fix."

What on earth did he expect me to say to that? Everything he'd said and done during the last six months of our marriage had shown me how little he cared about me. When he'd moved out, I had cried—but I'd been angry too. When he filed for divorce, I cried and languished in a blue mood for a week, but then I'd tried to get on with my life. Now he'd changed his mind. He wanted me back?

Oh come on.

I crossed my arms over my chest. "Why should I believe you?"

He knifed his fingers through his hair, letting out a long breath. Then he walked around the island to me, laying a hand on my shoulder. "I missed you so much, Mara. Not having you in my life for six months—eight including the separation—it made me realize how much I love you. I got scared, acted like a jerk, and fucked up everything."

"What do you expect me to say? You wanted a divorce."

"Because I was terrified you'd leave me for somebody better."

I tried to be angry. I should've been angry. But the look on his face, the tone of his voice, those things stopped me. He seemed so…sincere. Part of me wanted to believe him. The end of my marriage had been my worst screw-up ever, something my mom never let me forget. How could I let a catch like Nico get away, she'd asked over and over and over. I knew she'd been trying, in her own bizarre way, to help me with those comments. She honestly believed I would've been better off with Nico.

He had been a catch. An attractive, charming, successful man who owned his own restaurant. He'd been featured in the biggest restaurant-industry magazines as an up-and-coming entrepreneur and five-star-worthy chef. Of course my mom thought Nico Marshall was the perfect man for me.

"We used to be so good together," he said, rubbing my shoulder. "Don't we owe it to each other to give it another try? Come home with me. Please."

Yeah, Nico could be charming. But he was also the man who'd jabbed tiny pins into me with every sneaky little comment he made about my body, my enthusiasm for sex, the way I ate, and anything else that didn't conform to his standards for appropriate behavior.

"I've changed," he said. "Please, Mara, give me another chance."

My husband wanted my forgiveness. My ex-husband. I had loved him once upon a time, but I'd believed I'd gotten over that. Had I really? Did I still love him, even a little bit? God, I didn't know anymore. The week had been confusing and wonderful, almost like a dream.

This morning, everything had seemed crystal clear. Now I was trying to see through a fog of confusion.

Nico acted sincere.

What about Ollie? I adored him, but we'd met this week. I didn't know him that well, to be honest. I wanted to know him better, but now Nico had to throw this at me. Should I give in to his contrition and give him another chance? Should I tell him to buzz off and run back out there to find Ollie? All my old fears and anxieties came flooding back while I studied Nico's face. Maybe he would be different this time. Maybe Ollie would get sick of my neuroses and my hang-ups, and he'd leave me too. Maybe Nico was the best I deserved.

Dammit, that was Nico talking, getting inside my head.

And still…those doubts kept niggling at me.

"I don't know," I told Nico. "Give me some time to think."

"Sure. Take all the time you need."

Nico's smile seemed a little sad, but also a little hopeful. He wandered out of the house.

I waited a few minutes, standing there in the kitchen thinking about my life, the mistakes I'd made, the two men who wanted me. Was I a fling for Ollie? His ex-girlfriend wanted him back. They had history, while I was just the crazy girl who'd fainted in his arms.

Was fate trying to tell me something? If so, I had no idea what.

Finally, I went outside and looked for Ollie. I spotted him at the far end of the lawn with Damian—and the Kitten Brigade. They all seemed to be playing charades, so I walked over there.

The girl who had been making gestures to depict who-knew-what finished up right as I got to the group.

"How was that the Eiffel Tower?" Damian asked. "You looked like an uptight whooping crane."

Ollie snorted. "Like you've ever seen a whooping crane."

"I did see one. In a PBS documentary."

"Yeah, right." Ollie rolled his eyes. "The day you watch PBS is the day I join a monastery."

Ollie noticed me, smiled, and waved for me to come over to where he and Damian sat on the grass. I settled onto the ground beside him, my knees tucked under me.

He leaned in to whisper, "How'd it go?"

I shrugged.

"It's Heidi's turn!" one of the girls shouted.

Heidi trotted up to the spot the other girl had just vacated, positioned directly in front of the crowd. Another girl handed her a folded slip of paper. Heidi opened it and read whatever was written on the paper. Her brows crinkled, her nose too.

Must've been a hard one.

She crumpled the paper and tossed it into a large paper cup that seemed to be acting as a trash can. I could see other crumpled papers inside it.

Heidi began to pantomime. She waved her arms and tipped sideways, raising one foot off the ground.

Ollie watched her with a rapt expression.

A beautiful, naked woman showing off her body in front of her ex-boyfriend, the man I was currently sleeping with? No, that didn't bother me at all.

In the kitchen with Nico, I'd wondered if I should take him back. Now, I was jealous of Ollie ogling Heidi. I finally understood the concept of being torn between two men. Or maybe I was just crazy, like most people thought.

Heidi waved her arms with more enthusiasm, tipping left and right, making her breasts bounce.

Damian made a catcall.

The other girls clapped and shouted out silly things like, "You're a drunk astronaut!"

Ollie kept staring at Heidi, his lips parted and curved into a relaxed smile.

"Don Quixote," I called out.

Everyone froze and fell silent. All eyes turned to me.

Heidi's face blanked. "Wow, that's right. How did you know?"

"You were making like a windmill and tilting. Don Quixote tilted at windmills."

Heidi blinked several times, still seeming shocked. "You're really smart, Mara."

"Um, thanks."

Ollie looked at me, grinning.

And naturally, Nico appeared right then. He ambled over to the group and sat down beside me, sandwiching me between him and Ollie.

Nico patted my knee in a too-intimate way. "Hey, Mara. Thanks for listening, and I hope you'll think about what I said. It's not too late for us."

I scooted closer to Ollie.

And Ollie squinted at Nico, his lips flattened.

Nico smiled at me in a way an ex-husband should *not* be smiling at his ex-wife when she was with someone else. I wanted to deck him. Then push him into a colony of velvety tree ants. While he was naked. So yeah, I didn't want Nico anymore. His pleas in the kitchen might've made me doubt that for a while, but I was over it.

Ollie grabbed my hand, jumped up, and dragged me toward the guest house.

My heart pounded. My ears started to ring because I'd stopped breathing. Why was I letting men fight over me, like I was a prize heifer and they were in a bidding war over me? It was my life. A grown woman with a mind of her own did not let men make all her decisions for her.

I stopped dead halfway to the guest house.

Ollie tugged my hand.

I yanked it away.

We stood there staring at each other for several seconds, both of us breathing hard though we hadn't walked that far. His gaze burned into me, hot with lust and irritation, a potent combination that made me grow warm too—warm and wet. He clenched his fists, which made his biceps swell.

Peripherally, I noticed the other guests on the lawn, their attention glued to me and Ollie. But I didn't care what they thought.

I barred my arms over my chest. "Don't drag me around like a suitcase. If you want to talk to me alone, ask first."

He stared at me, his eyes narrowed, for a few more seconds while he took slow, deliberate breaths. "Please come with me, Mara."

The tone of his voice shivered heat through me. It was full of hunger, the dirty kind.

"Since you asked nicely," I said, "I'll go with you."

He claimed my hand and led me into the guest house, straight to the kitchen. It had stainless steel appliances and stainless steel counters, with pots and pans and utensils hanging from hooks above the counters and the stainless steel island. It looked industrial, but then, this kitchen did serve all the guests three times a day.

The kitchen was empty right now.

Ollie hoisted me up by the waist and set me on the island. "The cooks went to town to buy groceries. We've got the kitchen to ourselves."

His voice still sounded rougher, sexier, hotter.

"I'm not hungry," I said.

"Really." He pushed between my thighs and mashed his mouth to mine, plunging his tongue deep without waiting for my tacit permission to do it, making me moan and sag into him. When he pulled away, we were both breathing harder again. "Still not hungry?"

Gazing into his eyes, feeling his hard body between my legs, I couldn't deny the truth. "Starving."

"Thought so." His mouth slanted into a sexy smirk. "And here's how I'm going to feed you…"

Chapter Twenty-Four

Ollie

Maybe I got a little jealous when Mara went off with her ex. Maybe I didn't like it when she came back and Nico followed her, then he touched her like he still owned her. Nobody owned Mara. I didn't want to, that was for sure. But I loved taking possession of her body so I could give her exactly what we both wanted.

Okay, I might've been a touch jealous.

Not anymore. I was the one who had Mara alone in the kitchen, where the erotic possibilities were endless. I'd never done anything like this before. Girls knew I rocked the bedroom, but they didn't like my adventurous suggestions.

Mara was up for anything. Our time under that tree in the woods had proved it.

I grasped her hips and pulled her closer, our faces aligned. "I know you're not a suitcase. Sorry I hauled you away without asking first."

"Apology accepted." She glanced around the kitchen. "You still haven't finished that sentence. You said 'here's how I'm going to feed you,' but you trailed off instead of telling me."

"I know. Here's the rest of it." I placed my open mouth on the base of her throat, dragging it up, swirling my tongue over her skin that tasted faintly salty. When I reached her earlobe, I pulled it into my mouth and sucked, making her moan. "I'm going to fuck you so good for so long that everyone will see it on your face that you're mine and I'm yours. You'll come so many times you'll think you can't take it anymore, but still you'll beg me to do it again."

"Yes," she breathed.

I nibbled my way along her jaw, then flicked my tongue out to tease her mouth. "I want to feast on you like I've never done with anyone else. That's why we're in the kitchen."

Her pupils had blown, and her breaths came hard and fast. The faint blush that colored her cheeks made me even harder. I wanted this woman like I'd never wanted anyone, like I'd never known I could want anyone. While I'd been pretending to watch the charades game, I'd been plotting the hottest ways to make Mara shiver and moan and writhe and scream.

Nico had better find another woman. Mara was mine. By the time I got done with her, she would never want anyone else. Yeah, okay, maybe I was getting a little caveman-ish. So what? Mara seemed to like it. And I would never force her to do anything.

I moved my mouth to her ear again. "You know what I want. What do you want?"

She yanked my shirt out of my waistband and shoved her hands under the fabric, whisking them up my chest. "You, Oliver. I want you."

Her hands traveled over my chest, exploring and arousing me. But when she pinched my nipples, I lost it.

"Fuck," I hissed, and I ripped her shirt off over her head. "I'm gonna feast on you for real this time."

I tore off her bra, and she wriggled out of her pants and underwear, kicking off her sandals too. Then she stretched out on the island with her legs dangling off it, her arms raised above her head. Stainless steel shimmered around her, and her auburn hair feathered over the shiny surface, a dark halo around her face.

A dirty angel. That's what she was, and I loved it.

"Get naked," she commanded, running her hands up and down the metal surface beneath her like she wanted to make love to it.

I stripped off my clothes faster than I ever had in my life. Gazing down at her body, at the curly dark hairs below her hips, I couldn't resist licking my lips. The scent of her lust overpowered my senses. I fought the urge to spread her thighs and dive in, because I had plans for that body.

"Do you have any food allergies?" I asked.

"No." She sounded a little confused by my question.

Pretty soon, she'd understand why I asked.

I opened the big fridge and got out the items I needed for the appetizer—strawberries, whipped cream, and vanilla ice cream. I set those items on the island beside Mara.

She watched me with a puzzled expression.

Puzzled and aroused. I got the feeling no one had ever done what I was about to do to her. Damn sure Nico never had.

I returned to the island, standing between her legs, and tugged her hips to get her ass resting on the very edge. Her puzzled expression melted into a smile so sexy it made my cock throb. I took a breath to calm myself—*cut that out, little buddy, we've got work to do*—and leaned over her body, looking straight into her gorgeous green eyes.

"Your cream is the sweetest thing I've ever tasted," I told her, "but I want to feed you a different kind of cream. Open that luscious mouth for me, baby."

She opened her mouth.

I grabbed a strawberry, dipped it in the bowl of whipped cream, and held it to her open mouth. "Take a bite."

She bit off half the strawberry, closing her lips around it, chewing slowly, sensuously, and then she moaned like she'd never tasted anything so good in her life. Her eyes half closed, she savored the strawberry until it was all gone. Her lips curved up at the corners, but her eyes stayed hooded.

"Mm," she hummed. "That tastes so delicious, but not as delicious as you."

Her words, the sultry way she spoke them, it made my cock throb again. I devoured the rest of the strawberry, but fruit wasn't what I wanted to consume right now.

Take it slow. That's the plan, remember?

Yeah, the plan. What was it again?

Mara stretched her tongue out, licking the strawberry remnants off my lips. "Mm-mm-mmmmm. Food tastes better on you."

I could barely catch my breath, but dammit, I would do this the way I'd planned. I straightened my arms, putting a little bit of distance between my body and hers.

She picked up a strawberry, dipped it in the whipped cream, and smeared cream all over my chest.

"Mara—"

"Oops," she said in a sexy tone, her smile just as hot as her voice. "Let me clean up the mess I made."

She lifted her head to lap up the cream she'd smeared all over me. Every flick of her tongue made it harder for me to breathe, and harder for me to ignore what my dick wanted so badly that I might just lose it and come all over her belly.

Not that it wouldn't be hot to do that. But I had these plans.

I pinned her wrists to the table. "Do I need to tie you up? Or will you let me do my thing before you make me blow my top?"

"You don't need to tie my up, but that might be fun too."

"Maybe another time." I let go of her wrists, sliding my hands down her arms, loving the feel of her silky skin and the fine hairs that dusted it. "I've got lots more I want to do to you."

I got another strawberry, loaded it with cream, and painted a trail down her body with it, starting at her throat. Every time my berry-brush ran out of cream, I dunked it again and kept painting that path down to her belly until I reached her mound. Then I used the berry-brush to drop a dollop of whipped cream on each of her stiff nipples.

Mara squirmed and bit her lip.

Tearing the leaves off the berry, I spit them out and held the strawberry between my lips, leaning in until my mouth hovered inches above Mara's. I swept the berry across her lips until she got the idea and bit off a chunk.

I ate the rest of it. Juice clung to my lips.

Before I could wipe it off, Mara sneaked her tongue out to lap up the liquid.

Damn, she was the hottest lover any man could ever want.

I licked the whipped cream off her throat, laving my tongue over her skin in leisurely strokes, and followed the trail I'd painted down her chest. When I reached her breasts, I drew one nipple into my mouth, licking and suckling until I'd cleaned every last speck of cream off it—and until she was writhing and gasping under me. I switched to the other breast, giving it the same attention, making her squirm and whimper.

"Oliver," she cried out when I nipped her rigid peak. "Yes, Oliver, please."

She knew how much I loved it when she called me Oliver, but I also knew she wasn't doing it on purpose this time. I'd gotten her so wound up she probably had no clue what she was saying.

Getting her turned on got me wound up too. But I focused on my task, licking my way down her belly, swirling my tongue inside her navel, lapping up every last bit of cream until I reached her mound. I nuzzled the soft hairs, inhaling a deep breath through my nostrils, intoxicated by the scent of her.

"Fuck," I groaned, fluttering those hairs. She smelled so damn good, and I knew she would taste even better.

"Oliver, please hurry."

"Uh-uh. Not rushing." I forced myself to give up the scent of her and grabbed the container of ice cream. I tore off the lid and dug a chunk of ice cream out of the tub with my fingers, holding it in my fist until it started to melt. With my other hand, I urged her to spread her legs for me.

Mara watched me, her head raised, her brows cinching together.

I chuckled. "Ready for phase two?"

She nodded so vigorously her hair flapped against her face.

Opening my fist, I let the half-melted chunks of ice cream fall onto her mound. The thick liquid oozed down her skin, between her thighs. I parted her glistening folds, letting the ice cream drizzle down between them.

Mara was breathing so hard her breasts jiggled.

I lowered my head and dragged my tongue up her folds. The flavor of ice cream and Mara deluged my senses, the taste so incredible I couldn't stop myself from groaning and devouring her with more hunger. She opened her thighs for me even more, diving her fingers into my hair. Ice cream. Mara cream. Nothing better in the whole world. I licked my way up to her clit, closed my lips around it, and sucked every last drop of everything off her flesh.

Her body tensed.

Licking, lapping, suckling, so drunk on the flavor of her that I couldn't stop.

"Oliver!" she shouted as her climax rocketed through her. She clutched my head so tightly her nails dug into my scalp.

I kept going until she went limp on the island. Then I lifted my head to look at her, breathing hard, my cock demanding I feed it some of Mara too. She lay there sprawled on the cold metal surface, her eyes closed, her mouth open, an expression of pure satisfaction on her face.

God, I'd never seen anything so beautiful.

Voices echoed from down the hall.

"Shit," I hissed. "It's game time."

"What time?" Mara said, sounding as blissfully dazed as she looked.

"Game time. It's a weekly event where guests play board games in the entertainment room."

I could not go out there in my current condition.

The voices got closer, but then faded as everyone veered off into the entertainment room. It was two doors down from the kitchen.

Mara sat up, draping her arms around my neck. "I don't care who's out there listening. You need to finish fucking me. Right now, Oliver."

If she hadn't called me Oliver, maybe I could've said no.

Yeah, I didn't believe me either.

Mara took my dick in her hand and raked her thumb over the head. "Do it now, Oliver."

How did she make my name sound like the dirtiest word on earth?

I pulled away from her just long enough to get a condom out of my pants pocket. Once I'd rolled it on, I nestled between her thighs, feeling her heat penetrate the latex. The sensation drove me crazy. And I hadn't even gotten inside her yet.

"Now, Oliver, please."

With a long, guttural groan, I thrust inside her, pushing in all the way until I couldn't go any further. Her hot body molded to my cock, and she latched her legs around my hips. With her breasts mounded against my chest, I couldn't hold back for one more nanosecond.

I spun us around, pinned her to the fridge, and fucked her.

She squeezed her eyes shut, her mouth open, that blissful expression taking over her face again.

Thrusting, thrusting, harder, faster. The sucking sound of our bodies colliding echoed in the kitchen while she flung her arms around me, her nails digging into my back. I flattened my palms on the stainless steel fridge, pumping and pumping, the pressure inside me so intense I knew I'd blow any second. *Wait for Mara.* I tried to do that, tried so damn hard I was gritting my teeth.

Just when I thought I'd go off before she did, Mara came with a strangled scream. I sealed my mouth over hers to muffle her cries—and my own. I came so hard I swore I saw stars flashing behind my eyelids. A couple more thrusts did me in. I sagged against the fridge with Mara crushed between my body and the steel surface.

I let my forehead fall onto her shoulder. "Oh God, Mara."

She hugged my head and kissed my temple. "That was incredible, Ollie."

No idea how I managed to move, but I did. I raised my head and kissed her softly. Then I withdrew from her body, set her down on the floor, and discarded the condom.

A throat-clearing drew our attention to the doorway.

Damian stood there with his hand over his eyes. "Didn't see a thing, I swear." He peeked through his fingers, smirking. "Well, not much."

I expected Mara to get embarrassed and run away.

She surprised me again, laughing as she said, "Oh well, this is a nudist resort. Damian was bound to see me naked sometime."

"Thought you didn't want to go nude in front of the other guests," I said.

"I've been thinking I might give it a try. As part of my self-liberation campaign."

Damian snickered. "Yeah, Mara, you get as liberated as you want."

I flashed him a scowl, which he saw since the ass was still peeking through his fingers. Then I pulled Mara into the corner farthest from Damian and whispered, "He might've seen what we were doing a minute ago."

She glanced at Damian. Though her cheeks turned a little pink, she shrugged and said, "So what?"

"You're seriously okay with that."

"Uh-huh." She wrapped her arms around my neck and smiled. "You make me feel brave and sexy and safe."

"You don't need me for that. You *are* brave and sexy, all on your own."

Damian pretended to gag. "If you two are going to make out, I'll head back to the games before I hurl all over this nice shiny floor." He looked at Mara. "I really didn't see whatever you two were doing. I heard weird squeaking noises and thought I should check it out. You were both standing there naked when I walked in."

Squeaking noises? I kind of remembered something like that, but my brain had been offline at the time. Mara's skin must've squeaked on the stainless steel fridge.

"Get out of here," I said, waving for Damian to leave.

He grinned and skedaddled.

"What should we do?" I asked Mara.

She puckered her lips like she was thinking hard, then she smiled again. "Let's take a shower."

I scooped her up.

Damian ducked back into the kitchen. "I've got a sudden yen for cleaning a kitchen."

My best friend was offering to clean up after the mess I'd made with Mara, which I hadn't even thought to clean up myself. My brain still hadn't ramped up to full power yet.

"Thanks, man," I said. "You're an awesome friend."

"Not really. I just don't want to eat food that was made on the counter where you two got it on."

He smirked and winked.

I carried Mara upstairs to our room, where a nice, big shower stall waited for us.

Chapter Twenty-Five

Mara

After our shower, Ollie and I headed back outside. Ollie had started to put his clothes back on, but I assured him he didn't need to do that for my sake. I'd gotten used to spending my days surrounded by naked people, and seeing Ollie in the nude was hardly a terrifying experience. I didn't blame him for thinking he shouldn't go naked in front of me, considering how things had gone when we first met, but I didn't want him to change his ways to suit me.

So now, we were participating in a game of miniten—Ollie in the buff, and me wearing shorts and a tank top. I wore sneakers, but Ollie chose to go barefoot. The game pitted the two of us against Ruth and Sylvester Norris. That sounded like an easy win for us. Two fit twenty-somethings against a pair of senior citizens? Piece of cake.

Not so much, as it turned out.

Today I learned never to underestimate anyone because they're over seventy. Ruth and Sly—Sylvester asked me to call him by his nickname—beat me and Ollie, barely letting us score two points in the whole game. Miniten might be a more laid-back version of tennis, but the Norrises decided to turn it into an acrobatic performance. They leaped up to smack the ball with their thugs.

I wondered why Ruth had bothered with a bra when we were playing an easygoing sport, but she did more than leap to hit the ball. She also spun around, dodged right and left, and even dived for the ground to hit the ball when I got my angle wrong and sent it barreling straight for the grass. Sly did the same and more, leaping sideways with his feet off the ground to whack Ollie's shot before it flew out of bounds. The Norrises won and celebrated by cheering and giving each other high fives.

Ollie had chastised the young guys yesterday who had played rough. But then, one of them had slammed into me. Ruth and Sly didn't do anything like that, and they never went overboard in their enthusiasm to hit the ball and win the game.

After the game broke up, I needed a trip to the bathroom. When I returned to the lawn, I glanced around to search for Ollie.

He and Damian were relaxing on the grass, talking. Ollie lay on his side with his head propped up with one arm, his cheek resting on his palm. Damian lay on his back, hands linked over his belly. Both men wore sunglasses. The sight of Ollie naked still made me tingle, which was highly inappropriate when other people were around. I couldn't stop it, though. He was hot.

And so was Damian. But his sexy bod didn't affect me the way Ollie's did.

I caught sight of Heidi on the other side of the lawn, hanging out with her girlfriends. She kept glancing at Ollie. Staring at him, actually. How much history did they have? She sure seemed hung up on him. Ever since Heidi had arrived here, I'd wondered if Ollie still had feelings for her. I'd also wondered if I still had feelings for Nico.

No, I didn't. But the thought made me a little queasy.

Did that mean I had no feelings for him? I supposed I would always care about him in some way, in spite of all his wheedling comments that had made me feel small and useless. But we'd had good times too, and I'd known Nico a lot longer than I'd known Ollie.

Why, then, did I feel closer to Ollie than to anyone else? Why did being with him give me a sense of relaxation and freedom I'd never experienced before? He came from a normal family and worked at a nudist resort. I came from an uptight family of rich snobs who were horrified I was staying at a nudist resort. That wasn't quite accurate. Dad didn't seem to care, and though he'd always gone along with whatever Mom wanted, he had never been uptight. He didn't tell me to act like a proper lady.

And yesterday, he'd told me he was proud of me.

No, I did not want Nico back.

But I wasn't sure I belonged with Ollie either. Could people from two different planets make it work? I wasn't even sure how this thing between us could work. He lived here. I lived in Philly. He had a job here, one that he loved. I owned an apartment building, which I'd built into a profitable business. Would I give that up to be with Ollie?

He might get sick of me. I mean, I was an uptight city girl.

But he made me feel free.

I sat down next to Ollie, still wondering about all of those things.

"Hey, Mara," he said, smiling at me. He patted the grass. "Come closer, baby."

Damian lifted his sunglasses to peek at us. "Isn't that against the rules? Getting friendly with your girl while you're naked?"

Ollie kneed Damian in the side. "We aren't going to make out. Mara can sit right next to me without it getting inappropriate."

Yes, we needed to be appropriate, didn't we? I understood the need for rules at a nudist resort, but I hated that word. Appropriate. And its synonym, proper. Both words made me cringe inside.

But I scooted closer to Ollie.

We spent the rest of the afternoon just hanging out, first on the lawn, and later in the entertainment room in the guest house. Damian and Ollie taught me how to play poker, but when Damian offered to show me how to cheat at it, Ollie intervened.

"Oh no," he said, laying a hand on Damian's chest to push him away from me. "You are not corrupting my girl. She's perfect the way she is."

I got a glowy feeling in my chest when he called me perfect. But a pit soon formed in my gut when I considered the ramifications of that statement. Did he expect me to be actually perfect all the time? No, of course not. I was being ridiculous.

My parents invited me and Ollie to go into town with them for dinner at a steak house they'd heard about from Val and Eve. My parents wanted to get to know Ollie better, and in an environment where my mom would feel more at ease. That meant a clothing-required outing. Ollie accepted their invitation with more enthusiasm than I would've expected. I mean, my mom hadn't exactly welcomed him with open arms. Ollie didn't hold a grudge, which made me like him even more.

And I'd already liked him a lot. Like, really a lot.

I put on my favorite dress, the only one I took with me everywhere I went because it suited any occasion and looked pretty damn good on me. The black halter dress hugged my curves, but flared out into a swishy skirt that stopped just above my knees. I wore my black heels too, though not the stilettos I'd had on when I first showed up at the resort.

Someone knocked on the door to my room right as I finished getting dressed. I already had my makeup on and my hair fixed. Ready to go.

I swung the door inward.

Ollie's eyes went wide, then slid half closed while he drank in the sight of me. "Damn, Mara, you look hot enough to melt steel."

"Thank you." I spun around so he could see my dress swishing around my legs. "You look sizzling hot too."

He wore a suit that showed off his sexy physique without seeming too tight. It fit him so well that I swore my mouth actually watered when I saw him. Oliver Jackson was one gorgeous man.

How could any woman have called him her gay best friend? How could Heidi Mackenzie have dumped him to go back to her ex?

All his exes had to be insane. No other explanation fit the facts.

Ollie offered me his arm, like a Victorian gentleman escorting a lady to a ball.

I slipped my arm under his.

He led me downstairs, where we met my parents, and all four of us got into a waiting taxi.

The restaurant was very nice, but my mom had to comment that it wasn't "five-star quality" like her favorite restaurant back home. She also curled her lip when she saw the menu.

"Red meat?" she said with a hint of horror in her voice. "I'm a vegan."

"Since when?" I asked. "You love escargot, which is snails. Little creatures that died so you could eat them."

My dad patted Mom's arm. "Sher, don't be difficult. I know steak and potatoes isn't your usual fare, but you can make do." He glanced at me. "Your mother is not a vegan."

So she was just trying to be a pain. *Ugh.* Would she ever get over the fact I wasn't married to her favorite guy, Nico? And that I liked staying at a nudist resort? I was positive what bothered her the most was that I'd broken all her rules of propriety.

Well, almost all of them. I hadn't become a nudist yet.

I doubted I ever would do that. I loved being naked with Ollie, but the thought of having other people look at me sans clothing made my skin itch. Everywhere. Really itch.

"Something wrong?" Ollie whispered to me. He'd leaned in so my parents wouldn't hear, though they sat across the table from us.

Realizing I had actually been scratching my arm, I forced myself to stop. "No, I'm fine."

"You sure? I know your mom can make you kind of crazy."

"I'm okay, really. You're so sweet to ask."

He kissed my cheek.

Mom finally ordered a steak, despite claiming she'd become a vegan after sitting down in this restaurant. She even enjoyed her steak. Dad and Ollie told jokes and talked about computers. My father had never been adept with electronic devices, so Ollie gave him pointers on how to make his phone work better and how to optimize his home computer.

Mom said nothing. She stared down at her plate while she ate, and when she'd finished, she stared down at her lap.

I wanted to ask if she was okay, but Ollie and Dad were still talking. It would've been rude to interrupt.

When Ollie excused himself to go to the restroom, I finally asked, "Mom, are you okay? You seem…not quite yourself."

She jerked her head up, blinking at me. "What?"

Dad hooked an arm around her shoulders. "Mara thinks you're unhappy, Sher. She's worried."

"Why? I'm fine," Mom said.

I chewed on my bottom lip.

Dad sighed. "Our daughter can see you're not happy. So can I. Why don't you tell us what's wrong?"

She fiddled with the napkin on her lap. "I don't understand why Mara wants to stay at that resort. Mr. Jackson seems nice enough, but he's not the right man for Mara."

"How do you know that?" I asked. "You've barely spoken to Ollie."

"I know, but—" She raised her head to look at me, her lips pinched. "He's a nudist."

She spoke those words in such a soft voice that I almost didn't hear her.

Groaning, I said, "And nudism isn't proper, right? Nothing I've ever done has been proper or acceptable, even though I was doing everything you wanted and making myself miserable in the process. I married Nico because you thought he was the right man for me. Well, guess what? He absolutely was not."

"I never told you what to do." Mom slapped her napkin down on the table. "I tried to show you how ladies need to act, so you wouldn't be embarrassed. The level of society in which we live is not forgiving of rash behavior."

"Rash? I never did anything without first considering how you would feel about it."

"You're dating a nudist."

"Ollie is the sweetest, kindest, most honorable man I've ever met. If you'd taken the time to get to know him, like Dad has, maybe you'd realize how amazing Ollie is." I grabbed my napkin and wrung it with both hands. "I've never been good enough for you, so why should I keep trying? Might as well strip naked right here in this restaurant. Maybe if I get arrested, you'll realize how much I've hated my life, until I came here."

Tears streamed down my cheeks. My eyes burned, and my gut twisted into knots. I had never spoken to my mother this way. Never. But the words had come pouring out, and I couldn't take them back. Did I want to?

Ollie returned from the bathroom.

He stopped at his chair, laying one hand on it while his gaze flicked back and forth between me and my mom.

"The ladies had a little argument," Dad said. "Why don't you take Mara out on the balcony for some fresh air?"

"Sure," Ollie said.

I got up, and he clasped my hand, leading me across the dance floor and out onto the empty balcony.

Then he pulled me into his arms.

With my head on his chest, pressed against his warm body, I felt all the anxiety sluice out of me.

"You don't have to tell me what happened," he said. "But I'm here to listen if you need it."

I sucked in a deep breath, exhaled it in a rush, and told him everything.

There was something about this man that made me feel free and whole and like the best version of myself.

But could we work out in the long run?

Chapter Twenty-Six

Ollie

We hung out on the balcony for a while, with Mara cuddled up to me and the music from inside drifting out here to us. The balcony overlooked the river that wound through town, but we couldn't see it in the dark, except for the pale glow of the moon shimmering on its surface, like a ghost hovering below us.

Mara's argument with her mom had really upset her. I couldn't imagine arguing with either of my parents that way. I'd never needed to, because my parents trusted me to make my own decisions and my own mistakes. Mara's dad seemed like a cool guy, but it was obvious he'd let his wife run the show for a long time. Now Mara wanted to take control, and Sheryl couldn't deal with it.

I actually kind of liked Sheryl. Maybe that was weird, considering she wanted Mara to get back together with Nico, but Sheryl Kanda Severins seemed like a smart lady who loved her daughter—but who went overboard trying to protect her from the world.

Mara lifted her head off my shoulder. "Thank you."

"For what?"

"Being so sweet and understanding. It's been a crazy week, and that's all my fault."

I cradled her cheek in one hand. "None of it's your fault. Your mom and your ex-husband threw you for a loop, and I think you're doing amazingly well under the circumstances."

"See? I was right. You are sweet and understanding."

"Just don't call me your gay best friend. Not sure I can handle that right now."

"I will never call you that." She kissed me, her lips lingering on mine as softly as a feather teasing my skin. "I've had sex with you. Lots. So trust me, I know exactly how straight you are."

"Glad to hear it." I linked my arms around her waist, tugging her closer to me. "Want to make out for a few minutes before we go back inside?"

She smiled, the expression brightening her from the inside out. "Yes, please."

For several minutes, we kissed. And kissed. And kissed. Her lips were soft and warm and tasted like steak sauce. Maybe that should've been gross, but the savory flavor of it just made me want her even more. Since we were in a restaurant, I couldn't do what I really wanted to do. I settled for making love to her mouth since I couldn't make love to her the right way.

When we finally went back inside, Mara's lips no longer had any lipstick on them. Luckily, I'd brought a handkerchief, so I wiped her lipstick off my mouth before we headed back to the table where her parents waited for us.

Sheryl seemed surprised when I pulled Mara's chair out for her and waited for her to sit down before I took my seat.

Yeah, I seriously doubted Nico ever held a chair for a woman or held a door for a woman or any other polite things nice guys did. Were all the guys in the Severins family's "level of society" as dickish as Nico? Nah, they couldn't all be like him. I'd met nice rich people. Maybe the Severins family liked hanging out with asshats. It was more likely Sheryl insisted they hang out with those people so they could be a part of that kind of society.

Whatever kind it was, I didn't want to go there.

I glanced at Mara. Could I stay with her and not join her world? She said she hated her life, but it was all she knew. I couldn't ask her to give that up for me. We'd known each other for such a short time. I already knew I wanted to be with her for the long haul, but maybe she didn't want that.

Sheryl cleared her throat. "Mara, I'm sorry. I shouldn't have gotten short with you, and it's none of my business how you live your life."

Mara's eyes widened. "Mom—"

Her mother raised a hand. "Let me finish, please. I have a lot to say."

"Okay."

I laid my hand over Mara's on her lap, giving it a quick squeeze. She flashed me a grateful look.

"Your father and I had a long talk," Sheryl said, "while you and Ollie were out on the balcony. I don't mean to make you feel unworthy. It's time I told you why I've been so hard on you and pushed you to be a proper lady, or what I thought was a proper lady."

Sheryl had her hands clasped tightly on the table.

Peter closed his hand over hers, giving her an encouraging smile.

"When I started dating your father," Sheryl said, "my mother disapproved. Peter wasn't an appropriate match for me, since his family was middle class." She looked at me when she said, "The Kandas have owned a string of high-end furniture stores for decades. When my great grandparents started the business, it catered to everyone, not just the wealthy. Over the years, as my family became more affluent, the business changed too. We lost sight of where we came from and stopped trying to appeal to anyone who wasn't in the right strata of society."

Why was she telling me this? Since she didn't want Mara dating me, she had no reason to explain herself to me.

But she kept looking at me when she spoke again. "I refused to stop seeing Peter. My mother put her foot down and threatened to disinherit me. I told her to go ahead and do it, because I would not break off the relationship."

Mara's mouth fell open. "Mom, you never told me any of this."

"I know. I'm sorry, Mara, I should have told you everything a long time ago." Sheryl bowed her head for a couple seconds, then met her daughter's gaze. "I stood up to my family, but it nearly cost us everything. Your father and I moved in together and got jobs. I worked as a cleaning woman, and he found work as a carpenter."

"What?" Mara said, gaping at her mother. "I thought—You always talk about the big check Grandma and Grandpa gave you as a wedding gift. Half a million dollars, that's what you said."

"And they did give us that gift." Sheryl glanced at her husband and smiled with genuine, deep affection. "Six months after we struck out on our own, my mother gave up. She agreed to accept Peter as long as we got married and both worked for the family business. The Kanda family business. You know your Severins grandparents aren't wealthy. My parents welcomed Peter and his parents into the family. It took a long time for the 'right' people to accept my new family, but eventually they did."

I still couldn't figure out what Sheryl was getting at with her story. Sure, I got that she was admitting she and Mara had more in common than Mara had thought. They both decided to be with men their mothers disapproved of, but I sensed Sheryl was trying to make some other point too. Damned if I knew what.

Mara's mom fixed her attention on me again. "I apologize, Ollie, for the way I've treated you. Peter has been telling me for days that I should look to my past for answers about the present. My husband likes to say cryptic things and then wait for me to figure it out. It's how he shows me what I've been doing wrong."

Peter patted his wife's hand. "You need a nudge in the right direction sometimes, that's all."

She nodded. "That's why I adore you, Peter. You're more than the love of my life. You're my conscience too."

"No, you don't need me for that. You always do the right thing, eventually."

"Because you show me the way." Sheryl turned back to her daughter, and her eyes glistened with what seemed like tears gathering in her eyes. "I'm so sorry, Mara. I love you, and I'm more proud of you than you could ever imagine. Despite everything I've done, you have grown into a strong and capable woman. You run that apartment complex without any help from me or your father, and you stood up to me when I went too far."

Mara opened her mouth, closed it, opened it. She did that several times before she managed to speak. "Thank you, Mom. But I'm far from perfect. I've screwed up so many times—"

"No, don't do that. Do not dismiss your accomplishments." Sheryl leaned forward, and the tears pooling in her eyes shimmered even more. "You are a better, stronger woman than I could ever hope to be. Don't let anyone, not even me, tell you otherwise."

"You've never told me I'm not worthy," Mara said in a hushed voice. "I decided that's what you meant every time you told me how to behave like a proper lady. I was so afraid of screwing up and embarrassing you and Dad that I never did anything I really wanted to do. That's my fault, not yours."

"I made you feel that way. It wasn't my intention, but that doesn't change the fact I made you feel unworthy." The tears rolled down Sheryl's cheeks. "If I ever say anything about being proper again, don't listen to me. Listen to your heart, Mara, always. I let my mother convince me that being proper was the only way to survive in this world, but she was wrong. Find your own way."

Mara started crying too, wiping the tears away with her fingers.

Peter draped an arm around Sheryl's shoulders and gave her a squeeze. "It's okay, Sher. Everything's okay. Now that Mara understands why you are the way you are, she won't be afraid anymore."

"That's right," Mara said, sniffling. "I might have accidentally wound up staying at a nudist resort, but being there has made me realize I need more out of life than being accepted by the upper-crust elite. I don't care about any of that. Not sure what I do want, but I know I need to change my life."

Peter handed his wife a napkin.

She blew her nose delicately. "I want you to do whatever makes you happy. Promise me you'll do that."

"I will, Mom."

The ladies excused themselves to go powder their noses, which I figured meant they needed a few minutes to stop crying and splash some water on their faces or whatever women did to freshen up after a round of tearful confessions. Guys didn't do tearful confessions, so I had no idea what happened after something like that.

Peter and I talked about sports while we waited for our girls to come back. We were in the middle of a debate about which baseball team would win the World Series this year when I spotted a waiter leading two people toward an empty table across from us.

I froze. That was Heidi and Nico.

They couldn't be on a date. Heidi would never go for a jerk like Nico Marshall. Would she? Nah, she had to be trying to make me jealous or something.

Jeez, was I really that narcissistic? Thinking Heidi wanted me so badly that she'd hook up with Nico to get my attention. That had to be the dumbest thing I'd ever thought.

Nico settled onto a chair at the table, not more than fifteen from where Peter and I sat.

The waiter pulled out a chair for Heidi, who smiled and said something to him, probably "thank you."

Of course Nico hadn't bothered to get her chair for her. What a douche.

Heidi noticed me, her eyes flaring wide for a heartbeat, then she smiled and waved.

I waved back.

She waved at Peter too, who reciprocated.

When Nico saw me, he puffed up like a baboon who'd claimed his mate and wanted every other boy baboon to know she belonged to him. He aimed a smug smile at me.

Did he really think I'd get jealous? Did he think I'd care if he dated Heidi? Well, maybe I would—but not because I still had feelings for her. She was a nice girl, and I didn't want to see her get tangled up with somebody like Nico. Heidi deserved a lot better.

Mara and Sheryl came back to our table, giving me a great excuse to stop wondering what Nico was up to with Heidi. She was an adult who could make her own decisions.

The music started up again.

I guessed the band had taken a break, though I hadn't really noticed the lack of music. The conversation between Mara and her mom had kept the four of us distracted from everything else.

Nico got up and offered Heidi his hand. "Let's dance. You look so beautiful in that dress, it's a shame to waste it by just sitting here. I'm so lucky to have a date with a woman of your caliber, and I want to show you off to the world."

What a load of bullshit. I could practically smell it, that's how deep he'd shoveled into the shit to dig out that smarmy line.

Heidi blushed and took his hand, letting Nico lead her out onto the dance floor.

No, she couldn't be falling for his bullshit. Heidi was smarter than that.

"Ollie," Mara said sharply.

I realized I'd zoned out on the conversation at our table and smiled at Mara. "Sorry. What were you saying?"

Her gaze sharpened on me like a laser beam zeroing in on its target. "Dad asked if you've ever gone fishing."

"Oh. Yeah, sorry, I missed that." I faced Peter. "No, I've never gone fishing. Is that something you like to do?"

"Yes," Peter said, "I used to take Mara with me sometimes, until she got older and lost interest in it. Maybe both of you could join me and Sheryl on the boat sometime."

"Sounds awesome."

I couldn't stop myself from glancing at Nico and Heidi as they walked onto the dance floor and he took her in his arms, smiling and saying something that made her laugh.

Mara jabbed me in the side with her finger and whispered, "What are you doing? You haven't taken your eyes off Heidi since she walked into the restaurant."

Leaning in close enough her parents wouldn't hear, I said, "I'm worried about what your ex-husband is up to with Heidi."

"That's their business, not yours."

"I know, but Heidi's kind of…too trusting for her own good."

"Maybe you should go tell Heidi you're still in love with her."

"Why would I do that? I'm not in love with her."

"Are you sure about that?" Mara said loud enough for her parents to hear. "You haven't been able to stop looking at Heidi since she showed up the other day."

Nico was watching us and smiling like the smug baboon he was.

He must've noticed Mara's angry expression. I needed to calm her down and explain things, but I couldn't do that with Nico the Numbskull watching. He'd probably break out a bag of popcorn and munch on it while he enjoyed the show.

"Let's go outside and talk," I said to Mara. "Please."

"Fine." She hopped up. "Let's go."

She half walked, half ran toward the front doors.

And I hurried after her.

Chapter Twenty-Seven

Mara

What was wrong with me? I never got hotheaded. I cowered in corners and got so anxious it made me nauseous, but I never confronted anyone. Well, I had tonight. I'd confronted my mom, and she hadn't blown up. Instead, she'd confessed the truth to me, about how Grandma made her feel and how she did the same thing to me. But nothing my mom said had upset me as much as the way Ollie kept staring at Heidi.

I shouldn't be jealous. Right? It was dumb. Ollie wanted to be with me.

So why did he care so much about Heidi going on a date with Nico? He ought to be glad about that, since it meant Nico was losing interest in getting me back.

Unless Nico was using Heidi as a ploy to make me jealous.

I marched halfway across the parking lot, having no idea where I was going, before I stopped and spun around to face Ollie.

He raised his hands, palms out. "I am not in love with Heidi. I never was. We dated for five minutes last year, that's all."

Before I responded, I took a moment to calm myself with slow, deep breaths. "You were staring at her. And it was obvious you didn't like her being with Nico."

"Yeah, but that doesn't mean I want her back."

"Even if you don't love her, you're still attracted to her and still feel something for her. During that charades game, you couldn't take your eyes off Heidi."

"Because I couldn't figure out what she was supposed to be acting out."

"You looked like you really enjoyed leering at her naked body."

"Come on, Mara." He threw his arms up. "We were all naked. It's a nudist resort."

"And I'm the uptight city girl who won't take her clothes off." I hugged myself, suddenly feeling chilled. "Maybe you belong with someone like Heidi, someone who's not tied up in knots with all these hang-ups and anxieties."

Ollie strode up to me, grasped my upper arms, and looked me straight in the eye. "I want you, Mara. Only you. But Heidi is a nice girl, and I don't want her to get hurt as part of some scheme Nico's cooked up to make you jealous."

"I'm not jealous."

He leaned in closer, his lips hovering a hair's breadth from mine. "I'm not jealous either, not of Heidi and whoever she goes out to dinner with. The only time I get jealous is when Nico looks at you." One side of his mouth slanted upward. "I didn't like it much when Damian looked at you either, and he's my best friend."

"I get jealous whenever Heidi snuggles up to you. It's awful, and I don't want to feel that way, but I can't help it."

He brushed hair away from my face, his finger grazing my skin. "Heidi never snuggled up to me. She tried to kiss me once, but I told her I'm not into her anymore. She gets it, I think. But even if she doesn't, I have zero interest in her—except as a friend."

"Oh. Good." Having him so close was making me...tingle. I should've moved away, but I couldn't convince my body to do it. "I have zero interest in Nico, in any context."

"Glad to hear it." He slid an arm around my waist, drawing me closer until our bodies met. "Maybe I better show you how I really feel."

I couldn't catch my breath, with his body molded to mine and the heat of him penetrating me. "That's not necessary. I believe you."

"But I've always been better at show than tell."

He thrust his free hand into my hair, cradling my head so he could tip it back, curving my neck. With a soft groan, he dragged his tongue up the column of my throat, leaving a trail of moist heat on my skin. The air cooled the moisture, making goosebumps raise all over my body and my knees go weak. I clutched at his shirt to keep from collapsing at his feet, but every thought fled my brain when he danced his tongue over the sensitive skin just under my ear.

"Oliver," I breathed.

He pulled my lobe, and my diamond stud earring, between his teeth and licked it.

My knees buckled.

Ollie held me up with his strong arms and murmured in my ear, "Do you understand now?"

"Yes. I—" My voice failed me when he sucked on my lobe and tugged on the diamond stud with his teeth. "Oh, Ollie…"

He lifted his head to look at me. "Told you I was better at showing than telling."

"Mm-hm." I laid the back of my hand on my cheek. "You definitely know how to set me on fire from head to toe."

"Because you show me what you like, without saying a word." He pushed a hand between our bodies, cupping my mound. "I love finding every way to drive you crazy."

I tilted my hips forward, pushing his hand more firmly into me. "You make me feel wild and free, like I can do anything and nothing bad will happen."

"How wild are you feeling right now?"

"Like I want you to throw me down on the hood of the nearest car and fuck me."

He glanced over my shoulder and sighed. "Better save that for next time. Your parents are coming this way."

"Oh." For the first time ever, I didn't panic at the idea of someone catching me in an intimate moment with a man. Instead, I turned toward my parents and said, "We'll meet you at the car."

They veered in that direction.

Ollie held my hand while we made our way to the car. He kept holding my hand on the drive back to the resort, and he didn't let go until we walked through the door to my room. Our room. I wanted to make love with him, but he suggested tonight had been emotional and everybody needed a good night's rest. I had to agree. The evening's events had taken a toll, and I was ready to sleep.

Once we got in bed, he kissed my lips tenderly. "Not sure I can control myself. I might wake you up five times overnight to make love to you."

"I wouldn't mind that."

"You need to rest." He kissed me again. "There's always tomorrow."

After another kiss, a long and sexy one that made me tingle again, we curled up under the covers together, naked. I'd always wanted to sleep naked, but it had seemed like an improper thing to do, so I never tried it. I'd slept naked all night with Ollie once before, but going to bed in the nude still seemed wild and sinful.

And I loved it. The feeling reminded me of Ollie.

I woke in the morning in a fantastic mood, well rested and energized for the day ahead. Ollie had left me a note explaining he had to get up early to handle office duties, so I should go ahead and have breakfast in the dining hall with the other guests. He promised to find me later. And he signed the note, "Love, Ollie."

Once I'd done my usual morning routine—face washing, moisturizing, putting on makeup, fixing my hair—I got dressed and headed for the door.

Someone knocked on it.

Was it Ollie? He'd implied I wouldn't see him until after breakfast, but maybe he'd gotten his chores done earlier than expected. The prospect of seeing him again made me almost giddy, so I flung the door open.

Nico leaned against the jamb. "Morning, Mar-Mar."

"I hate that nickname, and you know it." I tried to push past him, but he thrust out an arm to stop me, so I glowered at him. "Out of my way."

"We need to talk."

"No, we don't."

He moved in front of me, forcing me to shuffle backward. "I didn't sleep with Heidi."

"She turned you down? What a shocker. I knew she was a smart girl."

"Oh, I could've fucked her if I'd wanted to. I can spot an easy lay at a hundred feet." He stretched an arm out to take hold of a lock of my hair, twining it around his finger. "But I was more interested in your reaction to seeing me with Heidi."

"Get out of my way."

"Not until you admit you got jealous." He leered at me, roving his gaze up and down my body. "You and Ollie got in a big fight after that. He's jealous of me being with Heidi, and you're jealous of her for being with me. We've still got a connection, Mar-Mar. Stop fighting it."

"Oh please." I tried to squeeze around him, but he managed to bar the entire doorway with his body by spreading his legs and arms. I glowered at him again. "If you don't move on your own, I'll make you do it."

He laughed. "Little Mara thinks she's a superhero. That's so damn cute. You can't even get in an elevator unless somebody pushes the buttons for you."

"You don't know me at all."

"I'm the only one you can be with. Ollie Jackson will get sick of you eventually, and you'll realize the truth."

Fisting my hands at my sides, I gritted my teeth and hissed, "Go. To. Hell."

Then I backed up a few steps and took a running start before swinging my leg up to kick him in the gut.

Nico flew backward, landing in the middle of the hall flat on his ass.

While he lay stunned, I rushed past him and down the hall to the office door. I knocked, but he didn't answer. I turned the knob, finding it unlocked, and swung the door open.

No Ollie.

I spun around just as Nico roused from his shock.

He lifted his head to look at me. "Damn, Mara, what's gotten into you?"

"Liberation."

I stepped over him on my way to the stairs. Just as I reached the landing, Nico called out to me.

At the bottom of the staircase, I swerved left to head for the dining hall. My feet stopped moving so suddenly I almost tripped over my own toes.

There, halfway between where I stood and the door to the dining hall, Ollie leaned against the wall with a naked Heidi plastered to his body. He wore his work uniform. Heidi was puckering her lips, leaning in for a kiss, all but begging for it. He held her head in both hands like he was about to lay one on her.

My heart pounded. My head grew light and wobbly, or at least it felt that way. My hand flew to my chest all on its own accord, and I couldn't breathe.

Ollie noticed me. His eyes bulged, and he shoved Heidi away.

She tumbled over backward, landing on her rump.

"Mara," Ollie said, hurrying toward me. "It's not what it looks like."

"What's going on?"

"She was trying to kiss me, but—"

"Looked like you were about to kiss her."

"No." He bracketed my face with his hands. "I was trying to push her away. Heidi's stronger than she looks, and she was really determined. I couldn't push her away too hard or I might accidentally hurt her." He glanced over his shoulder at Heidi and winced. "Looks like I hurt her anyway."

Heidi was sitting on the floor massaging her ass.

I guessed he had needed to be more careful pushing her away, but still, he'd taken who-knew-how-long to even try it. Was I being irrational? I had no idea. Nico had made me feel like a foolish, stupid girl for so long that I didn't know if I could trust my own instincts. They urged me to believe Ollie. I'd known him for such a short time. What if I trusted the wrong man again? Gave my heart and soul to the wrong man again?

The adrenaline from my confrontation with Nico had me wired. I knew that, but I couldn't do a damn thing to stop it.

Ollie gazed into my eyes with such earnestness that it made my chest ache. "I care about you, Mara, a hell of a lot. Please believe me, I don't want Heidi—or anyone else."

Heidi clambered to her feet and hugged herself, her attention on me and Ollie. She bit down on her lip so hard it turned white, veering her gaze away from us. Head bowed, she slumped her shoulders.

I had no energy left to feel bad for her. Why should I empathize with Heidi, anyway? She had repeatedly tried to steal Ollie away from me.

"Mara."

Ollie's voice drew my focus back to him.

I shut my eyes for a second, hauling in a deep breath and exhaling it slowly. When I looked at him again, I shook my head. "I can't do this. You've come to mean so much to me, Ollie, but I shouldn't have rushed into this thing with you. I'm fresh out of a bad marriage, clogged up with all these crazy anxieties and fears, and I had no right to drag you into my mess."

"What are you saying?"

Something I did not want to say but that I'd suddenly realized I needed to say—to do, for myself and for whatever this was between us. "I have to go home. Be alone, and try to figure out what I need and what I want. I haven't really lived my life on my own terms, what with my mom and Nico telling me how to behave and who to love. I get why my mom did it, and I'm not angry with her anymore. Nico's another story."

Ollie bent his head to level our gazes, his nose millimeters from mine. "What about me? Us?"

"I don't know. Honestly, I just don't know." I peeled his hands away from my face, though I loved his touch, because I had to start separating myself from him right now. "I know I love being with you, and I meant it when I said you make me feel free and wild and happier than I've ever been. But I need to live my old life, for real, before I can commit to anything else. I don't expect you to wait for me. I'll understand if you can't."

He stared at me for so long I wondered if he might be considering how to phrase "fuck you, bitch" in a polite way. But no, Ollie Jackson would never say anything like that. Maybe I was saying those words to myself. How could I walk away from an amazing man? Maybe I'd lost my mind, for real, but all I knew was I had to sort out my own life before I could share it with anyone else.

Ollie kissed the tip of my nose and rested his forehead on mine. "You go home and do whatever you need to do. I'll be here, waiting for you, for as long as it takes."

I took his face in my hands and kissed him. "You're a good man, Oliver. The best I've ever known."

Then I walked away.

Chapter Twenty-Eight

Well, at least Mara hadn't said I was like her gay best friend. This time, I got dumped the old-fashioned way—face to face, with apologies and explanations. I supposed that was better than getting dumped by text message. Yeah, that happened to me too. A brush-off text was bad enough, but a brush-off text full of crying emojis was even worse. I still couldn't keep a girlfriend, no matter how solid and hot the connection was between me and the girl in question.

Mara hadn't exactly broken up with me. Had she? Sitting on a little sofa here in the entertainment room, alone—everyone else had gone to the dining hall for breakfast—I replayed in my mind everything she'd said. I remembered all of it, word for word. She needed time. She needed to live her old life for a while. She didn't expect me to wait for her, but she clearly hoped I would.

How long did it take a woman to sort out her life?

Maybe I shouldn't wait for her, but I'd meant it when I said I would. I knew we had a connection, a strong one, and it was based on more than sex. I'd gotten to know the amazing, smart, strong woman behind all those hang-ups. She'd gotten over all of that, anyway. Well, most of it. Maybe she did need to go home for a while to figure out how to be herself—her true self, the one I'd gotten to know—without the complications of hanging out at a naturist resort with me, my ex, my best friend, and a bunch of other wacky but lovable people.

And then there was Nico.

I picked up a deck of cards and shuffled it, not really paying attention to what I was doing. The sound of the shuffling cards became kind of soothing, and I relaxed back into the little sofa. Shuffle. Shuffle. I needed patience if I wanted to have Mara in my life, and I knew she was worth it. But what if she decided being with me didn't fit in her new life plan? Shuffle. Shuffle. The cards poured out of one hand into the other, over and over. Nothing I could do if Mara wanted to leave. Unless I tied her to her bed upstairs. As hot as that sounded, I kind of doubted holding Mara hostage would convince her we belonged together.

My hand slipped, and the deck of cards flew out of my hand, spraying across the table, the floor, and a couple of chairs.

Shit. Maybe I was cursed.

Peripherally, I noticed someone stepping into the doorway. When I glanced up, I groaned out a long, pathetic sigh. "What do you want now, Heidi? You've screwed up my life enough for one day."

"I'm sorry, Ollie." She shuffled up to the table, where I had my feet propped on it, and only then did I realize she was wearing clothes. "I know I screwed up everything, and I want to fix it. Or at least try to."

Could I really blame Heidi for the fact my life had been dumped into a shithole again? It wasn't fair to pile all the blame on her shoulders.

I sat up and scrubbed my face with both hands, groaning again. "I'm sorry too. You didn't help matters, but my life would suck even if you hadn't tried to lay a big, wet smacker on me in the hall."

"Mara's packing. I saw her when I walked past her room. The door was open." Heidi perched her butt on the table's edge. "I need to apologize and explain myself. It won't take long, I promise."

"Okay, fine." I made a go-on gesture. "Get it over with."

"I need to say this to Mara too." Heidi got up, grabbed my hand, and tugged. "Please, Ollie, come with me. I won't do anything crazy, I swear. But we need to go upstairs to catch Mara before she leaves."

As much as I did not want to do it, I let Heidi lead me upstairs. Mara was just zipping up her suitcase. By the looks of things, she'd already packed her multitude of other bags. The dresser drawers hung open, empty.

Heidi and I stopped a few feet inside the doorway.

Mara swiveled her head to look at us, her focus veering down to my hand which Heidi still held and then up to my face. Her lips tightened.

I ripped my hand free of Heidi's. "She grabbed my hand to drag me upstairs, that's all. I am not having sex with Heidi."

"Yes, I can see that." Mara's lips twisted to one side, then the other, like she was trying not to smile. "At least she's not super-glued to your body anymore."

She was teasing me, right? That had to be a good sign.

Heidi stepped between me and Mara. "I need to apologize to both of you. I've done stupid, awful things. I'm so sorry, and you have my word I will never bother either of you again. Maybe some-day we can be friends, Mara, but I'll understand if that's never pos-sible. And Ollie, I understand if you don't want me around either. I won't come back to the resort again."

I shoved my hands in my pants pockets. "I can't ban you be-cause you dumped me and then tried to seduce me. Let's just forget that stuff happened and move on."

"That's really generous of you, Ollie." Tears welled in Heidi's eyes, and she sniffled. "Thank you. I don't deserve your forgiveness, but I'm grateful you can see a way to move past all my craziness."

"I forgive you, Heidi."

A single sob burst out of her. She flumped down on the bed, keep-ing her head down until she'd calmed her staccato breathing. Wip-ing at her eyes, she raised her face to Mara. "I am so sorry, Mara, for everything. I've been so horrible, trying to steal Ollie away from you. I convinced myself you two weren't serious about each other, that it was just a vacation fling. But now I see how much you two belong together. I swear I have never in my life tried to seduce a guy away from another girl. It's just not me."

"Yeah, it really isn't," I said.

Mara studied Heidi for a moment, her expression giving away nothing.

Heidi grabbed a tissue from the box on the bedside table and blew her nose.

Finally, Mara sighed and sat down beside Heidi. "I forgive you. I honestly don't know if friendship will ever be possible between us, but I won't rule it out. That's the best I can offer."

"It's more than I deserve. Thank you, Mara." Heidi blew her nose again. "I know there isn't any excuse for the way I behaved, but there is kind of an explanation. My boyfriend, Tim, he dumped me last summer. It was the fifth time he'd broken up with me. I kept going back because he kept swearing he'd never cheat on me again, that he loved me so much, that our relationship meant everything to him. And I kept believing him."

"Yeah, I know," I said. "You pushed me overboard so you could go back to him."

"But I regretted it almost immediately. It was too late, though, and I couldn't come crawling back here."

Mara handed Heidi another tissue.

Heidi dried her eyes with it while she said, "I believed I had to fight for my relationship with Tim, to keep trying over and over, because he's not a bad man. He cheated because I wasn't giving him what he needed. Which is bullshit. But I believed that for a long time, partly because he kept telling me it was true."

"I know what that's like," Mara said. "To have someone constantly saying you're not good enough, it hurts. And it burrows into your heart and soul, so deep it can be hard to get it out."

Heidi turned her head toward Mara and blinked rapidly. "How can you be sympathetic to me? I tried to steal Ollie."

"Yeah, but Ollie and I weren't officially a couple. Besides, I'm starting to think you tried to seduce him in public places because you wanted to get caught and be punished for it."

Heidi stared at Mara, her face blank. "How did you know? I just figured that out this morning, after I made myself the wedge that drove you and Ollie apart."

"Once I got over the anger, I realized you must have a lot of insecurities, just like I do." Mara laid her hand over Heidi's. "We have that in common. I understand how other people can mess with your head and make you feel like nothing you do is right. Maybe you should do what I'm doing. Live your life alone for a while and see what happens."

"That sounds like a good idea." Heidi managed a small smile. "You're a super nice person, Mara. I get why Ollie thinks you're amazing."

"He has nothing but nice things to say about you too." Mara patted Heidi's hand. "That's how I know your recent behavior isn't normal for you. And that's why I forgive you. I'm glad we had this talk."

"Me too." Heidi got up. "I'll leave you guys alone now. Please don't give up on each other because of what I did. You two are a perfect match."

She left.

And I was alone with Mara. My skin itched, but I knew it wasn't a physical problem. I had no idea what to say to Mara now. She was leaving. I didn't want her to go, but I couldn't make her stay.

"I get that you need time," I said, "but I meant what I said. I'll wait as long as it takes."

"Yeah, I know." She stood and surveyed her bags. "But I need to do this for myself."

"Let me help you with your luggage."

I reached for the nearest bag, but Mara shooed me away.

"You don't have to do that," she said. "I can manage."

"But it's my job."

"Okay, fine." She picked up one of the smaller suitcases. "I'd appreciate the help."

I picked up the biggest, heaviest suitcase.

Val had offered to drive Mara to the airport with her parents, so I said goodbye to her beside Val's big, super-expensive truck. I kissed her cheek, because anything more seemed weird when she was leaving me. Sure, we hadn't exactly broken up. We hadn't exactly been a couple either. I had no frigging idea what we'd been to each other, but I knew one thing for sure.

I would miss her.

Once Val's truck disappeared down the driveway, I walked over to the little house and knocked on the door.

Eve swung it open and pulled me into a hug. "Ollie, I'm so sorry. I thought you and Mara were perfect for each other."

"So did I. But she didn't really end things. She needs time, that's what she said."

Eve ushered me into the kitchen, waved for me to sit on one of the stools at the island, and took a seat on the one beside me. "Nico told everybody that you and Mara had a huge fight at the restaurant and that she told you to go to hell. I know that's garbage, but I thought I should make you aware of what he said."

"Is that jackass still here?"

"No, Val and I banned him from the resort for life." Eve smiled. "Val literally threw Nico into a cab, along with his luggage, and told Phil to dump him off at the airport."

"Wish I could've done that." I rested my arms on the island, my thoughts rewinding to the last thing Mara said to me before she climbed into Val's truck. "Mara says she needs to sort through all the emotional stuff that happened this week and that means she can't have any contact with me for a while. That feels an awful lot like I've been cut out of her life."

"She'll be back. I can feel it."

"I hope you're right." I drew random patterns on the butcher-block island with my fingertip, obsessed with the pointless task. "I don't have good luck with women. Don't have any luck at all, actually."

"This time it's different." Eve clasped my hand to stop me from drawing invisible lines. "I saw you with Mara. What you two have isn't a fling. It's real, and I know she'll figure that out too."

"Mara needs to learn how to stand on her own two feet, and I get that. But I can't help worrying she'll realize I'm not the right one for her, and I'll be out in the cold. Again."

"Give it time, but don't wait weeks like Val did with me."

I glanced at her sideways, smirking. "Yeah, I remember how you jumped on a plane to California so you could go smack some sense into him."

"When you love someone, you fight for them. That's what I learned last summer."

"First, I have to let Mara do her self-analysis thing. Right?"

"I can't tell you what to do, Ollie. You know Mara better than I do."

"Yeah, I guess." I checked my watch, groaned, and slid off the stool. "A new guest will be here any minute. Better get out there and greet them."

"Let me do it." Eve hopped off her stool. "You need a few days off. Go hang out with Damian and the rest of the gang." She tugged on one of the buttons on my shirt. "And get out of these clothes. That's an order."

"Yes, ma'am."

"Oh, and you're moving back into the guest room here." She tapped my chest. "That's also an order. You wouldn't leave me alone when I was down in the dumps about Val leaving, so I won't leave you alone either."

"That sounds vaguely like you'll be stalking me."

"Only if you try to get away from me." She smiled and patted my cheek. "Relax. I'll ask Damian to keep an eye on you when I'm not around."

"Great. I have a feeling I'll be stalked by everyone at the resort." I pumped my fists in the air halfheartedly and gave a phony whoop. "This is the awesomest vacation ever."

"We'll stalk you only because we love you."

She kissed my cheek and left.

I got my stuff moved into Eve and Val's guest room and got rid of my clothes, then headed out to the lawn. Damian and some of the other guests were playing badminton. I spotted Heidi slinking toward the driveway while lugging a wheeled suitcase.

So I hurried to catch up to her.

Heidi froze when she saw me. "Ollie? What are you doing?"

"Don't leave, Heidi. Not because of me."

"I'm not leaving because of you. Not completely. I need to go home and get my head on straight, somehow."

"Women are walking out on me all over the place today."

"Mara will be back. She's crazy about you." Heidi lunged toward me to give me a quick hug. "You deserve to be happy, Ollie."

"So do you. Promise you won't stay away from the resort on my account. You and the rest of the Kittens love it here."

Heidi rubbed her arms. "We'll see."

A cab drove up, but it wasn't Phil driving this time. He'd still have been on his way to the airport with Nico. I held the door for Heidi while she climbed in, then I bent to kiss her cheek.

"Have a safe trip home," I said.

She smiled a little. "You're a good man, Ollie."

I shut the door, then stowed Heidi's suitcase in the trunk. And for the second time today, I watched a woman I cared about disappear down the tree-shrouded driveway.

Chapter Twenty-Nine

Mara

Make sure the new sign gets put up today, and change those lights in the second-floor hallway," I said to Roger, the head of maintenance in this apartment building. "I don't want any gloomy areas in the public spaces. This building needs to be light and cheerful and welcoming."

"Will do." Roger smiled. "You're really on fire these days, aren't you? A new sign, new decor, new furniture in the lobby. You even hired full-time, on-call child care so parents can go out to dinner and a show without needing to search for a sitter."

"Everyone deserves to have fun. That's something I've learned lately, and I want to ensure our tenants enjoy living here." An idea popped into my head, and I said, "Oh, I also want to have weekly pool parties, weather permitting, with free food and beverages."

Roger scribbled on the almost-full sheet of paper clamped onto his clipboard. "Danny says the tenants keep raving about you and all the changes you're implementing. They love the suggestion boxes you've put on every floor too."

Danny manned the front desk during the daytime, while his twin brother, Dave, handled things at night. Twenty-four-hour concierge service was another new perk. The suggestion boxes on every floor meant nobody needed to feel self-conscious about voicing their opinions, since they no longer had to drop off their suggestion cards at the front desk. They could still do that if they wanted, but they had other options too.

"Thank you, Roger," I said. "I couldn't have done any of this without you and the rest of the staff. It's a team effort."

"With one very smart, very talented woman at the helm. You're our captain, Mara. We follow your lead—not because we have to, but because we love you."

He smiled again and strode off down the hall.

I walked back into my office. Sitting down behind the desk, I got back to work on the new marketing campaign. This one needed more oomph, since it would promote not only this complex but also the two new buildings I'd purchased and planned to refurbish in the same vein as this building. I hadn't asked my parents for money. I hadn't needed to. This apartment complex had become successful enough that I could get a loan from the bank, one I knew I could pay off swiftly once I got the new buildings up and running.

Two weeks had elapsed since I left Au Naturel Naturist Resort—and Ollie. He called me every day, twice a day, and we talked for hours sometimes. I'd told him all about the changes I was making to my business. He often told me how proud he was and how I amazing I was, which always made me blush. Ollie could see that, considering that we usually turned our calls in video chats.

Once, we even turned it into video phone sex. Yeah, that had been soooo hot.

He never asked when we would see each other again. Ollie was too sweet to pester me about that.

I wanted to see him in person. Wanted it so badly I dreamed about it every night. But I needed to finish what I'd started here first. How long could it take to get my chain of apartment complexes going full steam? It had taken months to get this one complex rolling along smoothly.

Waiting that long to see him…

Focus, Mara. You'll never get there unless you finish this marketing campaign.

For the rest of the day, I worked my brain to its limits. Then I headed home to my condo—the big, empty one. Sure, I had plenty of furniture and even artwork on the walls, but this place didn't feel like home anymore. The nudist resort did.

After ordering dinner in, I cuddled up on the sofa with my favorite fleece throw and an action movie on TV. Watching a hunky man fight the bad guys, getting sexily covered in sweat in the process, usually cheered me up. Tonight, it just made me think of Ollie.

Halfway through the movie, I heard the doorbell ring.

I paused the movie and padded over to the door, my fuzzy purple slippers dragging on the wood floor, and swung the door inward.

Nico grinned at me. "Mar-Mar, baby, I've missed you."

"Yeah, I know. I made sure you missed me every time you showed up at my work or showed up at my home or showed up anywhere within a ten-block radius of me."

Had I been running away from my ex-husband? Hell yes. I'd had enough of Nico at the resort, and I did not need to see him ever again.

"Come on, Mara," Nico said in a wheedling tone. "We can still work things out."

I laughed too loudly, because really, his statement was the dumbest thing I'd heard in ages. "Which part of me kicking you in the gut made you think I might ever want to see you again, much less get back together?"

"Thought you'd cool down and get back to being yourself. You know, now that you've gotten away from that freak show."

"I'm looking at a freak show right now." I flapped my hand in a go-away gesture. "Skedaddle."

"We belong together." He slid a hand up and down my arm. "You know I'm the only one who'll put up with your neurotic behavior."

I hadn't been neurotic since I left the resort. I'd found a new focus and a new determination to make my life what I wanted it to be instead of what others thought it should be.

"Go away," I told Nico. "Or do I need to get a restraining order?"

He grasped my shoulders and tugged me closer, lowering his lips toward mine.

I slapped both hands on his chest, stomped my foot down on his, and shoved him away.

Nico stumbled but didn't fall down. "Shit, Mara, what's your problem?"

"You, obviously."

The clacking of high heels made us both glance down the hall.

My mother was marching toward us, looking like a general about to kick the ass of her most derelict soldier. A general dressed in designer clothes. And wearing stiletto heels.

She rammed her stiletto down on Nico's foot and kneed him in the groin. "Get away from my daughter."

Doubled over, he gasped for air.

Mom bent to aim her glare straight into his eyes. "If you keep harassing Mara, I will call in every favor I'm owed to have you arrested and charged with stalking."

Nico finally caught his breath and straightened, though he cupped his privates like he thought Mom might nail him in the balls again. "You attacked me."

"Did I?" my mother said in her most frigid tone. "There's only one witness. What did you see, Mara?"

"Looked to me like he tripped."

Nico gaped at me. "And did what, hit my dick on the doorknob?"

I shrugged. "All I know is you fell before my mom got within ten feet of you. Maybe you had a few beers before you showed up at my apartment to harass and assault me."

"Assault *you*? I'm the one whose balls got burst like a balloon."

My mother dismissed his claim with a hand gesture and a soft snort. "You'll survive and still be fertile. Unfortunately."

"You two are crazy." Nico eyed us like he thought we might both jump on him and start tearing the flesh off his body. "I'm done with you, Mara. Done for good."

"Hallelujah," I said, raising my hands to the heavens.

Nico scurried off down the hall, practically flinging himself into the elevator when the doors opened.

Mom ushered me into my apartment. We both sat down on the sofa.

"Is that a Bruce Willis movie?" she asked, glancing at the TV. Her eyes lit up the way they often did at the prospect of a *Die Hard* movie. "Let's rewind and watch it together from the beginning. I love it when he takes his shirt off."

Yep, my mother loved her man candy. It was the one thing we'd always agreed on, and the one thing that always brought us together. Mutual appreciation of hot, sweaty men beating the bad guys to a pulp.

"Sure," I said. "Let's do that. I'll make popcorn."

"First, I need to talk to you." She stared down at her lap for a moment, then raised her head to look me in the eye. "There's something I've never told you, and it's time I did. I hope it will help you understand my behavior a little better."

I tucked my feet under me cross-legged style. "Okay."

"You know your father and I were married for four years before we had you, our miracle baby." She hesitated, biting her lip the way I often bit mine. "Two years before you were born, I had a miscarriage. The doctors told us I couldn't have children. Your father and I were devastated, and we even started talking about adoption. Went to an agency a few times too. Then the miracle happened. We found out I was pregnant—with you."

"Wow, I never knew that." Miscarriage? No hope of having a baby? God, I couldn't imagine going through something like that.

"The point is that I worried about losing you, while I was pregnant and after you were born. I smothered you because I was terrified something might happen to you." She sniffled and paused to dig a tissue out of her purse, dabbing her eyes with it. "Even once you were old enough that I didn't need to worry about your physical well-being, I still worried you might get hurt in other ways. Emotionally. So I tried to shield you from all of it and prepare you for whatever I couldn't see coming. That's why I was hard on you."

"I get that, Mom, I do. And it's okay." I clasped her hand. "You've always been there for me when it counted. Who stood beside me during the whole divorce court thing?"

"That was the least I could do, after the way I've mistreated you."

"Let's not dwell on the past anymore. I forgive you, and I want us to move forward and start fresh. That's what I've been doing."

"I'd like that. Thank you, Mara." She took my face in her hands and kissed my forehead. "I love you. All I want is for you to be happy."

Tears pricked at my eyes, but I blinked them away. "I love you too, Mom."

She blew her nose, rolled her shoulders back, and said, "You love Ollie too."

"Yeah, I do." An image of Ollie flared in my mind, and my chest ached. "But I don't know if we belong together. We're so different."

"I don't think you're as different as you believe. Besides, your father and I aren't the same, but it works for us. Our differences balance out and complement each other."

"Ollie lives in Oregon. At a nudist resort." I sank back against the sofa. "I want to be with him, and I've kind of been planning for that, but sometimes I think he'll be better off if I let him go. What if my new outlook on life doesn't last? I might slip back into Neurotic Mara mode."

"You have never been neurotic. I force-fed you my fears, and I regret it more than you'll ever know." She slipped an arm around my shoulders. "Don't let my mistakes taint your future. You know what you want, so go and get it." She gave me a quick, firm squeeze. "Go and get *him*."

"I can't fly to Oregon right now. I'm in the middle of re-branding my business."

She patted my arm. "Oh, you won't need to go as far as you think."

"What are you talking about?"

The doorbell rang.

My mother stood. "Get up, Mara. You have a visitor."

"I've had enough visitors tonight. It's probably Nico again."

She shook her head. "No, dear, it's not. I guarantee that."

"Ugh, Mom."

"Get up." She grabbed my hands and pulled. "He's waiting."

He? That single word made my pulse speed up and my skin tingle. It couldn't be.

I jumped up and ran for the door, flinging it open.

Ollie smiled, holding out a bouquet of daisies. "These are for you, Mar—"

He didn't get to finish saying my name. I threw myself at him, latching my arms around his neck and kissing him.

"I'll leave you two alone," Mom said.

The clacking of her heels told me she was walking away, but I didn't pay attention to anything else. Ollie was kissing me back with a hunger I'd never experienced before, and I responded with the same passion. God, he tasted so damn good. He felt so damn good too. With my body crushed to his, I relished the sensation of all his muscles flexing against me, and when he lashed his arms around me, I loved the way his biceps flexed and his hands splayed over my back.

He scuffled into the apartment with me clinging to him, my feet dangling above the floor. We didn't separate our mouths until he backed me into the sofa and I tumbled onto it.

We were both naked inside of one minute.

And he was inside me seconds later.

"Oliver," I whispered into his ear while he made love me to tenderly, taking his time, letting us both revel in the bliss of being together again.

After we both came, and we lay there with Ollie on top of me, I realized the curtains were still open.

Ollie followed my gaze to the windows. "Well, I guess any snoopy neighbors who have telescopes got a good show tonight."

"Let them watch. Who cares?"

He arched his brows. "You really don't care anymore, do you?"

"Nope." I skimmed my fingers up his back, loving the way his breath hitched. "I'm so glad you're here. I'd been planning to wait until I got the business going full steam before I begged you to take me back."

"Begging sounds hot, but it's not necessary." He brushed hair away from my eyes. "I told you I'd wait as long as it takes. I love you, Mara."

"I love you too."

He rolled off me, sitting on the edge of the sofa. "Are you going to stay here in Philadelphia?"

"Only until the two new apartment buildings are ready to go."

"You have two new buildings?"

I nodded. "This time, I bought them myself. Got a loan and everything, without any help from my parents. I'm sure knowing I'm the daughter of Peter Severins and Sheryl Kanda Severins didn't hurt, though."

He laid a hand on my thigh. "You get more amazing every day. How long will you need to stick around here?"

Now that he was here, sitting naked beside me, I had trouble remembering why I needed to stay in Philly. I had employees—lots of smart people who could handle anything that came up. I could work on the marketing plan from anywhere.

"Actually," I said, sitting up, "there's no reason to wait."

"What are you saying?"

"Let's go home, Ollie. Tonight."

He grinned. "Seriously? I don't know if we can get a flight out tonight. Your mom arranged for me to fly here, but the return flight isn't until morning."

"Can't wait that long. I don't care if we ride the bus all the way to Oregon." I wrapped my arms around him. "Just take me home."

He kissed me, long and slow and hot.

"You know," I said when we finally separated our mouths, "I bet my mom and dad can help us get a flight ASAP. They know people."

"How's it going with your mom?"

"We had another talk, and I told her I want us to start fresh instead of focusing on the past. She agreed."

"Glad you two made peace."

I couldn't stop myself from admiring his body, which I hadn't seen in person for two weeks. "Why didn't you tell me you were coming here?"

"Your mom called me this morning and said I should get my ass to Philly. She booked and paid for my flight." He glanced at our naked bodies. "Think we better get dressed if we're going home tonight. Airlines still frown on nude travel."

"Promise me one thing."

"Whatever you want."

"Never, ever wear clothes unless you absolutely have to."

Ollie chuckled. "You got it."

Chapter Thirty

Ollie

*L*ife was perfect. I had my girl, my best friend, and an amazing group of guests who had become like family to me.

Mara and I had gotten home early yesterday morning—pre-dawn early—and slept so late we had breakfast for lunch. After that, we had excused ourselves to spend time alone. Eve and Val didn't mind me taking a few days off. They were happy for me and Mara, and they knew better than anyone what a reunion meant.

Lots of sex. Lots and lots and lots of it.

But today, we were kicking back on the lawn with the other guests. Damian had gone home only long enough to quit his job and move his stuff here. I'd suggested to Eve and Val that Damian would make a great concierge for our expanding resort. They agreed but insisted Damian take today off and start his job tomorrow.

Like I said, life was perfect.

Mara and I were sharing a chaise, with me naked and her clothed. Well, since she wore tiny shorts and a bikini top, "clothed" was a relative term. God, I loved her body. I loved her, period.

"I'm ready for a walk," she said, getting up to stretch her lithe body.

"Yeah, sounds good." I got up too. "Better get some shoes."

She unzipped her shorts and pushed them over her hips, along with her bikini bottoms. They fell to her ankles. She kicked them aside and stripped off her bikini top. Stretching again, she said, "Mm, that's better."

I gaped at her.

Damian raised one brow and smirked.

While he was looking at Mara. Naked Mara. My naked girlfriend.

"Hey!" I said, smacking Damian's arm. "Quit gawking at my girl."

"Chill, Ollie," he said. "If you get bent out of shape every time a guy looks at Mara, you'll need serious therapy. Like, today." He glanced at Mara again. "Especially if she's becoming a naturist."

Mara nodded. "I am."

Pretty sure my eyes bulged like a cartoon character's.

She walked up to me and settled her palms on my chest. "Relax, Ollie. It doesn't matter how many guys look at me because I'm only looking at you."

"You really want to be a naturist?"

"I do. We both have to stay clothed while we're doing our jobs, but the rest of the time..." Her lips curved into a sexy smile. "I'll be au naturel."

"Mara's got a job here?" Damian said.

"Oh yeah," I told him. "Didn't you hear? She's our new marketing specialist. And she's also an entrepreneur in her own right, since she owns three apartment complexes."

"Damn, you really lucked out. Didn't you, Ollie?"

"I sure did."

Mara slipped her hand into mine. "So did I."

We ambled down the nature trail hand in hand.

Before I knew it, a month went by. Mara and Damian settled into their new jobs and excelled at them. I'd never doubted they would. Damian being...Damian, he couldn't resist bringing some of his Rom sensibilities to the resort. When he suggested he could offer our guests palm readings, I wasn't sure about it. I mean, that seemed awfully carnivalesque for a family-friendly place. But Eve and Val both loved the idea.

And of course, Damian ran with it. He convinced Val that he needed a special place to do his palm readings, and Val agreed. With Val's backing, Damian bought a freaking gypsy wagon, the kind that was usually pulled around by horses. And oh yeah, Damian suggested we offer horseback nature tours too. Eve and Mara loved that idea, but it meant we needed more employees to clean up the literal shit the horses left behind.

The gypsy wagon sat parked by the guest house, on the opposite side from the lawn, where all new guests would see it. The wagon had a blue, barrel-shaped roof and ornate decorations inside and out. The interior featured a small table with a gold tablecloth and lots of fringe hanging from it. Damian dressed up like a gypsy too, in clothes that Mara described as "hot Rom chic." His outfit seemed a little overdone to me, but the guests really did love his fortune-telling routine. He wore his uniform the rest of the time, while handling his concierge duties.

Today, I was greeting new guests—a married couple who had brought their kids with them. The twin boys looked about ten, but I'd never been good at guessing ages. Damian could guess anyone's age with surprising accuracy, which he claimed was "God's gift to the Ludar."

Maybe he did have mystical powers. Who knew? I kind of doubted it, but I had to admit his intuition was often spot on. He'd been wrong about me and Mara, but hey, nobody got everything right all the time.

Just as I was giving the new guests my standard spiel, reciting the resort rules and pointing out all the amenities, the door to Damian's wagon swung open and he hopped down the steps.

"Who is that?" the wife asked, her expression turning very, very appreciative.

Yeah, I'd seen that look a lot since Damian started up his palm reading schtick. Women salivated over him. Mara claimed it was the outfit, and his body. But mostly the outfit.

Damian wore black jeans and a black, long-sleeve shirt with the top three buttons undone, revealing a swath of his tanned chest. The chicks dug that. He also wore big black boots with chunky bronze clasps, a braided hemp necklace, and a big silver ring. He'd kept his hair long like before but purposely made it messy, giving him that "I'm a wild gypsy" look.

"That's Damian," I said to the new people. "He's our concierge, but he also does palm readings, tarot readings, and fortune telling."

"Can he speak to the dead?" the wife asked.

"Oh please," her husband said. "It's all a big show. A bunch of hooey to get more money out of the tourists."

"I can't swear he has supernatural powers," I told them. "But Damian is a genuine gypsy, though they prefer to be called Rom. Damian is descended from a line known as the Ludar."

"He's gorgeous," the wife said. "I'd love to have him read my palm."

"Uh, let's move on to the guest house." I shepherded them in that direction, hoping to defuse the jealousy bomb ticking away inside the woman's husband. I'd gotten used to handling the side effects of having Damian here. Swinging the main doors open, I waved for the family to enter. "Here we are."

The next day, my family showed up. Mara hadn't met my parents and my sister yet, but I knew they'd love her.

My sister, Bailey, marched straight up to Mara and said, "Liver's totally gaga over you, so you better not be mean to him."

"I would never do that," Mara said. "Ollie is my favorite person in the whole world. He's my best friend too."

"Cool." Bailey offered Mara her hand. "I'm Bailey Mariel Jackson, but you can call me B."

"Since when?" I asked. "Last I heard, you wanted to be called Bay, like you're a city or a port or something."

Bailey rolled her eyes and sighed. "When I was twelve, I wanted to be called that. Now I'm B. Get over it, Liver."

"Don't you want to be called BM, for Bailey Mariel? You know, BM like a bowel movement."

"Gross! Grown-ups are so totally retarded." Bailey took Mara's hand. "Come on, let's go someplace private and talk. I need to warn you about all the gross things Ollie does. Like when he eats baked beans and—"

I slapped a hand over Bailey's mouth. "Don't scare Mara away with your disgusting teenage humor."

"Okay, fine." Bailey caught sight of Damian and shrieked. "D-Man! It's you!"

My sister raced over to my best friend and high-fived him. They started talking and laughing, and I really hoped they weren't exchanging stories about baked beans and me.

"Ignore my sister," I told Mara. "She's insane. Teenage boys are supposed to be gross, but Bailey decided she's being a trailblazer by becoming a teenage girl who has a disgusting sense of humor."

"Well, you did start it by calling her BM."

"Yeah, I did." I pulled Mara snug against my side. "My family fell in love with you at first sight. I think I did too."

"I fell for you right away too, but it took me a while to admit it to myself." She latched her arms around my waist. "I'm not afraid anymore. The future isn't a scary, dark place these days. It's bright and full of potential."

"Yeah, it is." I scooped her up in my arms. "Let's go for a nature walk."

"Mm, I know what that means." She wriggled, smiling with excitement. "Naked fun time in the woods."

"And I know the perfect spot."

"I'm all yours, Ollie."

Oh yeah, my life was absolutely perfect.

Chapter Thirty-One

Mara
Two months later

I slid across the wooden bench to make room for Ollie, Bailey, and their parents. My mom and dad sat on the other side of me, leaving me sandwiched between the Severins and the Jacksons, with Ollie right next to me. There was nowhere else I'd rather be.

Ollie slipped his hand into mine, threading our fingers.

The ceremony would start in a few minutes. Eve Holt and Val Silva would tie the knot today, in this beautiful little church eighteen miles from Au Naturel Naturist Resort, with friends and family filling the pews. Lots of people loved Eve and Val. I'd come to love them too, the way I loved my family and Ollie's and all the guests, even Damian too.

Eve and Val seemed like opposites, but they shared important things in common and brought out the best in each other. She was a no-nonsense businesswoman, but Val encouraged her to take time to enjoy life and let go of her inhibitions. He had been a playboy athlete and still had an exhibitionist streak, but Eve brought out the softer side of him, the Val who loved his family and wanted one of his own someday.

Ollie and I had similar effects on each other. I'd been a tangled mess of fears and pent-up desires, but Ollie showed me how to embrace my passions and stop worrying about what other people thought. He had been a loser in love who thought he couldn't keep a girlfriend, until I proved him wrong.

Everyone finished filing into the church, and the first strains of the wedding march filled the air, played by a string quartet. A saxophone added a sexier vibe. The sax had been Val's idea, naturally.

We all twisted around to see the doors, waiting for Eve to emerge.

She moved into the doorway on her father's arm, revealing her dress that was a gorgeous combination of sleekly modern and lacy traditional, with a neckline that managed to be both sexy and modest. Her strawberry-blonde hair fell in loose curls around her face, and her makeup enhanced her natural beauty without overpowering it.

Eve looked so beautiful, so happy, so ready to join her life with Val's.

Her groom stood at the altar, waiting for his bride. He and Eve had decided not to have groomsmen or bridesmaids, since they had so many friends and relatives that it would've been impossible to choose who should stand up there with them. Besides, all they needed was each other.

Larry Holt led his daughter to the altar, kissed her cheek, and winked at Val. Then he took his seat in the front row beside his wife.

I clutched Ollie's hand tightly while we listened to the minister recite the opening lines. "Dearly beloved, we are gathered here today..."

But I stopped listening then. I watched the expressions on Eve and Val's faces, fascinated by the joy and love they evinced and the commitment they were making to each other. It was beautiful, magical, emotional. Some people might've said marriage was irrelevant these days, but the looks on this couple's faces told a different story. They loved each other with everything they had and pronounced their intentions to love and honor each other with so much conviction that it made my heart swell.

Love was real. Marriage meant more than words spoken before an officiant. It touched something deep inside everyone in this church.

Eve and Val exchanged rings, and then they kissed.

Cheers erupted inside the church. A few people whooped or whistled.

I started to cry.

And I wasn't alone. While Eve and Val walked back up the aisle, heading for the doors, I noticed other people crying too—including Ollie. He hid it well, but I saw the way his eyes glistened and he swallowed visibly. I loved that he could get choked up by seeing two of his closest friends tie the knot. I loved him, period.

Everyone walked across the street to the restaurant that would host the reception. I met Val's parents and his sisters, and I danced with so many men that I lost count. Ollie got the first dance with me, but Damian waited until much later, after I'd taken a whirl with everyone else, before he asked me for a dance.

While we glided across the floor, Damian said, "I've been to weddings before, but this one has made me rethink whether I want to get married."

"Have you been against it until today?"

"Yeah. It seems like a silly tradition, but now..." He shrugged. "Maybe it's not so silly after all."

Wow. Eve and Val had made a convert without even trying. Well, a potential convert.

"I've known Ollie for a long time," Damian said, "and I've never seen him so happy. You did that. So thank you, Mara."

"You don't need to thank me. Ollie did the same thing for me, and no words can describe how grateful I am to him."

"Ollie has an idea for how to express his gratitude." Damian nodded toward something behind me and stepped back. "She's all yours, man."

I turned to see Ollie standing there, holding out his hand to me.

"Come on," he said, "let's go for a walk. There's a nice little park a couple blocks away."

"Not sure my shoes are good for walking. They're strictly designed to look pretty."

"That's okay. I've got your sneakers in the car. We'll grab them on the way out."

I settled my hand in his, letting him lead me out of the restaurant. We both grabbed our sneakers from the car and strolled down the sidewalk past cute, touristy shops, until we reached the little park. Flowers overflowed concrete planters along the asphalt path that led through the park, beneath a canopy of trees.

Ollie stopped in a secluded spot and dropped to one knee.

My throat went thick. I knew what he planned to do, but still I couldn't breathe from the anticipation.

"I love you, Mara," he said, pulling a small velvet box out of his pocket. "I want to spend the rest of my life with you. After all the bad break-ups and 'you're like my gay best friend' bullshit, I finally found the one woman in the whole world who understands me and makes me feel like the best version of myself."

He flipped the lid open on the little box, revealing a sparkling diamond ring.

The tears flowed, trickling down my cheeks, and my lips trembled.

"Mara, will you marry me?"

I nodded, because I couldn't speak.

"Should I take that as a yes?" he asked with a lopsided smile.

"Yes," I managed to say, though the word came out choked and almost inaudible.

He slipped the ring onto my finger.

Then we just gazed at each other, with me crying, both of us too overwhelmed by the emotions of this moment to move or speak. I swiped at my eyes and sucked in a big breath.

"Oh Ollie," I said, "I can't wait to marry you."

"Good." He surged up to crush me in his arms. "Because I'm not letting go of you, not ever."

I wrapped my arms around his neck. "Not letting go of you either."

We kissed, and we didn't stop kissing until I was lightheaded from lack of oxygen. I loved kissing this man, and I could do it for the rest of my life.

"Let's go," I said. "We need to celebrate our engagement the right way."

"You mean while naked and screaming each other's names?"

"Absolutely. Take me home, Oliver."

He grinned. "You know how I get when you call me Oliver."

"Well, stop dawdling."

"Yes, ma'am."

He swept me up in his arms and took me home.

Epilogue

I loved my job. Working at Au Naturel Naturist Resort was the best thing that had ever happened to me, and I had my best friend to thank for it. Ollie had convinced me to quit my old job, since I was bored out of my ever-loving mind there, and join him here. He'd been pestering me about it for almost a year, ever since he quit his tech job to move to Oregon. I kept saying no. I mean, a nudist resort? How could I ever concentrate with all those hot, naked girls prancing around? Then I came here for a visit and suddenly understood.

Not that many hot girls on the premises. Well, except when the Kitten Brigade was here. I'd met those girls once so far, but they were coming back today. Most of our guests were families or senior citizens.

So yeah, no hordes of nubile hotties to distract me.

Too bad, but also good. I loved women, but this was my job now, not a sexy vacay at an adults-only nudist resort in the Caribbean.

Had I been to one of those? Absolutely.

I climbed out of my "gypsy wagon," as Ollie insisted on calling it. Since I liked playing up the Rom angle, I didn't care if everyone called me a gypsy. So what? It was just a word.

Hopping off the last step onto the grass, I stretched and closed my eyes while I soaked up the sunshine.

The rumbling of a vehicle's engine interrupted my moment of relaxation.

I glanced toward the driveway, about a hundred feet away, and smiled.

A big, pink RV was pulling up. The Kitten Brigade had arrived.

Hot, naked girls on demand. Wasn't I the luckiest jerk on earth?

I watched the Kittens disembark from their RV, all of them wearing pink T-shirt dresses. All but one. The blonde who exited last wore cargo pants and a baggy T-shirt, with a baseball cap covering her hair. I remembered that hair. Golden blonde, silky, glistening in the sun. She'd let it grow out, so now it tumbled over her shoulders in lustrous waves. I also remembered her breasts. Spectacular, they were. I'd seen all of her nude body, but I had never even flirted with her, much less kissed her. I didn't want to be the rebound guy.

Heidi Mackenzie had been hung up on Ollie the first time I'd met her. Maybe she still was.

One way to find out.

The other Kittens shed their dresses, tossing them high in the air while whooping with joy.

Heidi hunched near the front bumper of the RV. She didn't undress.

Weird. She'd been one of the most fervent devotees of nudism.

Eve, Val, Ollie, and Mara all emerged from the little house to greet the newly arrived guests. Mara approached Heidi, and the two women shared a brief conversation that ended with Mara hugging Heidi.

Even weirder. Heidi had tried to seduce Ollie away from Mara a while back. Now they acted like old friends. There had to be a story behind the change, but I'd need to ask Ollie about that.

While Eve and Val helped the Kittens carry their tents and bags to the camping area on the other side of the guest house, I snagged Ollie and Mara.

"Hey, lovebirds," I said. "What's the deal? I thought Mara and Heidi would have an epic throwdown when they saw each other again. I was hoping for a down and dirty girl fight, with mud wrestling and everything. Preferably in the nude."

Ollie rolled his eyes at me. "The girls made up a long time ago. They've been trading emails."

Mara nodded. "We've talked on the phone a couple times too."

I really didn't get it. If I had a girlfriend and some dick tried to steal her away from me, I wouldn't forgive the guy and become his BFF. But Mara and Heidi had become friends. Seriously? Had I stumbled through an invisible portal into *The Twilight Zone*?

Ollie clapped a hand down on my shoulder. "Mara and Heidi are being adult about it. Besides, Heidi's been bummed out and needs all the friends she can get."

Well, if sexy little Heidi needed a friend...I volunteered for the job.

"Leave her alone," Ollie said, giving me his stern face that always looked silly to me. He wasn't the tough-guy type.

"What?" I said, pretending to be clueless. "All I want to do is help her through this transitional period."

Transitioning into my bed. That would cheer her up, for sure.

"You're my best friend," Ollie said, "so I'm asking you bro to bro. Give Heidi some space."

"What if she jumps my bones? It would be rude to reject her. It might damage her self-confidence."

"Are you really going to wait for her to make the first move? If she does."

"Fine, yes, I'll wait until she's ready. I'm not a total dick, you know."

"Yeah, I know." Ollie put his arm around Mara. "We should go help the Kittens get set up."

I glanced toward the guest house and saw Heidi going inside. "Isn't the home-wrecker staying in a tent with her girlfriends?"

Mara rolled her eyes at me this time. "Heidi is not a home-wrecker. She's actually very sweet. And no, she's not staying with the other Kittens. She'll be in the guest house."

Ollie kissed Mara's cheek. "We'd better get going if we want to have time for today's Japanese lesson too."

"Can't miss that," Mara said with enthusiasm.

Yeah, Ollie and Mara were learning Japanese online, through one of those language websites. It didn't sound like fun to me, but they seemed to like it.

The lovebirds ambled off to assist the Kitten Brigade.

I wandered into the guest house to find Heidi. Not that I planned to hit on her. Not yet, anyway. But I was curious why she'd dressed like a female version of a college guy. I'd never dressed that way, but cargo pants had been the uniform of choice for a lot of the guys I'd met in college. Some of the girls too.

But not girls like Heidi. She had a beautiful face and a killer body, and last time I'd seen her, she wasn't shy about showing it off. She clearly loved stripping naked. So why hide all those curves now? And that creamy skin, with those cute little freckles sprinkled around just enough to make me want to count them all with my tongue.

I found Heidi loitering at the bottom of the stairs, her head tipped back, seeming to admire the carpentry or something.

"Hey," I said. "Remember me?"

She startled, her wide blue eyes swerving toward me. "Oh, it's you. Damian, right? You're Ollie's friend."

"Yeah, but I don't think we were ever properly introduced." I held out my hand. "Damian Petrescu, proud Rom and descendant of the Ludar line."

She shook my hand, though she looked skeptical of me. "Right. I remember now. You're the guy who loves to put on gypsy airs. I'm Heidi Mackenzie."

Airs? Hey, I might've enjoyed playing up the gypsy stuff, but it was no act. Not entirely.

Heidi raked her gaze over my entire body, and her tongue sneaked out to moisten her bottom lip. "Why are you dressed like Dracula's low-rent cousin?"

"Women love the way I dress." I smirked. "You do, that's for sure. I can tell by the way your pupils dilated when you saw me and the way you licked your lips."

"My lips are dry, and it's kind of dark in here. It makes everybody's pupils get bigger."

"Have dinner with me."

She blinked slowly, her brows hiking up. "Excuse me?"

"You heard what I said. Have dinner with me. I give awesome dating."

One side of her mouth tried to smile while the other side wanted to frown. "Yeah, I'm sure you think you're awesome at everything to do with women. But I'm not interested."

I leaned against the bottom post on the staircase, cocking my hip. "I bet you'll change your mind after a date with me. What have you got to lose? I'll buy you a nice meal, we'll have some laughs, and then you can decide how badly you want to get me naked."

"Oh please. Does that kind of talk really work for you?"

"Usually." I slanted toward her and lowered my voice. "I can give you the best time of your life, and I'll even talk dirty if you beg me for it." I grinned. "Actually, you won't have to beg. I love whispering filthy things into a woman's ear."

"I'm not into that." She crossed her arms over her chest, elevating her tits. "I'm not interested in dating or sex at all."

"Come on, you must be joking. Aren't you the girl who loves to be naked and loves to suck every ounce of marrow out of life?"

"I'm not a silly, wild girl anymore. I've changed, for the better."

Right. In the space of a few months, she morphed from a party girl into a serious, cargo-pants-wearing woman. Sure, she'd humiliated herself with Ollie last time they saw each other. But that was no reason to shun hot sex and wild times.

"Don't you miss having a good time?" I asked. "I guarantee I can make you feel good."

"I'm not having sex with you."

"We can start with a date, then."

She shook her head, trying to frown but not quite accomplishing it. "You really are persistent, aren't you? Maybe I'm not being clear enough. I'm done with men, at least for a while."

"Have you defected to the other side?"

"What?" She shook her head again, almost smiling. "Oh, I get it. I'm not a lesbian. I'm taking a break from dating, that's all."

"Hmm." I inched closer to her. "We can start with getting it on, and upgrade to dinner once you're over this no-dating thing."

"Do you have concrete for brains?" She made exaggerated lip movements to match her exaggerated enunciation when she said, "I am celibate. No sex. No dating. No men, except for platonic friends. Get it?"

"I can read lips, you know. You could've just mouthed all that, and I would've understood."

"You're so pigheaded, I figured you needed extra emphasis."

Heidi Mackenzie was off dating. Off men. But I wanted her *on* me. Something about her frumpy clothes made me want to rip them off even more than if she'd been wearing a skimpy outfit. And her celibacy vow only increased my lust for her.

Seducing her into breaking her vow could be lots of fun.

"How about a kiss?" I asked.

"No, Damian. We can be friends—platonic, which means no sex, no kissing, no fondling—but that's it."

I sighed with all the melodrama in my Rom soul. "Have it your way."

"Thank you."

"We'll be friends, until you drag me into the woods and ravage me."

Heidi smiled just enough to create dimples. Her eyes twinkled too. "You're going to be a handful, aren't you?"

"Oh yeah. I always am."

I kissed her hand and walked away.

Life at the Au Naturel Naturist Resort was about to get wild.

Damian and Heidi will return in *Natural Satisfaction*.

*A*nna Durand is a bestselling, multi-award-winning author of contemporary and paranormal romance. Her books have earned bestseller status on every major retailer and wonderful reviews from readers around the world. But that's the boring spiel. Here are some really cool things you want to know about Anna!

Born on Lackland Air Force Base in Texas, Anna grew up moving here, there, and everywhere thanks to her dad's job as an instructor pilot. She's lived in Texas (twice), Mississippi, California (twice), Michigan (twice), and Alaska—and now Ohio.

As for her writing, Anna has always made up stories in her head, but she didn't write them down until her teen years. Those first awful books went into the trash can a few years later, though she learned a lot from those stories. Eventually, she would pen her first romance novel, the paranormal romance Willpower, and she's never looked back since.

Want even more details about Anna? Get access to her extended bio when you subscribe to her newsletter and download the free bonus ebook, Hot Scots Confidential. You'll also get hot deleted scenes, character interviews, fun facts, and more!